Unexpected

By

Amy Marie

AMY MARIE

Copyright © 2014 by Amy Marie
Self-publishing
AuthorAmyMarie@yahoo.com

ALL RIGHTS RESERVED. No part of this book may be reproduced or transmitted in any form without the written permission of the author, except by a reviewer who may quote brief passages for review purposes only.

This book is a work of fiction. Any resemblance to actual persons, living or dead, or actual events is entirely coincidental. Names, characters, places and incidents are the product of the author's imagination or are used fictitiously.

Cover Design: Louisa Maggio @ LM Creations

Editing by Elizabeth Froelich

Formatting by Angel's Indie Formatting

Dedication

This book is dedicated to my two best friends.

To my husband Josh...You are my rock and there is not a day that goes by that I don't know how blessed I am to have you in my life. I love you with all my heart.

To my best friend Valerie...This book would not be in existence if it weren't for your love, support, and pushiness. Thank you. I adore you...HARD. Real hard.

UNEXPECTED

"Miss Decker, I'm in the Pen 15 club now!" I hear over the chatter of my 6th grade students walking into my classroom. "See? All I had to do was let Aaron write it on my arm," Jeffrey, one of the more naïve kids, says sticking out his left forearm to show me. Shaking my head I am horrified to see the word "penis" prominently displayed there in permanent marker.

"Ha! I can't believe you fell for it Jeff!" Aaron yells from the back of the classroom. "Pen 15 looks like penis! Jeff has penis on his arm!"

I glare at him and point towards the door signaling him to go to the principal's office. Aaron hangs his head as he makes his way out of the classroom. He has spent one too many afternoons in detention lately and it seems he's just earned himself another. As he exits, giggling erupts and I turn my attention back to Jeffrey.

"Alright mister, let's get this cleaned off your arm as best we can," I say, ruffling his sandy hair.

Being a math teacher at Hudson Middle School has its good days and bad. I don't really know why I chose that subject except I did well in my high school and college courses and figured it would be easy enough to teach. Little did I know that I would be shaping the young minds of prepubescent, hormone driven tweens. When they aren't fighting, laughing, or talking, they are sleeping, in class no less. I wouldn't change it for the world though. I really love my job. Well, I love it minus the parents, like Jeffrey's, who will most likely blame me for this most recent incident even though I wasn't present when it occurred.

I love my life too. It's taken me a long time to get where I am. At 27 I have an established career, a great starter home that I share with my completely crazy best friend, Noelle, no credit card debt or student loans, three months off during the summer, a nice car, and Robert, the sweetest boyfriend that anyone could ask for. I'm not bragging. I fought hard to get here and I'm very proud to have done it by myself. My parents had three kids to worry about. After studying like crazy in high school I earned a fifty percent scholarship to Northern Illinois

University. The other half came from what little my parents did give me and from working my ass off at a restaurant on campus. I walked away with my degree and without a cent owed.

The final bell brings me back to the present. Glancing at the clock I realize I've let most of the class pass while I daydreamed and allowed the kids to chit-chat the whole time. Out in the hallway chaos ensues. Papers are flying everywhere, kids and teachers are high fiving each other, yearbooks are quickly being signed and I'm almost on my way to celebrate the end of another successful year of teaching, after I speak with Jeffery's parents in the pickup line.

I am NOT looking forward to this conversation. His mom and dad are the type of parents who never hold their kid responsible for his behavior. Was it Jeffrey's fault? No, but he is 12 years old. He really should know better than to let someone write on him with a Sharpie, especially when it's Aaron, a known troublemaker, whose parents are just as bad. *I guess I just better get it over with.*

~~

Returning to my classroom thirty minutes later, I feel deflated. Not exactly the way I wanted to end the school year. I'm just going to do a quick clean up before I head out the door. I'm planning to come back tomorrow when it's quiet and pack up the rest of my things. I'm locking up my classroom when I hear someone calling my name.

"Erin! ... Erin, are you leaving so soon?" I finish locking my door and turn around to see Rosie, the other 6th grade math teacher, calling to me from her classroom directly across the hall. "Is your room already packed up?"

"It's not Rose," I reply. "But I'll be back tomorrow to finish up. How about you? Excited to retire?" I'm silently hoping this conversation is short since I had to endure getting chewed out by Jeffery's parents. I have a glass of wine, scratch that...a bottle, calling my name.

"I don't have much left to do. But I wanted to give you a hug and tell you it's been great being across the hall from you for the past four years. It was such a blessing to have a young person who brings some energy around this place." She says wrapping her arms around me just a little too tightly.

"Why, thank you." Her vice grip loosens allowing my blood to flow freely again. "But it's not like I won't see you," I continue. "We should get together for lunch. Just because we won't be *working* together doesn't mean we can't still *get* together."

"That sounds wonderful," Rosie says, with a smile.

"Great! I'll call you next week," I say, giving

her a quick squeeze on the arm as I turn to head out the door.

As I'm running to my car I keep my head down. I really don't want anything else keeping me from getting home. I know I said I love my job but I love Pink Moscato just as much...if not more, and it *IS* the last day of the school year. I want to celebrate!

The house is quiet when I get in. Noelle hasn't returned home from work yet. Dropping my keys in the bowl on the counter, I throw my bags on the table making a mental note to pick them up before she gets here. Noelle is very anal and if she saw my bags on the floor she would shit...and then pick the shit up, shampoo the carpet, dry it, shampoo it again and curse my name without getting a speck on her. Neat freak is an understatement.

Noelle and I met freshman year at NIU when we were assigned the same dorm room. I hated her at first. In the beginning of the year I would come back from classes only to find my dresser, desk or even my closet rearranged. She was always reorganizing my space and we fought over it constantly. I wanted to strangle her, but more than that, I wanted her to stay on her side of our room. After I realized how persistent she was, I gave in, letting her arrange my stuff. Once she had exercised her anal retentiveness over my belongings, we found out that we actually had a lot in common, having both grown up in the northwest suburbs of Chicago.

    I still remember the day I realized she had become my best friend. In the middle of finals week, a few days before we were both heading home for winter break, one of the frat houses was having a Finals Finale party. Darren, a guy she was casually dating was a brother there and she begged me to go. The minute we got to the party I regretted it. Adrienne, Darren's younger sister who thought I was trying to steal her boyfriend, was in my face. I wanted nothing to do with him, except finish the project we were assigned together. I tried to reason with her, but she was insecure and apparently livid about the amount of time I'd spent with him recently. Loudly calling me a slut in a room full of partygoers was the last straw. Fed up, I raised my fist, but before I had the chance to punch her in the face Noelle stepped in and beat me to it. I tried to tell her I could have done that but she insisted that was what friends were for. We were on our way out the door when Darren tried to get her to stay by grabbing her arm. He wouldn't let go, and he was holding her upper arm so tight that she couldn't get enough leverage to shove him off of her. Infuriated by his actions, and with my pent up anger towards Adrienne, I punched him in the face, knocking him back. He stumbled and actually fell to the ground. As we were both running back to our room laughing,

Noelle used my line, saying she had it herself, but I repeated her earlier statement. That's what friends were for. *Cue corny 80's song.*

That is one thing best friends do; stand up and stand by you through your ups and downs, to make sure you come out breathing on the other side.

Smiling at the memories of our early college days, I fill my wine glass to the brim with pink goodness and start a lavender bubble bath. I deserve it. The conversation with Jeff's parents was tough. Even though it happened during lunch, it was, of course, my fault. What a way to end the year.

As I slip into the warm bubbles my cell phone rings. I fumble to answer with wet hands, putting my mother on speakerphone and laying it down on the ceramic edge of the tub.

"Hey Mom, what's going on?"

"When are you going to get married to that handsome hunk of meat you have and give me some grandchildren?"

Sigh. Meet my mother. Mrs. Decker was married at 22 and had three kids by the time she was 30. She thinks my eggs are drying up more and more every day. My older sister Nicole apparently has no TV because she's had 4 kids (Hannah, Marie, Jack, and Nick). My younger brother, Trent, has little Jason, who just turned one, and ever since he was born my mother has been on my ass to start popping them out. I am not in a rush. My nieces and nephews are amazing birth control.

"I'm great! Thank you for asking," I say, rolling my eyes, and taking a sip from my glass.

"Oh, Erin. I'm just messing around with you...don't be so serious. But, how *is* that Robert of yours?"

She doesn't even bother to ask about my last day or if it's a bad time to call. I love my mother but she drives me crazy when it comes to my future. She sometimes forgets how independent I am.

"He's good Ma; working late again tonight. I'm going to head over there after a bath and surprise him with dinner."

"That's great honey. Show him what a good wife you would make." I can visualize the smirk that must have spread across her face. I can't win.

We hang up after a quick recap of the day and I climb out of the bathtub since there is no way it will relax me now. Plus, the water is cold, my wine is warm, and I'm feeling cranky. I slip into my favorite pair of jean shorts and a new yellow tank top, before tying my short brown hair up into a pony tail, throwing on some light makeup and walking towards the door to head to Robert's apartment. Spotting my bags still on the floor I run and throw them in my closet so Noelle doesn't defecate on our new carpet.

    I stop at the grocery store and run in to grab some ingredients I'll need to make dinner. From the store to Robert's place takes about ten minutes. It's 6:30 now, and since he said he works until 7 this evening, I have plenty of time to have the chicken parmesan ready by the time he arrives home. My flip-flops clang on the metal steps as I dig through my purse trying to find his key. The door creaks softly as I open it and instantly I become breathless.

    Candles and flower petals fill the entire living room and the sounds of Toni Braxton filter through the speakers. This was the first song we danced to at his fraternity's welcome back mixer. We have been dating since my senior year in college, 5 years ago, and lately I've been dropping hints that I'd like to take the next logical step. Engagement.

    My eyes fill with tears as I realize tonight might be the night Robert will ask me to be his wife. My mother will shit herself.

    I place my purse and grocery bag on the kitchen table and look around with new perspective. The scent of the vanilla candles warms my insides and I wipe the tears falling from my cheeks. Robert is nowhere in sight. My nerves are running rampant when the thought occurs that I may be too early. Stopping in my tracks I realize he couldn't know I was coming over. He didn't ask me to come.

    I sneak down the hall quietly, on instinct alone. He is obviously expecting me. My excitement gets the better of me and my pace picks up until I get to his half opened bedroom door at the end of the hallway.

    "Oh God, yes!" A female voice calls out. *What the hell was that?* "Harder Robby, harder!" The voice continues.

    Slap.

    "You like that baby, huh? I bet you love it," a muffled male voice, that sounds eerily similar to my Robert, says.

    Peeking through the doorway I feel my heart shatter into a million pieces. The last five years circling the drain like the frigid water of my earlier bath. Gone! If I could turn back the clock 15 minutes I would've never come into this apartment. No, I would have, because if not, I would be blind to what is going on behind my back. My eyes focus on the betrayal. It's like a car accident you can't look away from even though it's bloody and brutal. It doesn't seem real, but it is.

    Robert, my Robert, is screwing his secretary on the bed we picked out together at

Sears. Their two bodies become one on the sheets we decided on because of the thread count. And he is not just screwing her, oh no. He is pounding it into her from behind with a firm grasp on her blonde ponytail while aggressively smacking her ass. A far cry from the sweet passionate love making we had this morning before he left my house for work.

"I'm coming!" Anna screams and rage consumes my body.

"THE HELL YOU ARE!" I yell with a voice I don't recognize and push the door all the way open, hitting the wall with the door knob. "GET THE HELL OFF OF HER NOW ROBERT!"

They both jump at the sound of my shriek and she uses our 400 thread count sheets to cover up her fake breasts. Robert just stares at me expressionless and quiet. I'm hoping he has the worst blue balls imaginable.

"Go home Anna," he finally says. "Erin and I have to talk."

Awkwardly Anna gets up, never letting her eyes leave mine.

"Yes, go HOME Anna, to your husband and two kids, you whore!" I spit.

Scowling at me, she scrambles to get her pencil skirt and button up blouse on and runs out of the room. I follow behind her, not yet able to stand looking at Robert or 'Robby' as she calls him. She slams the door as she exits, leaving me alone in his living room. The candles and flowers that not 5 minutes ago gave me false hope of a future with him now leave me feeling alone and uncertain of what lies ahead. I know it's over. There is no coming back from this, no second chances.

"Baby. I didn't mean for you to find out like that," Robert says walking into the room.

The music suddenly ceases and my heart beats faster as I begin shaking with anger.

"How did you *MEAN* for me to find out Robert? Or were you hoping I wouldn't?"

The blood rushing to my face makes me dizzy and I have to sit on his couch. I immediately jump back up when I think of them screwing there too. *Disgusting!*

"I didn't want to hurt you Erin. We've been drifting apart for a long time and I feel like I'm...I'm getting bored. I know you think marriage is our next step but I'm just not ready for that. I want to experience other things, other people, and other...positions." He sits down running his hands through his shaggy black hair in frustration.

"What are you saying?" I ask. "That I'm not adventurous enough in bed? I lost my virginity to you Robert! I loved you and I thought you loved me...and now you are telling me that because I haven't role played with you or let you fuck me from behind that the last 5 years meant NOTHING to you?" My hands shake as I pick up my purse and throw it over my shoulder.

I pull open his door and whip back around towards him again, saying my last words to the man who will probably be the reason I won't ever be able to trust another. "I'm glad I caught you, you dirty bastard. At least my last image of you matches what you are. A DOG!"

"ERIN!" He starts towards me as I slam the door and run down the stairs.

As I near the bottom my traitor flip-flop catches on the step and I stumble across the sidewalk scraping my left leg. As blood arrives at the surface of my skin I feel Robert's hand wrap around my arm gently, trying to help me up.

"Are you ok?" He asks.

"No! I'm not ok. Don't touch me!" I yell, trying to yank my arm away. "Just stay away from me. Don't call me, text me, or email me. Just lose my number and forget you ever knew me, or that you ever loved me. That's what I plan to do." I glare into his soft brown eyes that I used to trust, hoping to make my point clear. "I. Hate. You."

The hurt in his eyes tells me I hit my

target.

Good.

His hand releases its hold and I pick myself up and stomp off to my car. Once in my seat, I drop my head onto the steering wheel. The pain throbbing through my leg is a stark reminder of the pain in my heart. As my tears begin to overflow, my vision blurs. *Why would he do this to me?*

Getting myself together before I have a complete breakdown, I search in my bag for my phone. I text Noelle knowing she will see these three words and drop everything for me.

Me: I need you.

"That son of a BITCH!" Noelle yells, as she plops down on the leather couch. "After all the two of you have been through how could he do that to you?"

I am shaking uncontrollably and can't stop replaying the events of the past hour over and over again in my head. After Noelle responded to my text, I can't remember anything else. I am lucky to have made it home. She was already here when I arrived, with a bottle of tequila opened and waiting. She knows me so well!

Noelle is right to say Robert and I have been through a lot. Some of the toughest times either of us has gone through have been over the past few years. Robert lost both his parents in a drunk driving accident 4 years ago. I held his hand from the minute he found out until the caskets were lowered into the cold December ground. We've even mourned a miscarriage together. Although it wasn't a planned pregnancy, it was a child, and we were very excited about the prospect of starting a family. My dad passed away last year from lung cancer even though he didn't smoke a day in his short 55 years. It hit me pretty hard and Robert was there to help me pick up the pieces. The two of us went from scared, early twenty something's, looking to start a life for ourselves, to an established teacher and architect with the world at our feet. It tears me up inside to think the whole relationship ended because Robert thought we weren't compatible in the bedroom.

    We waited a year after we became exclusive before I gave him the most sacred gift I could give; my virginity. My mother taught me from my early teen years that I didn't necessarily have to be married but that I should choose carefully and give it to someone I love. After 12 months I was sure that Robert and I were going to be together forever. I guess I was naïve to think that sex was about making love, and showing the other person how much you care about and trust them.

    When I really think about it, I should have seen the signs. After college graduation we were lucky enough to find jobs near my hometown. Robert insisted that we didn't move in together noting that we should leave something for when we got married. I agreed, wanting a chance to explore my independence. I bought a house with Noelle and he got an apartment. Once that happened things changed drastically. I didn't see Robert as much. I attributed it to his new job and working late. I guess he was working alright. Every time I called the office directly Anna would answer and I would never be able to get to him. According to her he was always busy.

    Last December I had become suspicious when I found them coming out of his office. She looked as though a tornado had whipped through her hair and he was adjusting his suit. I never brought it up, trusting that he was faithful to me. It seems love truly is blind.

    "Erin, maybe this is the best thing that could've happened to you," Noelle says, bringing me back from my thoughts. "I know you loved him...that probably won't ever go away but he was a real douche. He never wanted you to go out and have fun with your friends and you were so hesitant when I wanted to plan a trip to Cozumel this summer, just the two of us. Maybe it's time to start being selfish and do things for you. There are no kids to hold you back, no one to answer to, and 90 days of paid vacation. It's time to live and it starts with booking our trip!" She grows more animated with each sentence, practically jumping up off the couch. I guess I'm glad someone is happy about the break up.

I'm not happy at all. I just want to sulk until the pain goes away, if it ever will. Is it wrong to want to finish this bottle of tequila or eat my 130 pound weight in cookie dough? Thinking of all the "fun things" we can do is not something I'm currently focused on. But if I know Noelle, and I do, she is going to push and push until I give in.

"Let me think about it," I say, clumsily making my way up from my comfortable position on the recliner. I watch her face fall, but I can't be concerned with that right now... I need another shot.

~~

"Wakey, wakey, eggs and bakey!" Noelle's sing song voice sounds like she is talking into a bullhorn directly next to my ear. Did I mention that she NEVER gets a hangover? Whereas, I have 4 shots of tequila and I can't function the next day.

"I don't think my stomach can handle eggs and bakey at this moment," I say covering my head with the comforter and praying that she goes away.

"Ok! Well I just wanted to put your credit card back in your purse. You don't need to be awake for that. I know where it goes." Her ramblings sound muffled through the blanket.

Now I'm up! Her nonchalant announcement has me throwing my blankets off and squinting to find her in the brightly lit room. When my eyes adjust she is closing my wallet back up.

"My credit card? Why did you need my credit card, Noelle?" I'm seeing red. She never goes through my personal stuff without asking.

"So you won't change your mind." She shrugs like it's not a big deal and continues, "I just finalized plans. We're going to Cozumel in July!"

My mouth drops open and I'm sure my face has turned from a creamy pale peach to fire engine red.

"Tell me you're joking, Noelle! I swear if you aren't kidding me then I will NEVER speak to you again."

She hesitates at the door and turns her body back around to face me. The glare from her crystal blue eyes tells me she is going into "take no crap" mode.

"Erin Melissa Decker. You have six weeks to get over it and start talking to me. I could care less if you mope around until then but that boy, and I say boy because he is NOT a man, has held you back from living your life for the past five years. You need some fun and I'm going to make sure that you have it, whether you want to or not! So, put your big girl panties on and suck it up because we're going and that's final!" She whips her long blonde hair around, walks out, and slams my door.

"YES, MOMMY DEAREST!" I yell through the closed door and stalk to the bathroom, hangover almost forgotten. What greets me in the mirror is nothing short of scary. Mascara is caked on my tear streaked face from the previous night's endless sobs. I remember that in my hasty search to find my bed and not the floor last night, I didn't take my make up off. Taking a deep breath I brave a second look and really focus on what Noelle said.

As much as I hate to admit it she *is* right…again. Robert controlled my every move. My last year of college was spent practically glued to his side. If I wanted to go out alone he was always threatening to break up with me. The trip to Cozumel was something Noelle and I had wanted to do since the end of last summer when a friend of ours talked about the amazing snorkeling adventures she'd had. There was no discussing it with Robert. He had said no. I've always wanted to do a lot of traveling and being a teacher allows me the time. Plus, I hadn't done all that hard work paying off my student loans and never maxing out my credit cards for nothing! Screw him! I've decided I'm going, to spite him, even if only after the fact. This summer is going to be life changing. I can just feel it!

I still need to go and clean out my classroom so I wash my make up off and prepare to get in the shower. Then, as if Robert leaving me wasn't bad enough I notice that I got my monthly visitor.

Damn it!

Well at least the cheating bastard didn't get me pregnant.

~~

My life changing summer wasn't off to a great start. I was planning to spend day one post breakup cleaning and packing up my room at school and ignoring Noelle after I arrived home. I know I said she was right, but the woman didn't flinch when she charged a $550 flight and $400 for a hotel room, plus excursions, on my credit card. So if my share of the mortgage is a little late, well then that's fine with me. I'll just have to pay that off with my next check.

~~

On day three I tell Noelle she had had me at "get your big girl panties on." We laugh about the whole thing and since it is the 1st of June I also take care of the trip expenses with my first summer paycheck.

~~

Day five I decide to collect all my belongings from Robert's apartment. I haven't heard from him, not that I expected to, and decide to let myself in using the key he gave me to gain entry. I walk in with Noelle at my side. Armed with her same "screw him" attitude it doesn't take me long to get all of my things packed up and leave his key on the kitchen counter with a note saying I've been there and to continue on with no contact. A text came in later that day.

Robert: Came home to all of your stuff gone. I miss you Er-Bear. Let's talk.

Me: Go to HELL!

Less than a week shouldn't be enough time to get over such a long term relationship but I knew it was done. I had given him a lot of my firsts but someone else was going to get my lasts…and my bests.

~~

Over the last week or so I have been lounging around the house reading a book, hitting up the beach to work on my tan and avoiding my mother's calls. With no boyfriend and no job I am starting to get cabin fever and Noelle can tell.

"You're like a dog," she says. "I come home

from work and you're at the door ready to hump my leg and lick my face." Noelle laughs, as she walks back to her room, most likely putting her briefcase down exactly where she likes it.

She works as an event planner for a well-known establishment in town and it's perfect for her. Her boss Lisa wouldn't know what to do without Noelle. When Lisa forgets something or needs a task done Noelle is the one she turns to. She was once told she was Lisa's better half and has been known to be mine. I'm sure part of it is her mad organizational skills, which I'm also sure, stems from her being so precise about everything. It definitely keeps her very busy.

"That's not nice, Noe." I say following her into her room. Then, shaking my head I realize *I am* acting like a dog. "I just miss you is all."

"Go get dressed Erin. We're going out."

Her voice carries out from her bathroom as she is taking her work clothes off and throwing them in her hamper.

"I don't want..."

She comes out of the bathroom in her bra and panties and interrupts me by pinching my lips between her thumb and forefinger.

"Shut it! We need to go out, have some drinks and relax. I've let you mope long enough. It's time to have some fun and maybe get laid! It's been like 3 weeks for me."

Three weeks is a long time for Noelle. She *STILL* rocks all the hot genes. Blonde hair, blue eyes, and perky little breasts all perfectly put together on her 5 foot 6 athletic frame. I guess she's earned it after countless spin classes.

"Fine! Pick out my clothes!" I say around her fingers, which are still pinching my mouth closed. I won't try to deny her requests any longer. I do need to get out. The getting laid part though, not happening.

Two hours later I am staring at what can only be described as an illusion. I try to take pride in how I look but Noelle has transformed me into an unrecognizable woman that even I would switch teams for. My short brown hair has been curled and my bangs, which I'm trying to grow out, are braided to the side. The metallic gray eye shadow and black eyeliner on my lids make my brown eyes pop and smolder. Now for some very red lips and lengthening mascara and I'm almost complete. The little black dress she chose for me hugs me in all the right places. It's an A-line strapless pleated dress that lies across my mid thighs. Just short enough that I look sexy but I can still bend over without flashing my lacey boy shorts. The whole outfit is finished off with silver wedge shoes that have a strap around the ankle. For the first time in a long time I feel beautiful.

"You look hot, Erin. You are definitely going to get some tonight!" Noelle winks and pulls me out the front door.

"That isn't happening," I say, letting her drag me into a waiting taxi cab.

McKinley's is packed from wall to wall and the dance floor looks like it's one big orgy with sweaty bodies grinding on one another. The heat from outside seems like fall compared to the temperature inside. Thankful, in this sauna, for the small scrap of material that I call a dress, I push my way through the crowd and over to the bar where drunken patrons are waiting three and four people deep. Noelle and I decided on our earlier cab ride over that we would let it all go and just have fun. I hoped I had made it clear there would be absolutely no sexual encounters of any kind where I was concerned. She just raised an eyebrow at me.

"What'll you have sweet thing?" I'm asked by the over confident mixologist after fifteen minutes of being groped by drunk people in line.

"Two shots of tequila and a couple of Jack and Cokes," Noelle calls from over my shoulder. It's not difficult considering that even in 3 inch wedges she towers over my 5 foot 3 frame. I'm borderline vertically challenged.

Handing the $40 in cash over to Mr. Cocky she takes in my "what the hell" face. "What, Erin?" Noelle asks.

"I thought we were going to take it easy and just have a good time. I don't want to get trashed in the first hour we are here," I say as the bartender places the shots in front of us with our change. Noelle leaves the money on the bar and hands me my shot.

"We are! This is just to start us in the right direction." Her glass meets mine with a clink. "To looking for Mr. Right while having fun with all the Mr. Wrongs!" She says as I roll my eyes.

~~

My body isn't used to this much alcohol. The few glasses of wine I normally drink don't have me in the middle of a dance "orgy" without remembering how I got there. Sweat is dripping down my neck and tickling the space between my breasts. After the third round of drinks, bought by three different men just wanting to get in my pants, I feel relaxed yet out of control. Noelle is nowhere to be found and in my drunken state I'm not even the least bit concerned about it. The music has taken over my body and I can feel myself letting go of all the stress and anxiety that Robert has caused me. I don't care who is watching because at this moment I feel like the sexiest person in here.

With my eyes closed I rub my hands along my hips all the way to my hair, pulling it off my neck into a makeshift ponytail. The beat of the music moves through me like an electric wave. When a cool puff of air passes over the back of my neck it feels like water in the Sahara. Larger hands than I've ever felt before unexpectedly come around my waist and pull me back into a rock hard chest. My breathing becomes more ragged as the mystery man whispers in my ear.

"Are you hot, baby?" He asks, his hot breath sending shivers down my spine.

My senses are on high alert and despite the fact that I haven't a clue what he looks like, those four words turn me on instantly. If his voice can do that to me I'd love to see what his enormous hands are capable of. Our bodies connect and sway to the music as his mouth continues to hover just above my shoulder causing tingles to radiate through my body. I can feel his lips grazing the crease of my neck and when he nips my skin my knees go weak. My head falls back involuntarily giving him more access to continue his sensual assault. He smells delicious, and the soft suctioning kisses he places up my neck cause me to moan in anticipation. I have to see the man who is releasing all my inhibitions.

    Reluctantly I turn my heated body around feeling the loss of his soft lips, but what I'm rewarded with is a vision of godliness. Standing at what appears to be well over six feet tall is the most panty-dropping specimen that I have ever laid my eyes upon. I should have turned around sooner! His plain black t-shirt hugs every single slender muscle in his sexy ass arms. The faded blue jeans he wears are snug, even more so where his zipper lies, showing me how much he is turned on. His dark brown hair is a styled mess; short on the sides but longer up top. I can't help but wonder what it would feel like to grab hold of it and tug. Hard. A grin flashes across his face, as if he's read my mind, and I see a hint of just one dimple on the right side of his mouth. His green eyes appear hungry as they shamelessly take me in from my toes to my own starving eyes. I swallow hard and try to catch my breath.

    "I thought you looked good from behind but damn if you don't look heavenly from this angle," he says loudly, over the music.

    He grabs both of my hands, circling them around his neck. With our height difference my forehead falls into his chest perfectly, as if we are two pieces of a puzzle. I try to control my breathing; the alcohol is coursing through my veins now. Freeing my hands from their hold, they find their way down and softly graze over his pecs and then the ripple of his abs. They falter as they come in contact with not a six pack but, a ...1,2,3,... eight pack! I see his chest rising and falling rapidly. I think he must be as turned on by me as I am by him. *Impossible.*

His hands caress my body as we dance. I feel heat gathering at my center, and not from the dance floor. Robert never had this affect on me from barely a touch. If the setting was a bedroom and not a bar I wouldn't hesitate to strip this man down and do things to him Robert only dreamed I would do. His loss. Robert was wrong. I'm amazing in bed.

Maybe I've been going about this the wrong way. Why should I wait to be in love? Clearly that doesn't seem to mean a damn thing. Why can't I just ask this man to take me home and have his way with me? I can, but then I realize I've said nothing to the amazing masterpiece that is, from what I can feel, very well equipped.

Hazy thoughts run through my head about the first words I should say to him. Tell him my name. Ask him what he does. Anything but what actually leaves my tequila infused brain and comes out of my mouth. I stand on my tip toes and say into his ear, "I caught my ex screwing his secretary from behind and he told me it was because I'm not adventurous enough in bed."

Holy shit! I'm *way* too tipsy. My face burns with embarrassment and I am thankful for the dimly lit dance floor.

He looks at me like what I said makes no sense and runs his finger along my lips. "What's your name pretty girl?"

"Sally," I blurt out. There is no way in hell he is getting my real name with *that* pick up line. Even if I am drunk.

"Sally, huh?" He asks in a way that makes me think he knows I've lied. "Well 'Sally', my name is Walker. Would you like to come back to my hotel room and see what kind of adventures I can take you on?" His mouth is a breath away from mine.

I instinctively lean towards him, closing most of the distance between our lips. "Let's go," I say, before venturing a look into his eyes. They burn into me with an intensity I can feel down to my toes. I step back, steadying myself under his unwavering gaze. My hormones are on high alert and I'm starting to feel like a one night stand is exactly what I need. This can be the new start of my life changing summer. With the alcohol still clouding my judgment, I grab his hand without hesitation and pull him through the throngs of people on the dance floor before I have time to sober up and bolt in the other direction.

I barely stop as I pass Noelle on the way out. A confused look flashes across her face until she sees the man I am pulling behind me.

Giving me the best friend nod of approval she motions with her fingers to text or call her and then turns back to the man who practically has his hands up her skirt.

~~

Walker's hotel is adjacent to the bar and I'm thrilled that I don't have to walk too far in my wedge heels. Now he is the one who is taking the lead, pulling me through the lobby.

As soon as we enter the elevator he pins me into the corner bringing my hands above my head with a growl.

"You sure about this?" He asks. "I can't be held accountable for my actions if you let me get you into my room, but I promise it will be a night you won't ever forget."

My chest rises and falls rapidly as I nod how sure I am. He swiftly crashes his mouth onto mine, softly biting my lower lip. An embarrassing whimper escapes me as his tongue invades my mouth, first slow and then becoming more aggressive, and greedy. The ding interrupts, letting us know we've reached his floor and he sweeps me off my sore feet and carries me into the hallway, never letting our lips part. My back meets the door and with the swipe of his key card it flies open, propelling us into the darkened room.

"So, your ex fucked around on you because

you weren't willing in the bedroom, huh? Let's see how true that is," he says while I nod my consent. I have never let a man talk to me like Walker is, but his voice is so seductive I don't even care.

He throws me down onto the bed on my back, first going to work on my sandals. Slowly unclasping the right one he caresses my foot before bringing his lips to the arch and licking it. Then I find myself bowing off the bed as he takes my toes into his mouth. It's erotic and like nothing I've ever felt before. After repeating the same on the left one he has me breathing heavily and yearning for more.

"Walker," I call out, barely a whisper.

He reaches back and pulls his shirt over his head gracing me with his abs of steel. I want to stare at him so I don't forget an inch of his beautiful body, but he comes towards me, his naked torso covering mine as he climbs onto the bed forcing me to move backwards until I meet the headboard. The muscles in his biceps flex as he grabs my ankles and pulls me hungrily underneath him. My thighs tingle where his hands graze my body, from the bend in my knee up to my core. He then moves to my hips gripping the edges of my lace panties. His emerald eyes look to mine for confirmation that I still want this. I don't think I have ever wanted anything so much in my life. I dig my heels into the bed lifting my backside and giving him the go ahead to slip my panties off.

He pulls down gently and the feel of silk combined with his body heat sets me on fire.

In a matter of seconds my panties disappear into the darkness of the room followed by my dress. Without warning his head is between my thighs making me scream out in unexpected pleasure. The combination of tequila and Jack Daniels are bringing noises and words out of me that I will be red faced about in the morning, except I hope to never see him again. He switches from sucking on my clit to sliding his tongue effortlessly up and down through my folds. My hands, having a mind of their own, delve into his brown hair that less than an hour ago I had dreamed of pulling on.

"You taste so damn sweet. I could feast on you all night," he says while swirling his tongue around me as if I were a goddamn ice cream cone.

The hot pressure is pooling between my legs, drawing my breath out in gasps. Grabbing his hair tighter I'm teetering on the edge and shamelessly rubbing myself against his mouth. When his tongue slips inside of me I lose all control, screaming out his name in pleasure. Waves of bliss take over my body as he deftly continues his assault.

"That was so fucking sexy," he whispers as he places gentle kisses up my body. I can feel his jean clad hard on against the continual throbbing between my thighs.

In my drunken euphoric state I'm motionless. His lips circle my right breast biting at the nipple, giving me pain that teeters on pleasure. My chest rises up to push further into his mouth. When he releases me he lightly blows over my incredibly hard nipple and I cry out when he clenches down on my left. I can't take it anymore. My body is greedy for more.

"Fuck me, Walker!" I shout through clenched teeth.

Holy crap! Did I just say that out loud?

Bringing my arm up to cover my eyes in embarrassment I turn to pull away.

"Don't hide those pretty eyes, baby," he whispers in my ear. My tiny arms are no match for his strength and he pulls them off my face and sweetly pushes a renegade strand of hair behind my ear. "You are so beautiful. Let me help you forget."

I don't say a word. I just stare at this man, who I barely know, and will probably never see again after tonight, who wants to help rid me of my memories of Robert. And I'm willing to let him. If Robert can have meaningless, no love sex, so can I.

"Ok. Make me forget," I relent. With my resolve stronger than ever I surrender to what my body so desperately wants. Forget the cheating. Forget the betrayal. Forget who I am... even if just for tonight. I feel myself letting go, letting Walker's expert ministrations take away all my thoughts. All I can do is feel.

"Turn over," he commands and I immediately comply. The anticipation of what he is going to do next has my body tingling.

My stomach pressed onto the crisp white hotel sheets, I can feel heat scorching from his body into mine as his moist lips find my lower back. His hands explore my sides and grip tight making me squirm. His mouth moves lower. I can't breathe. I'm so turned on that if he even grazes my core I will explode again. His tongue finds my backside, licking along my cheeks and nibbling in between. I find it erotic.

"Please," I beg. I cannot believe I've resorted to begging, but I'm wound up again and ready for release and for him to end this sweet torment. His presence is all consuming, filling up my senses, and putting my body in overdrive.

"What do you want, baby? You want me to touch this?" He asks bringing his hand around to the front. Lifting up I give him the access he needs to slip his fingers along my swollen clit.

"Yes! Oh, God yes!" The scream that fills his room can't possibly be mine.

"Jesus, you are so wet," he practically

shouts into my ear.

He circles his fingers around my sensitive core holding another orgasm hostage. I can tell he is teasing me and I try to push onto his fingers, eager for release.

"Oh Sally. You won't come again until I am balls deep inside you. Do you understand?" His harsh tone coming from next to my ear and then his body lifts off me.

I'm naked, face down, in a strange hotel room, half way to my second orgasm of the night with a man I barely know. Within seconds he has returned to my back, but now I feel his arousal at my entrance teasing and taunting as his knees spread my thighs apart. Had he gotten rid of his pants that fast?

His lips are back by my ear, whispering. "I didn't go to the bar tonight expecting this, but I'm so fucking glad it's happening. You think my tongue and fingers can make you feel good? Wait until I get inside you. I'll make you want to be more adventurous."

Anger consumes me as the words leave his mouth, seemingly mocking. Robert made me feel worthless in the bedroom, but that ends tonight. I will never see Walker again, so what does it matter how I act?

I aggressively prop myself up on my knees and he has no choice but to do the same. I turn around letting liquid courage take over and push him so that he is now the one flat on his back. I'm in charge. I give him the same amount of notice he afforded me earlier, trailing my eyes down across his tanned abs, taking in the sharp V below his hip bones to his dick. He is much larger than Robert was, and I wonder how it will feel to have him inside me. I return my eyes to his and slowly, holding his gaze the entire time, I wrap my mouth around him.

"Damn it!" Strong hands grip my hair and, if possible, he gets harder when his tip meets the back of my throat. My naughty girl side coming out, I roll my thumbs over his balls again and again making him beg. "Don't fucking stop."

But I do, and tease him with his own words. "You won't be coming until you are balls deep inside of me either, big boy."

I give him a saucy smirk and when his eyes meet mine the sexual tension explodes. Sitting straight up, he grabs me at my waist pulling me on top of him. Reaching over he grabs a condom from the table and rolls it over himself. Straddling his hips, I move up until I'm lingering just above his rock hard member. He's in for a ride. Literally.

I push down slowly allowing the tip to gain entry. Even this much feels amazing and I resist the urge to take him in fully, teasing him

with just that small taste of me and then
pulling back up. He loses all control. Fingertips
dig into my hips and he slams my body down
on him. We both cry out in pleasure as he fills
me completely. I have to take a second, my
breaths coming in erratically. I am not used to
the massiveness that now has my insides
throbbing. Robert never stretched me out this
much. It feels amazing. *What have I been
missing?*

    Once I catch my breath and adjust to the
fullness inside of me, I slide my body forward
letting my breasts graze over his face. His
hands come up and squeeze my nipples while
he brings his face between them, slowly licking
up and down like he is savoring every moment.
I sit back and a shot of pleasure courses
through my body. I race to feel it again and
again.

    Over and over I rock my body into his,
yelling out things that don't normally come out
of my mouth. I have never felt pleasure like this
before and I know he is ruining me for anyone
else.

    "Let go, baby. Use me. Forget all about
him," he says from beneath me bringing his
thumb just above where our bodies meet,
circling my most sensitive nub, and setting off
every nerve ending in my body.

    The sensation has me feeling so
uninhibited and I am rocking back and forth so

violently that my head is spinning. I run my hands along my stomach and up to my nipples rolling them between my thumb and pointer finger. I'm spiraling out of control and I want to take him down with me. "Oh God!" I scream out as the orgasm begins to tease me, encouraging me to ride harder.

"Faster. Let that sweet pussy come for me. FASTER!"

His command has me grinding harder onto his dick. It's like two logs rubbing together trying to start a fire. I see the spark and then all of the sudden it ignites inside me and soon a shower of flames is raining down around me.

My screams of pleasure are loud enough to wake the neighbors but I don't care. I'm free and I'm forgetting. Leaning back I ride the waves of ecstasy as he comes with a growling "FUCK!" and falls back onto the sheets.

"Holy shit, that was incredible," I say breathlessly, laying my head on his smooth chest.

"In-fucking-credible," he whispers.

UNEXPECTED

4

My eyes squint as the sunlight beams through the windows and onto my eyelids. Turning my head away from the intrusion, a sharp pain radiates through my skull. *How much did I drink?* With a moan I lift my body off my stomach and take in my surroundings. I'm in a hotel room, alone. Last night's events go from hazy to crystal clear within seconds.

Tripping over the sheets, I scramble off the bed frantically searching for my clothes. A scrap of black catches my attention and I grab my dress and panties. Just as I'm about to slip into the safety of the bathroom, the door to the room opens and hungry green eyes linger over my completely nude body. I try to cover up what I can.

"Oh, sweet girl. I saw it all last night," he

says, throwing his key card and wallet down on the desk and raising up two white bags in his other hand. "Breakfast?"

"Uhm, no?" *Was that question?* "I, ah. I need to get going. I have a...meeting...with a client. I'm an interior designer. So, you see. I have to go. Yea." I rush into the bathroom, locking the door and sliding down to the floor.

What the hell did I do? I wanted to be free. I wanted to forget and look what I've done. I screwed a guy whose name I can't remember and I probably look like a complete child running away, and lying...again.

Getting up off the floor, I use the toilet, throw my dress and underwear back on, and wash off what I can of last night's make up.

After 10 more minutes of grabbing the door knob and then chickening out, I finally take a deep breath and open it up. *I can do this.*

"Hey. You ok?" He calls from his seat on the bed, lazily leaning back on his elbows. His body language showing he is clearly fine with the fact that I'm about to do the walk of shame.

"I'm cool." *Cool? Really? I'm so lame.* "Ok, so I'm just going to head out. Nice to meet you..." my voice trails off. *Damn, what IS his name!*

"Walker," he reminds me, a slow smirk spreading across his face revealing that one sided dimple that I still find myself wanting to lick. "I would think with how many times you screamed my name last night you would remember, Sally."

I am never drinking again. Grabbing my shoes from the foot of the bed, I try not to get too close to him. "Yes, Walker. Well thanks, for everything." I turn and walk to the door.

In a flash he rolls himself up to stand and stalks towards me before I can get the door open, towering over me and pinning me against the wall with his stare. I am forced to look up to meet his eyes. Goosebumps spread over my skin as his hand skims up my arm and gently cups my cheek. My eyes close feeling his face close to mine. Thoughts of how amazing last night was have me panting and wanting him all over again. His breath is hot and just millimeters from my mouth. I close the distance, raising my chin to find his lips.

This kiss is unlike last nights. It is slow, and sensual, making me rethink my exit. Both of his hands now hold my head firmly, thumbs on my cheeks, pulling me deeper into him. His tongue breaks the barrier of my lips. The sweet taste of sugar invades my mouth making me hungry for more, but he unexpectedly stops. Deep green irises greet mine when my eye lids flutter open.

"Your ex is stupid, you know? You're so beautiful, and sexy. Give me your number." His authoritative tone almost has me giving in. I didn't plan on a one night stand but it happened and it needs to be left at just one night.

"No." I slowly unwind my traitorous arms from around his neck and pull his hands away from my face bending down to retrieve the shoes I didn't realize I dropped.

"Well let me give you my number. That way if you change your mind, you can call me." Walking over to the table he retrieves a pen but I'm already opening the door.

"No. I'm sorry. I needed last night, and it was amazing, but I just got out of a relationship. I don't think starting up something new is a good idea right now."

I push the door open more and see his unsure eyes watch me go. He is so hot. As my feet lure me towards the elevator I assure myself that I will regret not getting his number.

~~

The lobby of the hotel is quiet and lonely. The front desk clerk hardly acknowledges me as my bare feet walk across the washed out green carpet. I know she is silently judging me in my wrinkled dress and messy hair. As I plunk down into a chair by the coffee station I wish I brought a hair tie or at least a brush. I called Noelle from the elevator and told her where to come get me. I hold her responsible for all of this. She fed me my first couple of drinks and after that the others were more than welcome. I didn't have to drink them, but who am I kidding, being wound up I needed to let go. The last few weeks I have been walking around feeling sorry for myself. Letting out a small aggravated breath I think about how much I don't want Robert's cheating on me, with a married woman no less, to define me. It will hurt for a while. The knife to my heart came when he said that I was uninteresting in bed. Making love was the most sacred thing to me. I gave all of myself to him and let myself be exposed. I trusted Robert and if there was a problem he should have talked to me, told me how he felt or showed me what he wanted. After last night I know that I would have enjoyed all that with him. It's not that our sex life was so vanilla but there was never any raw passion. Maybe you just can't talk that one out.

Leaving Walker's room I thought I would regret last night but the more I am left to my own mind the more I realize I won't. He promised me I would never forget it and he sure as hell is right. I never felt so sexy in my life. My body rising and falling on top of his made me feel like a woman in control and not someone who lets others make decisions for her. I've spent most of my 20s letting another person dictate where I can go, what I can do and who I can and should hang out with. He may not have realized it, but Walker showed me I can make my own choices. Even if that choice was to ride him like a cowgirl.

My back straightens when I think I've made a mistake. Maybe I should have some fun with him and screw the entire "wait until you are in love" nonsense, because that is what it is. Nonsense. As I'm about to jump up and go back to his room I remember where I am. A hotel. He must not be from around here. I don't see the point in having meaningless sex with someone over and over if they are just going to leave. Knowing me I would fall in love with him and be heartbroken all over again. No thank you. A new and improved Erin is on the way and another man letting me down is not in my future.

"Let's go slutbag! I've been waiting for five minutes at the curb." Noelle's raspy voice echoes in the lobby.

"Oh my God, shut up!" I whisper-yell, standing up, directing her attention to the clerk giving us a death glare.

"He must have been huge, Erin. You're walking funny," she calls out, louder this time.

A small chuckle escapes from behind the desk and my mouth drops open. Leave it to Noelle to completely humiliate me. As if that wasn't mortifying enough she rubs my head like a dog and says, "Awe, my little Er-Bear is growing up. Your first one night stand. After years of dating a douche you finally get your vagina some real action."

Walking out into the warm June air after I lovingly push her out of the hotel we jump into her waiting SUV and drive away from the most awkward morning ever.

"What exactly is a slut bag?" I ask Noelle while slipping my seatbelt on.

Looking over from the driver's side she glares at me as though I should know. "A bag full of slut, which is what you are, although I strongly support it. So, how was it? That man looked like he could rock your world multiple times."

Staring at her in disbelief I plead the fifth. As close as we are I've never been the kind of woman to talk about sex, even with her. Besides my mother teaching me to wait until I was in love, she also taught me to keep my private life, well, private. There was no way I was going to tell her about last night, though I wanted to scream from the rooftops how amazing it was. He showed me how a real man can make me feel and what he can do.

Robert rarely, if ever, went down on me. Walker's tongue had been like lightening, crashing into me and shooting electricity through my body, awakening feelings in me that I never knew existed. He had almost come apart in my mouth too, which surprised me since every time I tried to give Robert oral he would chastise me, saying I was doing it all wrong. I loved the feeling of wielding that much power over a man, and Walker had appeared content to let me be in charge. I'm starting to think that maybe I was never in love with Robert. He was safe, comfortable, and trustworthy, or so I had thought. Walker seemed dangerous, and mysterious, but I still felt more of a connection with him than I ever had with Robert. I just don't know if I could ever let down my guard enough to give all of myself to a man again.

"You're not going to give me anything Erin?" Noelle's voice brings me out of my thoughts. I shake my head side to side as she blows out a puff of air. "Ok then. Well you can be enlightened by hearing about my fuck fest with Zack last night. Let me tell you, if I thought you were walking funny you should be surprised I can stand. That man's dick was…"

"STOP! Oh my God stop!" I interrupt her, placing my hand over her mouth as my ringtone fills the car. Saved by my big sister.

"Hey Nic," I say rolling my eyes at Noelle as I pick up.

"Erin! You need to call mom. She is freaking out saying you haven't returned her phone calls in two weeks. What's going on?" She yells over my nieces and nephews shrieking in the background.

Leave it to my mom to send Nicole after me. Avoiding Eden Decker has been quite a task. I'm not ready to tell her that I won't be walking down the aisle anytime soon or immediately popping out grandkids. How do you explain to your mother that the man you gave your heart to for the past five years, the one that she had treated like her own son since his parents passed, the one who sent her flowers on Mother's Day and her Birthday every year, put her daughters heart into a shredder?

"I'll call her tomorrow. I just can't today, alright?" I close my eyes thinking how hard that conversation will be.

"Not alright. What the hell is wrong with you? You know how it's been since dad died. She needs to hear from us and know that we are doing ok. Now, tell me. Why haven't you called her, or me, for that matter? We usually talk almost every day," her motherly tone is evident through the phone.

Blowing out a deep breath I prepare to tell her about the epic failure of my relationship.

"Robert and I broke up, ok? I caught him in the middle of having sex with his secretary the day school got out. He told me I was a lame lay and that he wasn't ready for marriage," my voice cracks at the last word as I finally realize how angry I am.

Noelle puts her free arm around me as my body shakes with frustrated sobs. I don't speak anymore when Nicole tries to comfort me. After a few more minutes of our one sided conversation we pull into our driveway and I finally promise to call her and my mom back later.

"I'm fine, Noe. I promise. The whole situation just sucks."

"It will be ok, Erin. I promise. I really and truly believe everything happens for a reason. Maybe you can't see it right now, but there is a reason. You are meant for love that is extraordinary and you will have it. You deserve to have that and I know something big is coming your way. I can just feel it."

As per the rules of operation Big Girl Panties, or BGP as Noelle likes to call it, I had started taking care of myself not only mentally, but physically. Mentally, I needed to clear the air and do the one thing that I should have done in the first place: talk with my mom about what occurred between Robert and me. It went a lot better than I could've expected. I'm sure talking about my sex life made her uncomfortable but she never seemed as though it was too much to hear. She listened to all the details and apologized for always pushing my relationship with him to go to the next level. She even said she hoped that my lack of communication after the incident wasn't because of her insistence on us getting married. Out of the three women I confided in, she was the one who gave me the clarity I had desperately needed. I should have gone to her first.

"Lots of people come into your life, Erin," she had said. "Some for good, some for bad but all for one purpose; to send you in the direction you are supposed to go. Robert was there for his purpose and though his exit from your life wasn't ideal, his presence was necessary. Soon you will figure out why."

That was something I wasn't too concerned with just yet.

I have the mental part under control now, but physically, Noelle is ruling that transformation. For three weeks now she has been dragging me to the gym every other day. I'm not over weight by any means but I am not toned either. Every class has made me feel stronger and the more I go, the more I realize that getting fit is part of my healing process. There is something about working out that sets your mind straight and makes you happy, and I was starting to smile more and more.

"My vagina hurts," I whisper over to her in the middle of spin class. "It feels like it's taken a good pounding!"

"Your vagina needs a good pounding. Since big man Walker, you haven't given it the attention it needs, unless you've been taking a spin with the vibrator," she yells just as the music is changing to a new song.

Every set of eyes zero in on me as my face turns a brilliant shade of red. Noelle giggles and the next song comes on cueing them to pay attention to the instructor again.

"Thanks Noelle."

"Thank me after your newly toned body is donning that sexy black bikini in Mexico next week." She wiggles her eyebrows up and down making me flush again. I don't think my body is built for a bikini but I bought one just for the trip. Operation BGP obviously needed a new bathing suit, or so I was told.

The temperature has steadily risen in the few weeks since the night I went out to the bar with Noelle and I was ready for a trip to crystal clear blue waters. Winters around Chicago can be brutal but the summers are just as bad with temperatures above a hundred. We have beaches around Lake Michigan and they are great for tanning, but when that sun is beating down on you and your only option is to jump in the murky water, you look for another source of relief, or swim at your own risk.

My relief was coming in 8 days. Beautiful scenery, relaxation, a pool, sandy beaches and an umbrella drink were within my reach. I can almost taste that strawberry margarita right now. This trip is going to be something I will never forget.

~~

The hot Mexican sun beats down on us as we arrive at the Occidental Grand Cozumel. When we step out of the taxi we are greeted with brilliant yellows, blues and greens in the open air lobby. After checking in, we head to our room and slip into our bathing suits and flip-flops.

Agreeing we need a drink first we head to the poolside bar. We pass couples, families and hotel workers on the long wooden bridge, with beautiful landscaping, leading to our destination. Drinks in hand we find a cabana on the white sand next to the crystal clear ocean.

"This is amazing Erin. I'm so glad you came," Noelle says lifting her piña colada to my strawberry margarita.

"Thanks for forcing me to go. I really needed this." I clink my glass to hers and take a sip looking out to the endless miles of water. I can't believe I was originally planning to miss out on all this.

Hours later, after we dined at one of the many restaurants they have to offer, we are dressed up in our sexiest outfits ready to check out the onsite dance club...or as they call it, the Disco.

It's small and holds just one bar but the music is lively. Since I've had a few drinks I am ready to dance and have a good time. Noelle and I start towards the dance floor, fresh drinks in hand, pushing our way past the many couples. Staying at an all-inclusive resort means lots of newlyweds and not a lot of single men, but we don't care. We just want to enjoy the time away from our stresses.

They play a lot of songs that I hear back home and when Usher's *Yeah* comes on I find my rhythm and close my eyes, enjoying the beat. Large hands grasp my hips and I have a flash back of Walker. Thinking back to our encounter on the dance floor, I am turned on and hoping to find his emerald eyes staring back at me when I open mine. I'm instantly disappointed. To say he is older would be an understatement. With white hair, blue eyes and large framed glasses he is probably 65 or 70. A denture smile breaks out across his face and I try my hardest not to laugh. Not wanting to be rude I oblige him with a dance, but once the song is over I excuse myself to the bathroom and take off towards the bar, desperate for another drink.

A hysterically laughing Noelle beats me there, ordering for both of us. "Did you have fun, Er?"

"Stop it. He was sweet, and think of it this way: he can go tell all his friends at the senior home that he danced with a hot piece of ass!" I giggle but bend at the waist as a sharp pain invades my stomach. "Noe, I think we should go. I don't feel so good."

"Oh, come on Erin. He won't bother you again. You don't have to make an excuse to leave."

Another sharp pain hits me and I take off towards the door and practically run to our room with Noelle right behind me. I make it to the bathroom just in time to empty the contents of my stomach into the toilet.

"Jesus Christ, Erin! Are you ok?" Noelle asks with concern in her voice.

"I'm gonna die!" I say between dry heaves. "I shouldn't have eaten that shrimp. I knew it looked sketchy."

It's only been 12 hours on our trip and my body decides to reject the first and only solid thing I have eaten. My stomach tightens and with only the lining it left to puke up I start crying.

"Oh, baby. It's ok. It'll be over soon," Noelle soothes. "It's probably just food poisoning. Let me help you into the shower." She tries to comfort me by rubbing my back and pulling my hair to the side.

I allow her to help me up and strip me down the moment I feel the nausea has passed and she throws me into a hot shower as she sits on the edge of the sink. The steam helps me to breathe right again and I drop my head so that the water cascades down my back. It feels heavenly on my body after I just went through thirty minutes of hell.

"You ok in there?" She asks and I grunt a yes. "Good. I know you hate throwing up. Just imagine when you finally meet prince charming and get pregnant. My cousin had morning sickness throughout her entire pregnancy. She couldn't eat a damn thing."

As her words seep into my foggy brain, I snap my head up trying to do the math. *Come on Erin, you're a math teacher for Christ's sake.* Hastily I jump out of the shower to go locate my phone inside my purse. What feels like arctic temperatures meet my heated body on the other side of the bathroom door.

"What the hell are you doing?" Noelle's shocked voice yells at my bare form racing past her.

My mind is whirling at the thought that I messed up. *It can't be. It's just not possible.* Putting in my security code and tapping on the app, one look at my phone's calendar tells me it is. Drops of water drip from my hair and fall onto my phone as reality comes crashing down. They begin to mingle with my tears as I look at Noelle's confused expression.

"You need to sit down, Erin. You just threw up all of that retched food and ran out of the shower like the room was on fire." She retreats back into the bathroom.

"Oh my God," I say, barely audible.

"What Erin? What's 'Oh my God'?" Bringing a towel in from the bathroom she makes her way back to me sounding annoyed.

"Oh my God!" I say, much louder this time. Dropping the phone onto the floor I can't take my eyes off of Noelle. "I'm two weeks late, Noe. TWO WEEKS!"

Her face falls when she finally realizes what I am saying.

"What? No. Erin, NO! That cheating, lying, ignorant asshole knocked you up?" She rushes to me with the towel, wrapping it around my body and hugging me as I crumble to the floor.

Thoughts race through my mind quicker than I can process them. Remembering back to the day after school was out; I come to the stark realization that it can't be Robert's baby. "No, not him. Walker, the guy from the club. It's Walker's."

6

Although physically I was present for the rest of our vacation, my mind was in a different place. The first few days after I found out I was late were filled with trips to the store buying test after test, but I'd spent the last few watching Noelle drink enough for the two of us as I sat by the pool trying to figure out what to do next.

Searching my memory of that night I try to recollect if he used protection or not. Of course, it won't do me any good. What's done is done and a life has been created. Daydreaming about the way his hands felt on my body isn't helping me see clearly either. The way he instantly transformed me into an outgoing lover, encouraging me to take control. How my body felt on top of him. I lick my lips and squirm in my chair just thinking about how he felt moving underneath me.... moving inside me. I find myself wishing, for more reason than one, that I could see him again.

    The entire plane ride back to Illinois I am silent. Home will bring a reality that I don't think I am prepared to face. Noelle knows I need to get it together before we touch down. I am having a hard time believing that I left the state single and carefree and now I am coming back pregnant, with a man's child whose last name I don't even know, and the dreaded task of telling my family. Though I'm thankful the baby isn't Robert's, it would be easier to deal with than admitting to everyone I had a one night stand with someone I can't seem to contact. It's not for lack of trying. My numerous calls from Mexico to the hotel he was staying at were met with dead ends in light of the fact that they refused to give out guest information. The bar manager tried to help, even though he warned it was illegal to give out personal info of customers, but he still found no credit card receipts with the first name Walker. I just needed his last name and maybe I could track him down. Noelle and I even went as far as using the business center's computer to scour Facebook for hours in search of any guy named Walker that was residing in Illinois, if that is even where he is from.

    Dropping my bag at the front door, and earning a huff from Noelle, I race to the bathroom to take the test I forced her to stop at the drug store for. I know it won't change the result, and that thinking maybe an international pregnancy test could be wrong is dense, but for my sanity, I have to do it anyway. Three tense minutes later my heart sinks again as two lines pop up and I'm left slumped down on the floor with thoughts of single parenthood racing through my mind. When my cell rings I crawl over to the vanity, reaching up not caring to see who it is.

Before I can finish saying hello my mother's cheerful tone fills my ears. "Erin! You're home! I'm so happy to hear your voice. How was your trip? Was it fun? You'll have to tell me all about it when you come over tonight. Even Trent and Jason are coming over."

Crap! Dragging my hands down my face I realize I forgot about going over there for dinner tonight. With my family's busy lives, it's hard to get us all nailed down to one gathering. Knowing there isn't a chance in hell I can cancel on her, I reassure her I would see them all tonight and share all the beautiful details of the trip along with pictures. It's going to be tough to keep the baby a secret until I see a doctor. As if the 10 pregnancy tests weren't verification enough the doctor's tests should do it.

Hoping to cleanse away the awful mood I am in so I don't alarm anyone, I take a warm bath closing my eyes and letting my body relax. Washing with pear scented body scrub, I stop when my hands come to rest on my stomach, tears break through the barrier of my lids. To my surprise I speak to my little one for the first time. "We'll be ok. We'll make it through. I promise." And I know we will.

~~

    My mom lives in Buffalo Grove, a city in the northwest suburbs of Chicago, in the same house I was brought home to when I was born. The 3 bedroom ranch house sits in a quiet middle class neighborhood. The beautiful park diagonally across the street brings back memories of countless carefree childhood days, long lost and of running around the lake in high school. The driveway is full with my sibling's cars, forcing me to park on the street and walk up the sidewalk. Over the past year every time I walk up the three steps leading to the door I am saddened that my father isn't behind the glass with his megawatt smile and welcoming kiss to the cheek. Instead I'm cheerfully greeted by my 6 foot 2 brother and his mini me.

    "Erin, nice of you to finally join us," Trent says wrapping me in a hug. One year old Jason takes the opportunity to latch onto my hair and pull himself into my arms.

    "Hey Trent! And how is my handsome fella?" I ask when Jason grabs me around my neck making a face at the taste of my hair.

Screams of my name explode in the house when my sister's kids come barreling down the hall, knocking me down and pinning me to the floor.

"Auntie Erin!" My 7 year old niece Marie excitedly yells into my ear. "Guess what! Nick threw up all over mommy and she said 'shit'."

"Marie! Don't say 'shit'," Nicole scolds from the kitchen. Giggling I pull all the kids off me, give them each their own bear hug and send them back to the basement to play.

The short walk from the front entrance to the kitchen is filled with pictures of all three of us as kids growing up and now yearly pictures of all five, soon to be six, grandkids. A hint of a smile breaks out when I think about having my little bean's picture up there soon. The unexpected notion shocks me.

The moment my foot hits the kitchen threshold the smell of chicken invades my senses and a wave of queasiness comes over me. Both women twist around just in time to see me cover my mouth, and turn to run to the bathroom. I am met with a hard as stone chest when Trent grabs my arms stopping me. "Where ya goin' so fast sis?"

Fighting back the bile rising in my throat, I run around him to the bathroom, slamming the door, and barely making it to the toilet to void the four crackers I ate on the way here.

My sister's tiny fists begin to beat on the door just as the dry heaves begin. "Open the door Erin! Are you ok?"

"Go away!" I bellow, trying to catch my breath.

The door flies open anyway, and Nicole, who looks to be just an older version of myself, bends down feeling my forehead. "Are you sick? You don't feel warm."

"What's going on?" I hear my mother's anxious voice say from behind us.

"Nothing. Just give me a minute, please." Reaching for some toilet paper, I wipe the excess saltines away.

Everyone clears out of the bathroom and the looks on their faces tell me they don't believe that it's nothing. They shouldn't. I don't think I'll be able to hide it any longer since there is no way I can eat that chicken, or even be anywhere near the smell.

I splash some water on my face and swish some in my mouth hoping to get the wretched smell off my breath and pull my hair back into a pony tail. As I open the door, ready to try and lie to everyone, my mom is standing there crying.

"You're pregnant," she surmises. Not able to say it to her out loud I just nod, giving her the opportunity to continue. "What does this mean for you and Robert? You aren't going to take him back after what he did, are you?" She asks quietly looking around to make sure no one can hear us.

"It doesn't mean anything, mom. There is no reason to get him involved." Nerves begin to shake my body knowing I'm going to have to tell her what I did, and soon. I was hoping to break it to her after I figure out the best way how. But I guess there is no time like the present.

"What do you mean, Erin? Are you not going to tell him?" Alarm is evident from her expression.

"There isn't a need to." I can't figure out why I'm stalling. Air whooshes out of my lungs pushing the truth out just as fast. "The baby isn't Robert's mom." My eyes stare at the floor, no longer able to look at her puzzled expression any longer.

"I'm not sure I understand baby."

Lifting my head back up, I take another deep breath. "About six weeks ago Noelle and I went out to a bar. I just wanted to forget about what Robert did and I met a guy named Walker there. We slept together. I know it was wrong, and you always say to love the person you give yourself to, but I wasn't thinking, Mom. I just wanted to let go and forget myself for just one night. That's all. Just one night."

"Erin, baby, I would never judge you. Lord knows I had my fair share of indiscretions before I met your father." The warmth of her arms surrounds me in the narrow hallway. "So, have you told this, this Walker? What did he say?"

This is it; the point where the judgment comes in and disappointment takes over. "No, I haven't told him. I can't. I don't know his last name or even have his phone number. We went back to his hotel and I left the next morning. I'm sure he is from out of town and I've tried searching, but I can't find him. And even if he wanted to come and find me I didn't give him my real name."

A sad look flashes across her face which turns to what I can only assume is understanding. "You had a one night stand?" She asks and I nod my head yes.

"Oh, baby. That's kind of a rite of passage. I too fell for a sexy, no strings attached, night of passion. Mine just turned into a sexy, spend your life with me, night of passion."

"Mom please tell me you aren't talking about my father." I shake my head completely mortified at where this is going.

"Yes, actually. He was the one night stand that never went away. I was looking to have a good time and I was so good," she winks at me, "that he came back for more."

"I can't believe Daddy was a one night stand!" I say, covering my eyes.

"What's a one night stand?" A sweet little voice, belonging to my nephew Jack, asks. "I want one? Mama, I want a one night stand!" He yells all the way down to the kitchen.

"Mom, what about all that advice about waiting to be in love and finding someone special?" I call her out.

"What was I supposed to tell you Erin? 'Go out, have meaningless sex and you too could find your soul mate'?" She laughs.

My mom and I start a fit of laughter before Nicole interrupts us. "Please tell me that my son meant night stand and not ONE night stand. I'm glad Brad got called to the hospital tonight because he would have flipped his shit if Jack asked him that!"

My mother leaves Nicole and me alone and we walk into the living room taking a seat on the old green couch. Hand in hand I tell Nicole the same thing I told mom but with a little more detail. She assures me that everything will be ok and that if I need anything to let her know. Trent joins us as I start to cry again, relaying the story to him. He is the one who will be able to relate to me the most. After Jason was born, his girlfriend Alex, of four years, left him and their newborn baby boy. He hasn't seen or heard from her since, and her parents won't tell him where she went. He is a great father, amazing uncle, and one of the best and biggest shoulders to lean on. I'm lucky to have them in my life.

Conversation over and stomach settled we stand to go check on the kids when Marie walks in holding Jason up. "Uncle Trent. Jason shit himself."

"MARIE!" We all scream in unison, making Jason cry.

"It's a crazy life Erin, but I wouldn't trade it for the world." Trent says, patting me on the shoulder, and taking his son from our niece. "Let's go freshen you up little man."

Watching him walk away with a smiling Jason, hope fills my heart thinking that someone in my future will accept me and my little one. I only hope they are at least half the father Trent and Brad are. If I never find that, at least I know there are some amazing men in my life that will gladly step up and be role models.

"Let's hope it's a boy Erin," Nicole states, rubbing her hands over my flat stomach.

"Why?"

"You know what they say. With a girl you have to worry about all the dicks, but when you have a boy you worry about just one." She winks and walks away.

7

The beds of my nails are in shambles. I continue to bite at them, anxiously waiting in the pristine lobby of Dr. Gale's practice.

"Erin Decker." The overly keyed up nurse calls from the open doorway leading to the exam rooms.

Picking up my purse, I stroll towards her, nervous about going from a gynecological patient to an obstetric one. The long hallway is filled with nurses and doctors going in and out of rooms. A baby cries inside the first room to the right, raising my panic up a notch. What if I can't calm my child down? Swallowing the bile rising up in my throat I quietly follow the nurse to exam room four.

After a short greeting she takes my vitals,

weight, collects a urine sample, and then follows up with countless questions about why I think I'm pregnant. At this point I am three weeks late and eleven pregnancy tests sure. I don't think I'm pregnant. I know.

"Dr. Gale will be with you in a few minutes. Just slip on the robe and climb up onto the table when you are finished." The door closes behind her, leaving me alone in the cold room. Looking around, I spot the robe next to the chair and walk to the changing area they have secured behind a curtain.

With my clothes folded up nicely and ass firmly on the bed, hands folded, yet fidgety, I am tortured by the sound of every tick from the clock on the wall. Impatience turns to annoyance, which turns to rage when 15 minutes turns into 45. When I feel I cannot take another minute in this room a hard knock comes on the door, instantly relaxing me. *Finally!*

"Erin! So glad to have you back. I apologize for the wait. How have you been? How's your mother doing?" His glasses, which are slipping down his slanted nose, make him look ten years older than his age of fifty five. He has grayish brown hair and such blue eyes that you feel as though you are looking into the depths of the ocean. Although he is far from overweight, his protruding belly pushes at the buttons of his grey dress shirt and pulls out of his black slacks.

"My mother is doing fine, thank you. She sends her best."

Dr. Gale has been my OB/GYN since I was eighteen Even after I left for college I would always schedule my yearly visits with him. He has known me since I can remember. He and my father were close friends, and Dr. Gale has remained a calming and steady force for my mother, helping her cope with the loss of my father. Most women would choose a female gynecologist but I prefer a man. They always look at you as a patient and not some whiney girl who is complaining about something they have gone through. Don't get me wrong, some of the greats are of the female persuasion...it's just not my cup of tea. His warm demeanor and professional attitude have comforted me in some of the most uncomfortable positions. He was also the shoulder I cried on when I miscarried with Robert's and my baby. I was alone that day too. Robert was starting his internship at a big firm and apparently couldn't miss the first day.

Remembering the events makes me feel like the walls are closing in. Protectively I place my hands on my abdomen. Even though I am scared to death, I don't want to lose this baby too.

Dr. Gale can sense my unease, and places a comforting hand on my shoulder. "I understand you think you might be carrying a little person?"

There's that "think" word again. "Yes, I took a million tests Dr. Gale. I'm pretty sure I am." A nervous laugh slips from my mouth even though I hardly think anything about this is humorous.

Opening my chart with a "hmm" and an "ah" he begins. "Well I'm happy to be the first to say congrats! Your urine test came back positive and based on your last menstrual cycle you look to have a due date of March 4th. Would you like to take a look? You'll get to see your little miracle and we can make sure everything is running smoothly."

I am left speechless, unable to answer his question. It's one thing to have a stick tell you you're pregnant but now it's confirmed, and very real.

"Erin?" His question tugs me from my thoughts.

"Yes, I'm sorry. I'd like to see," I state, wishing someone was here to witness this with me. I didn't tell my mother about the appointment and Noelle couldn't miss a work meeting this morning.

"Alright, well let's get it set up for you, shall we? Is Robert in the waiting room? I can have the nurse go get him so he can see as well." He places his hand back on my shoulder.

"Uhm, no. Robert isn't here. This baby isn't

his." Looking down at my hands I let out a sigh. "And the father, well, he won't be here either."

"Oh, I understand. Well, Erin you are a strong independent woman who is going to thrive as a mother. I'm sure of it. I'll be right back." His voice cuts off when the door slams shut behind him.

The same nurse from before, who I now know as Carla, returns to the room, as does the doctor, with the internal ultrasound machine. They inform me that the baby is still too small to see using the external ultrasound. Placing my legs in the stirrups he warns of the pressure before pushing the long wand inside me. I didn't need the warning, having done this once before, but that time it didn't end well.

In an instant the black screen fills with the image of what looks to be the shape of a lima bean.

"There he or she is." Dr. Gale's heavy tone shakes me out of my reoccurring trance.

My hand involuntarily comes up to my mouth in shock. "That's my baby?" I ask, fascinated.

"Yup, that's it. And see the little flicker in the middle? Usually it's too early to see but that is your baby's heartbeat. A strong one at that."

That's what was missing when I lost Robert's and my baby. The heartbeat. The same image was on the screen but the flicker was noticeably absent. Seeing it now brings goose bumps to the surface of my skin. It's there. It's really there and strong. I lose all sense of control and cry, again. *Damn hormones.*

After Dr. Gale extracts the wand and washes his hands the machine next to me comes to life spitting out image after image of the little bean. Ripping it at the end he hands me 3 pictures with "Baby Decker" typed out at the top.

"Everything looks perfect Erin," he assures me. "There is no need to worry about this pregnancy. You are well on your way to having a healthy baby and I meant what I said. You are going to be just fine."

"Thank you," I say, and try to smile as the nurse hands me tissues to clean up my face.

"I'll write up a prescription for prenatal vitamins and a print out of what you can and can't do now that you have precious cargo in your tummy. Some important things to remember though, are no drinking, no smoking and no drugs, and remember Erin; you can always call me even if you think what you are concerned about is nothing."

After I agree to follow his instructions both of them leave me to change, but I am held captive by the pictures in my hand. My hormones take control, creating more tears that I can't manage to stem, and they free fall down my cheeks. Grabbing more tissue to wipe them away is pointless. They won't stop.

This thing, this little person inside me, is going to change my world and nothing will ever be the same again. Light breaks through the last few weeks of darkness. Night has now turned to day. My previously hazy visions are crystal clear. I, Erin Decker, am going to have a baby. I'm going to be a single parent and for the first time since I found out, that thought doesn't scare the crap out of me. This child will have more love and affection than any other child in existence. I am strong. My support system is steady and willing to stand by me.

Pushing past the glass doors out into the hot July sun I dig into my purse and pull out my phone finding that I have a missed call and a text from Noelle.

Noe: FREEDOM! Lunch after your appt?

Me: Portillo's at 12:15?

Noe: See you then, slutbag.

In the past week or so my appetite has returned and made me into a nonstop eating machine. The doctor said 25 to 30lbs was okay to gain and as of right now I am still at 130, thankfully. My mouth waters as I think of the amazing burger and French fries waiting for me. Portillo's is a staple in Chicago. It houses the juiciest burgers and Chicago style hot dogs you can imagine. The shakes are sinful and have you moaning from the first sip. *So. Freaking. Amazing!*

Noelle beats me there and already has a table for us. Lunchtime is insanely busy and they put their restaurant style food out quicker than a fast food place. To see she has already secured a spot amazes me. There have been plenty of times we've had to stand while scarfing down our food but it's so worth it.

The drop of my purse on the table barely makes a sound over the noisy patrons but it gets her attention. "Can you stop referring to me as a slut bag? I've only slept with two guys in my entire life, which is like 1/20th of the amount you have."

Her blue eyes lift from her smart phone while her fingers still type out whatever message she is sending and look up at me. "So, you are saying I slept with 40ish guys?" She asks.

"Uhm, give or take."

"I'm insulted!" She stands up quickly motioning to her svelte body covered in a sophisticated light blue dress shirt and white pencil skirt that brings out her 20's pinup figure. Her hair is pulled back into a low bun and her make-up enhances her high cheekbones. "This hot body has had way more than 40 men beg for it! At least 60."

Hysterical laughing erupts from me as one of the three business men at the table adjacent to us spits his drink out all over the food in front of him. "Now, who is the slutbag?" I laugh.

"Let's go get our food before one of them starts getting on his knees worshipping me."

The lines are long but in no time Noelle and I are back at the table, spitting men long gone. She asks me about my appointment and I tell her about all the tests, questions, my due date and that I am almost seven weeks along. The entire room goes silent when I pull out the pictures and she screams out, telling anyone in earshot, she is going to be an aunt.

"How are you feeling about all of this, Erin?" She asks as we throw away our trash and exit through the revolving doors.

Stopping just outside I look out into the midafternoon and tell her exactly how I feel. "I'm scared Noe. I'm 27, I'm single, and besides my nieces and nephews, who I can send home at any minute, I don't have the first clue on how to be a mother. What scares me the most, I mean really scares me, is that this child won't have their own father in their life. My dad played such an amazing role in my upbringing. He made me the woman I am today and I don't know if I can be both mother and father. So, I'm petrified, but besides all of that I am thrilled beyond words. The second I saw that little flicker on the screen my perspective and my world changed. That heartbeat is a little piece of Heaven residing in a tiny body. I love this baby so much already and I cannot even imagine what I am going to feel once they are here."

A single tear falls down Noelle's face. Smiling, she pulls me into a hug. "I am so proud of you. So proud. I know you are going to be a great mother and please know I am here for you." She pulls back but still holds onto my arms. "I will always be there. I can be the other parent. I'll get up in the middle of night, hold them while you shower, and hold you when times get too tough. I love you so much Erin and I'm going to love that baby just as much if not more."

"Thank you." I say bringing her back into an embrace.

"That's hot ladies, you should make out!" Some young kid from the nearby high school says from behind us. Noelle lets me go and spins around.

"Oh, yea little boy? Are we giving you a stiffy? I bet you can't wait to get home and pull out old Rosey Palm and give that small dick a few tugs since that's all the action you will probably ever get. Get a life loser."

His friends shove him through the revolving door making fun of him more and we head to our cars and say goodbye, making plans to have dinner together tonight.

Alone in my car I start to think about how things are going to be. In just under two months I will be back at school teaching. Who would have thought from the last day of school, to the upcoming first day of the new year, how much my life would change? I knew that this summer was going to be different from the moment I walked into Robert's room that day, but I would have never thought this. Thinking back, I wonder if I had the chance to do it over, would I not sleep with Walker. The answer is quick. *No.* I would still do it. It was the most amazing night of my life. I only regret not having a way to get a hold of him, which I knew would happen the moment I left his hotel room. I don't know if he is the type of guy I want to spend my life with but I'm sad that he won't know he has a child out there and that our baby won't benefit from his presence.

8

My body is on fire. His hands reach down between my legs and I can't help but scream out in ecstasy. "Walker!"

"I'm here baby. Give in. Give it all to me." His growl resonates through the room.

I'm almost there. My body craving the release his hands are holding back, torturing me. "Please Walker, let me come." I say hoping he will comply.

"What do you want? Faster, sweet thing? You like it fast? And hard?" He asks, his hands moving at a rapid pace bringing me to the brink before he slows down, causing a frustrated groan to escape my lips.

"Walker, NOW!" I yell.

His fingers glide in and out of me. I'm there. Just a few more times and the release I am longing for will be mine. My body is glistening with sweat, bowing off the bed, pushing further onto his hand. Waves of ecstasy wash over me from my toes to my fingertips as I try to ride the orgasm out, but it's out of reach. My body screaming, I search for Walker but he is no longer there. I move my body in sync with the penetration I was just feeling but it's gone. "No!" I say aloud to the darkened room. "No!"

The bright sun awakens me from my dream. This is the sixth one this summer. Every time I wake up in a sweat and heatedly reach for the vibrator. My pregnancy hormones are out of control and these dreams aren't helping. I want sex and I want it now. My body craves it. But not just the act. It wants Walker, and I can't fulfill its needs. He is gone and my body will never feel his touch again.

Flipping the switch to "on" I replay my dream getting release that is only half fulfilling.

~~

The week before school starts is always my favorite. The hallways buzz with teachers excited to start the new year and get rooms ready for the young minds we will start molding the next week. I haven't really spoken to any of my coworkers since the end of last year, except a few lunch dates here and there with Rosie. After filling her in on all the craziness my summer brought, she offered to help with the baby anytime I need it now that she has a lot of time on her hands. I told her that I wouldn't want to put that on her, but I would be more than happy to bring the little one over. Looking at her empty room makes me sad that I won't have my mentor just across the way.

Principal Callow has us all meeting in the gymnasium for a welcome back lunch on Wednesday, our first day back. This is something the staff hates but I find myself absolutely starved and ready to take an hour of torturous reminders of rules and ethics just to get my hands on a sandwich or three. I unconsciously place my hand on my stomach while walking in a herd with the rest of the faculty and into the gym. The sweet smell of coffee causes me to grimace, wishing I could still drink it. The doctor told me one cup a day was okay, but why tease myself? And decaf is definitely out of the question.

Shoes scuffle on the newly finished floor making me curiously look down and check it out. The feedback from the microphone pulls me from the lame thought of how beautiful it looks and the Principal taps on the end of it. I find a seat in the second row close to the tables of food.

"Welcome back staff. I hope you all had a wonderful summer and are as excited about the new year as I am. We have a lot of changes coming our way here at Hudson and I want to start with our two fresh faces." One of the seventh grade English teachers, Emma James, sits down next to me commenting on how much she cannot stand these little "parties." Saying she is beautiful is an understatement. Her long curly auburn hair is laying halfway down her back and I'm instantly jealous. Even though she has next to no makeup on she is utterly flawless. Her green eyes smile my way and I am distracted by how they are the shade of a perfectly manicured lawn.

"Holy shit! Good thing you have Robert because I'm calling dibs on that right there." I watch as her pools of green become lust filled at what lies in front of them.

Ignoring her Robert comment I follow her line of vision to her object of desire. I land on Callow who is still speaking loudly into the microphone. "This is our new 6th grade math teacher, who will be mentored by Ms. Decker. Let's welcome Walker Prescott, newly graduated out of Southern Illinois University."

Walker.

My mind races. How many men have that name? It can't be him. Panic seizes me and I can't focus. When I finally lay my eyes on the man who was just introduced, he is zeroed in on me, his green eyes burning into my skin as his smile spreads so wide I think his face might split in two.

"Erin, would you come up here and introduce yourself to Mr. Prescott?" Principle Callow motions to me.

Emma huffs next to me shoving her shoulder into mine. "Lucky bitch! I guess I'll be on your side of the school more often."

I drag in a deep breath and hope my legs don't give out on me as I stand up, about to face the father of my unborn child. His eyes never leave mine, and as I slowly walk toward the stage, they widen when he realizes that I'm going to be his first year mentor. Terror at the thought of speaking to him consumes me and I drag my gaze down to the floor. The steps seem steeper and higher, my legs struggle to climb them. When I am finally within arm's length I raise my chin, sticking my hand out to shake his. His hand covers mine, and the electricity between them is profound. I can't help but remember how those hands felt elsewhere.

"Nice to meet you Mr. Prescott," I say, stomach rising to my throat. *Please don't throw up on him.* "Welcome to the team."

"Thank you…what is it again? Sally?" A knowing smirk greets me and I now know for sure, he remembers.

"Uhm, it's Erin actually. Erin Decker," I say, my words barely a whisper.

"Well, it's nice to finally have a face to a name." His words roll like silk off of his tongue.

I force a smile and walk back to my seat. The introductions and meeting continue and I feel his gaze lingering on me. As soon as we are dismissed my mortification takes precedence over my hunger and I bolt for the exit.

My room is still very much empty but that is the least of my worries. I need to get out of here and fast. I had come to grips with the fact that I would never find him, that my child would grow up without a father, but now... Now, he is right in front of me and I just want to run. Grabbing my belongings I head to the bathroom since my bladder can't contain itself any longer. Washing and drying my hands I use a paper towel to open the door and am met with a face worth a thousand melted panties. His tongue brushes over his lips, mine doing the same.

He takes a step forward forcing me to retreat back into the bathroom. One more step and we are behind the privacy of the door and my back is against the wall. Both of his hands rise up to my cheeks, as he plants them on either side of my head and that earth shattering tongue glides over his plump mouth again. As he inches his way closer and closer my eyes slam shut and my lips part waiting for his mouth to be on me, for all of those hormone induced dreams to become reality.

Heated breath hits my right ear. "Oh, Sally. I've thought so much about you since our night together. The way you felt on top of me. I've never come so hard in my life. Then you leave me with no way to find you. Until today, Sally. Until today when I saw you walk into the gym. Beautiful and glowing. This job is going to bring you and I closer and I hope we can get to know each other deeper. Tell me...Sally, can we get any deeper?" His teeth nip my ear causing a familiar ache between my thighs. His hold drops and before I can open my eyes he is out the door. Anger surges through me at how quickly he had me almost bent over the sink. Throwing the door open I shout to his retreating back, halfway down the hallway to the gym. "IT'S ERIN!"

"I know," he yells, waving a hand without looking back, and still continuing to walk away. Mustering up the strength not to run from him I stomp towards the gym.

The door hits the wall when I throw it open and I immediately scan the crowd to find Walker next to Emma, with her wandering hands. Jealously carries my legs to them.

"Erin, I was wondering where you went. I was just telling Walker here how available I am." Her arms rub up and down his forearm. "Maybe we could double date, huh? Walker and me, you and Robert. It would be fun!"

"Robert? Well that sounds *adventurous*,"

he says, mocking me. Walker's tone tells both Emma and me that the idea doesn't suit him. "Don't you think Sal...I mean Erin? A night out with you and your *boyfriend* wouldn't be unadventurous at all."

I look him directly in the eyes. "I've been known to be very adventurous," I retort, running my tongue along my lips and biting the lower one.

"I don't doubt that, at all," he says pushing Emma's hands off his arms, looking straight at me. "I'm sorry, Emma. I am seeing someone at the moment."

True to Emma's form, she lets out an audible huff and leaves me alone with my child's father. *Shit.*

His words suddenly sinking in that he is dating someone. How am I going to tell the man, who only shared one night with me that he is going to be a dad? I'm not sure how his girlfriend will handle Walker having a child with someone else but thinking about another woman in my little bean's life scares me. There is no way I can tell him right now. I know I have to tell him, but I have to figure out how to do that. Blurting out that he knocked me up won't go very well, even though he seems like he can be pretty blunt.

Realizing I've zoned out I find him standing there, sexy hair and all, staring at my hands which have subconsciously made their way to my stomach.

"You feeling ok, baby? Maybe remembering how I felt inside you? I can make that happen again." His voice oozes seduction, and though the question pisses me off, the clothes he is wearing are now my focal point. It's nothing close to the sexed up god look from that night. It's even better.

The dark forest green polo shirt is slim on his torso, and showcasing the pecs I used for support as I rode him almost three long lonely months ago. The ironed khaki pants are tight and hiding the beast that almost split me in two. My pulse quickens at the thought. Raising my eyes up to his one dimpled smirk, and swallowing the lump in my throat, I know he has caught me. "Like what you see?"

"You are so egotistical, you know that? And didn't you say you were seeing someone, Walker? Don't make those kinds of comments to me and then go home to someone else," I say in a hushed tone, finally breaking my silence.

"I don't think she would mind, Erin. In fact, it's you that I'm seeing. You're *all* I see. All I've seen for months now. I can't get you out of this goddamn head of mine." He taps the side of his temple to make his point. "Every time I close my eyes I see your beautiful brown eyes, hovering above me, using me for pleasure."

I can't breathe and my mind is processing thoughts faster that I can comprehend them. My brain and my mouth aren't in sync and the time I needed to think is apparently over because I blurt out, "I'm pregnant."

His eyes bore into mine searching for the truth to my words and trying to take in the bomb I just dropped. "You're..."

"Mr. Prescott?" Principal Callow interrupts before this earth shattering dialog continues.

"I apologize about interrupting your conversation with Ms. Decker but I'd like to introduce you to the Superintendant." Once Walker reluctantly allows himself to be dragged away, I fall into the chair next to me, watching as he walks away. Right before reaching the Super he turns, anger in his eyes. My body can't move fast as I stand up to run out of the gym. Keeping the tears at bay, I make it to my car in record time.

In the comfort of the front seat, I let them fall freely, not caring about holding them in anymore. "FUCK!" I scream louder than I ever thought possible. Pain shoots through my right hand as I hit the steering wheel repeatedly.

"FUCK, FUCK, FUCK!" I say, each time slamming my palms down.

How could I tell him like that? I should have waited a little longer. Sat him down. Told him I had some news. Not blurt it out like a moron in the middle of the gym for Christ's sake!

I start the car and put it in reverse gliding out of the parking spot. A loud bang on the roof shakes me to the core. "ERIN!" Walker's muffled yell hits my ears.

Not looking at him I put the car in drive and leave him standing there. Blindly searching in my bag, I find my phone and attempt to call Noelle.

A honking horn blares and I slam on the breaks just in time to stop at a stop sign. The angry driver passes through the intersection shaking his fist at me. I can't hear him but I'm sure he is yelling obscenities and giving me the middle finger.

I inwardly scold myself. I need to keep this baby in mind at all times. No more stupid moves. Looking behind me, I make sure no one is there, and I pull up Noelle's number just in time for a text to pop up.

Unknown: We need to talk.

Me: Who is this?

Unknown: Mr. Prescott. Meet me. Tonight.

Mr. Prescott? So formal now, and pushy. *Jeez.* I can't meet him alone; if he touches me I will probably not be able to make him stop. *Or want him to.* We need witnesses. Quickly I save his number and change his name in my phone. Something I should have done months ago.

Me: Not tonight but we can meet at the school in the morning to set up our rooms. We can talk then.

Walker: 8am. No later.

Another honk from behind prevents me from texting him back. I drop my phone into the passenger seat and finish the short drive home.

That night nerves consume me. I realize tomorrow is "make it or break it" time. Not knowing if Walker will accept the fact that I am having his child has my stomach in knots. I hope he can at least agree to be there for the baby. I want nothing else from him. As much as I would have loved to be married and in love with my child's father, that might not happen. I just don't think I could ever trust another man so easily. Robert ruined that for me, made me gun shy, and I still hate him for it.

According to my reflection I look like crap. My half assed make up job does nothing for my bloodshot eyes or the dark circles beneath them. The three restless hours of sleep seem like zero and I would give my left leg for a cup of coffee...or three.

Noelle never came home last night and she wasn't answering my texts. Normally her long hours don't bother me but I needed to talk all this through with her. Get some clarity. So, I did the next best thing; I called my mom. After giving her all the details of the day's events she went silent. I thought maybe the line cut out. It's happened before in the middle of my rants and then all the sudden it's ringing right next to my ear.

She finally spoke but with so much

excitement that I had to try and calm her down. She said this was my chance and was spouting out her "everything happens for a reason" boloney. When I reiterated that he looked angry after my confession she toned it down a bit, got her head on straight, and started to think clearly and give some better advice. Her attempts to calm me down were working until she said something that completely freaked me out.

"It is your responsibility to give him the option to be there for his child. It's his choice whether he wants to be," she said, just before hanging up, providing the reason for my insomnia.

So, I tossed and turned and waited for Noelle to get home and maybe put my mind at ease. I never texted why I wanted to talk to her so she didn't know how dire the situation was. She finally replied at midnight saying she was out "with a friend." Which means she was getting some action...I was more jealous than disappointed. I had a steady boyfriend for so long that the most we had gone without making love was a week, maybe ten days. Then I got a taste of Walker, leaving me desperate for MONTHS without it. *I'm going to have to buy a new vibrator soon.*

I throw some concealer over the bags under my eyes and settle for the zombie look. I want to have the upper hand and be prepared for when Walker arrives so I leave at 7:30.

When I finally get to my classroom I am far from ready. My hearts stops when I find him sitting at my desk leaning back with his hands casually behind his head, eyes closed, leaving me the opportunity to shamelessly check him out. His hair is disheveled and looks like it did after our one intense night. The day old stubble has my hormones running wild and I can't help thinking of how it would feel on the soft skin of my thighs. His biceps strain against the short sleeves of his white polo shirt. Both legs are up on my desk covered in dark distressed jeans with tan construction boots. My eyes make their way back up and embarrassingly meet his now open ones.

"Erin, Erin, Erin." He places a palm over his heart. "I'm starting to feel like a piece of meat."

I throw my bag down on one of the desks in the back row, crossing my arms over my chest. "Your ego is huge, Walker. MASSIVE in fact."

As soon as those words come out of my mouth I blush, knowing he could turn that around. His eyebrow raises, he stands up and walks down the center isle towards me.

"There is a lot about me that is massive. You should know." As the distance between us gets shorter my knees start to get weak. His hand reaches for mine and as I take it, he pulls me into a seat.

"I'm sorry," he relents. "Let's start over. I have some things I want to say to you." He takes the next seat in front of me, keeping his grip firm.

"I have some things I want to say too," I tell him but he waves his hand as to signify that he wants to go first.

"Erin. Please let me apologize for my actions yesterday. That wasn't right. I know I come off cocky and egotistical but I'm a good guy, I promise. I couldn't stop thinking about you all summer. You just walked out of that hotel room and I thought it was no big deal, but I couldn't get you off my mind. I've never had someone take over my senses and consume my thoughts like that...and after just one night. You had me... But I feel like a jerk. I cornered you yesterday and I goaded you and made you uncomfortable. And again, I'm sorry." His face drops to look at our entwined hands and he finally lets go of mine. A flurry of emotions run over his face, before he gathers his breath and says, "Robert is very lucky to be having a baby with you."

Robert? He thinks this is Robert's baby. There are few times in your life where you have two choices; do the right thing or do the easy thing. I said all summer I could do this alone. I could take care of my little bean by myself with the love and support from my family. No complications. I never thought Walker would be in the picture. I could stick with my plans, and avoid the heartache that comes along with being tied to a man indefinitely through a child. Especially a man like Walker, who makes me so angry one minute and so hot the next. I can move on from this point and raise my child alone. My mom's last words run through my thoughts. As easy as it would be to let Walker think the baby is Robert's, I just can't do that.

"He's not," I barely manage to get out.

"Who's not what?" His eyes meet mine again with confusion and bewilderment.

I speak up and say, "Robert is not the father. We haven't seen each other since a few weeks before I met you."

The walls close in and I feel as though I'm in the desert, searching for a glass of water. Or wine. At this point I don't care. He is quiet, seemingly searching for words, and I am desperate for him to say something.

"Erin," he says cautiously, grabbing my hands once again like he is talking to a suicide jumper. "How far along are you?"

Here it is. The point of no return. My search for him didn't work and my plans had changed but he is here now. It's my responsibility to let him choose to be an active or inactive father. I hope he wants to be a part of this small life, for the baby's sake. "Thirteen weeks," I answer.

Silence follows as I stare at him. He says nothing. The ticking of clock on the wall gets louder and louder with every minute that passes by.

"I just need a second." He stands, dropping my hand again, and races out of the room like it's on fire.

My head falls forward onto the desk and I start to cry. I don't think I have ever cried as much as I have in the past three months. My tear ducts should be dried out by now.

I should be relieved to finally get it all out there and off my chest. But I am not. I'm still petrified of the road my life is going to take when Walker decides what he wants to do. Either way, it changes the plan I had in place just 24 short hours ago. The door flies open making me jump and Walker strolls in half paying attention to me while looking at a book he has in his hands. "Last period, Erin?" He demands.

What? Is he crazy? "Walker, I don't think..."

"DATE OF YOUR LAST PERIOD ERIN!" He commands looking up from the book.

"May 28th. Jesus. What is the matter with you? You can't just come in here yelling questions and demanding answers like that," I yell back at him, standing up.

His finger flips the pages over and over until they land on their target and then his emerald colored eyes look straight at me.

"Mine? This baby is mine?" He asks with little emotion, using his index finger to point towards my belly. "Are you sure? Because I used protection. I am certain of it."

I look at him trying to read between the lines, and realize that I need to be clearer.

"Yes, it's yours and I'm sure. I got my period the day after Robert and I broke up. You are the only man I have been with since," I verify, trying to appear strong.

His gaze looks at what I've figured to be a calendar, then at me, back to the calendar, and then down to my stomach. Throwing down the book on a chair he takes the few steps needed to be right in front of me and brushes his knuckles over my abdomen. "Mine," he repeats more as a statement than a question. .

He wraps his arms around my waist and picks me up so my eyes are level with his. He places a soft lingering kiss on my cheek.

"You're happy?" I ask, unsure if I am delusional.

Setting me back down, he places both hands on either side of my cheeks. "Happy? Baby, I'm thrilled. This wasn't planned, but of course I am happy. THRILLED! I want to scream it from the rooftops, Erin. I found my girl and we have a baby on the way."

"Wait. Walker, I don't want you to feel obligated to me...or this baby. You can be as involved as you want but I don't expect you to jump into a relationship with me. I can't even think about throwing a relationship into the mix right now. I'm still in shock that you are even here in front of me. I looked for you all summer. I checked the hotel, the bar, Noelle and I even stalked pictures of men named Walker on Facebook. Not in my wildest dreams did I expect you to want me. I just wanted you to know about the baby. He or she needs you."

"Are you kidding? Did you not hear a damn word I said yesterday... or today? I want *you*. I spent three months dreaming about you, wanting you, and thinking I would spend the rest of my life without finding you. And now you're here and I can touch you and talk to you. Of course I want you, and now that I know about the baby, I want to make it work that much more. " He moves even closer to me, if that's possible, and places a kiss on my forehead. "I want this so much, Erin. All of it..."

"Let's take this one day at a time," I say as I grudgingly push us apart. "Besides one night of sex we know nothing about each other. Let's take the next six months to get to know one another, and when the baby is born, we'll figure out the rest."

He dips his head so he is eye level with me.

"I agree that we need to learn more about one another, but know this Erin, by the time that baby is born I can assure you that you will be mine. One night of sex, *amazing sex*, was all it took for me to be hooked on you. There's no one else for me but you and now this baby. Please don't shut me out. Let me in."

His words tug at my heart. It's more than I could ever dream of hearing him say. But, everything is still so complicated. It can't be that simple, can it? How can he be so certain when I'm so confused?

"Okay," I concede. "I'm open to letting you in but I can't make any promises."

I spend the next hour telling him what happened since our last encounter. Talking about my summer seemed a lot easier than deciding what would happen with the two, well three, of us. I share the experience of my first two doctor appointments with him and extend an invitation to the next one in a few weeks. He doesn't hesitate to say yes, flashing me a huge grin that makes me warm inside. He tells me that my due date, March 4th, is also his birthday. He will be the ripe old age of 24 when the baby is born. I'll be 28 by then, my birthday being in November.

He tells me all about his family, how his sister lives in the area, and his parents used to, but had recently moved to Michigan when his father got a promotion at work. He had come back to town after graduation to look for an apartment, visit with his sister, and interview for the job at Hudson. His sister was apparently doing some major home renovations, so he had decided to stay at a hotel while he was visiting, and the day after his interview at the school, we met. After that he went to visit his parents in Michigan for the summer and help his mom out who had just broken her ankle. To my surprise, I learn his new apartment is down the street from my subdivision. That will certainly come in handy when the baby arrives. I'm also informed that he isn't a stalker but got my phone number from his welcome packet.

"So, I was thinking," he says after he finishes the last slice of pizza that we had delivered. "If we are going to see where this could go, maybe we should go on a date. Say, this Saturday? Maybe the Cubs and Brewers game at Wrigley."

"Oh, no. I'm sorry. I'm a White Sox fan," I say, trying to respond with a straight face.

"You're what? How could I have ever thought there could be something between us?" He jokes. "I'm kidding. I can think of something else no problem...since you like the White Sucks. I mean Sox."

Slapping him playfully on the chest I tell

him, "I'm joking. Die hard Cubs fan here. For life."

"Oh, thank God," he says, visibly relieved. "I was thinking of all the disgusting White Sox onesies you would put on our baby." He laughs and I'm stunned. He said "our baby". *Our baby.*

Taking a look at him I smile as my heart flutters a little. The father of my child is now within reach, happy about having a baby with someone he barely knows, and he wants to make it work between the two of us. A vision of the future plays out before me. Walker pacing back and forth in a yellow nursery kissing the forehead of our child, and smiling at me. *I can do this. I can try to make this work.*

10

Noelle finally made it home Thursday night after Walker's and my talk at the school. I think she popped my ear drum squealing with delight after I told her what happened. She started telling me how happy she was that he manned up and was going to take responsibility. She couldn't help pointing out how different Walker's response was from Robert's less that pleased one when I had become pregnant years before. I still had yet to call my mom back. She called numerous times wanting details on what Walker said but with trying to get my classroom in order on Thursday and Friday, lesson plans finalized, and being utterly exhausted every night from growing a fetus, I have held that off for two days. My text stating "he's in" was going to have to be good enough for now. She would have to wait one more day because today was Walker's and my first date.

Last night's dream was more intense than any dream I had of him so far. This one resulted in an in-dream orgasm that woke me up sweating and needing him more than ever. Needless to say, I was both loving and hating that I would have to spend all day with him.

With my stomach starting to show a small hint of a baby belly, I put on my too tight for my belly capri jeans and an old Mark Prior jersey. Slipping a pony tail through my red and blue Cubs hat, I take one last glance in the mirror as the doorbell rings. My heart skips a beat.

I pull open the door and am blessed with the sight of pure hotness. Walker is leaning into the door frame with his arms folded over his ripped chest and legs crossed at his ankles. His incredibly tempting backside is fit into snug jeans and paired with a vintage blue Cubs t-shirt that is just a bit too small for his upper arms. I nonchalantly squeeze my legs together to keep the lust at bay, thinking back on last night's fantasy. A fitted blue Cubs hat sits backwards on his head hiding his dark brown hair. Lowering my eyes back to his, he flashes me a "make your panties wet" smile that I definitely didn't need to see. I lick my lips and try to calm my pulse as he moves towards me and places his hands on my hips.

"You look beautiful, Erin," he compliments me, licking his own lips as he looks at mine.

I want them on me. Pulling on my ponytail, I will myself to glance away. "I look like a boy in this getup."

"You look nothing like a man." He steps forward and cups my face bringing his closer. "You look like an enticing woman. I think a female is sexiest when she wears jeans and a t-shirt. Especially, when she is carrying my child."

"Well then I'm glad I didn't throw on a red dress and heels!" I joke. My mouth runs dry and I can't help but lick my lips again.

"I wouldn't say that. Easier access!" He wiggles his eyebrows up and down. My hands, with a mind of their own, gravitate to his chest. *Holy Hell!* He pulls me up against him and places a chaste kiss on my lips before setting me back down.

"Are you ready to go? We can catch the train and get dropped off right at Wrigley," he informs me dropping his hands back to my waist. I'm not thinking straight.

"Uhm, what? Oh, yea. Train. Wrigley. Let's go." I sound like a complete moron. I grab my keys off the table shoving them into my pocket with a small wallet.

Get it together Erin.

I love the mass transit system in Chicago. There are so many different varieties of people. Sitting at the train station at Dempster waiting for the El to arrive, we see a man wearing a hot pink halter top, skin tight cheetah print pants and Sketchers. He's currently singing "Baby One More Time" by Britney Spears. Walker sees him at the same time I do and we both quietly chuckle.

No sooner than the train arrives, it is packed and Walker takes the opportunity to flush his body to mine. I can feel his steady breaths and his manly scent has my pulse racing. After my most recent dream, I'm not sure I can handle being this close to him for long without needing release. At Addison we all herd out like cattle, giving me a brief reprieve from the sexual tension I am experiencing. Walker puts his arms around my shoulders protectively, and I notice again how well we fit together. We walk down the stairs and look up at the amazing view that is Wrigley Field. It is absolutely beautiful. You wouldn't think someone would describe a baseball stadium that way, but I do.

Bypassing the entrance to the stadium we cross the street to The Cubby Bear, the famous bar and restaurant, and find it crowded with wall to wall fans. Since the price of beer is insane inside the park, most come here beforehand to drink.

"I think I see a table in the back," he points out pulling me by my hand.

When we finally get to the table it's dirty and a busboy is busily cleaning it off. We sit and the waitress comes over to take our drink order. I notice she can't stop staring at Walker and she looks over her shoulder at him repeatedly as she is leaving us to peruse the menu. Walker picks up my hand off the table and rubs his thumb over the top of it. Setting his menu down, he brings my fingers up to his mouth and gently kisses them one by one.

"What are you doing?" I ask fascinated by how good it feels.

"I'm just so happy that you are here with me and I want to kiss you, really kiss you, but I don't think you're ready so I'm settling for your fingers," he says, taking my other hand and giving it the same attention. I'm so past ready that I barely notice when the waitress is back.

"What can I get ya?" The waitress asks us while poking her perky breasts out towards Walker. He doesn't seem to notice but I can tell she could care less that I am sitting right here.

"I'll take a cheeseburger, well done with fries," I interrupt her Walker-gazing, and wave my menu in front of her face directing her attention to me. *Bitch.*

"I'll have the same, thanks," Walker smiles and hands her his menu. He looks at her without seeming to notice that she is easy on the eyes, but doesn't stare, which impresses me. .

"Erin, thanks for coming today," he says, turning his attention back to me as he takes a swig of his beer.

"Of course. We need to get to know each other and knowing you're a Cubs fan too is a huge turn on!" Raising my eyebrows and slapping a hand over my mouth, I can't believe I just said that.

His beer stops halfway to his mouth with my confession. "A turn on, huh?"

"It's the pregnancy hormones, Walker. I'm constantly turned on. Stupid dreams." I didn't realize word vomit was real, until that moment.

He takes another sip of his beer, contemplating my admission. His eyes are smoldering as he asks, "Dreams? Like sex dreams? About who, Erin? Me? Was it as good as you remember?"

"You ask a lot of questions." Hoping to avoid the rest of this conversation I look around the room, and pray he won't notice the crimson color rising into my cheeks.

"Well I think I know the answer anyway." His hand brings mine to his mouth and slowly places a lingering kiss on it again. The smile that crosses his face is raw, primal, and promising.

"With that grin you look like the big bad wolf hunting little Red Riding Hood. What a big mouth you have, grandma," I say, giggling at my little joke.

He leans in closer causing my lungs to gasp for air. I am wet and I want this need to go away. *I need it to go away.*

"The better to eat you with, my dear," he whispers suggestively.

"Here ya go! Two cheeseburgers. Anything else?" The waitress drops our plates down in front of us and I shift uncomfortably in my seat, hoping Walker won't notice my rapid breathing.

"Thanks. Another beer and some more water, please," he says. She acknowledges Walker's request and walks away.

"Did I tell you how sexy you look?" The question comes just before he takes a bite of his cheeseburger.

"Nope. You told me I look like a slob and you didn't want to be seen with me in public. It kind of hurt my feelings, but I'm trying to get over it," I say straight faced, making his jaw drop.

"You're funny. Eat your food so we can go see our Cubbies."

It makes my heart flutter anytime he uses the word "our". It almost feels as though we are a real, normal couple. Not two people shoved together for a lifetime over what was supposed to just be a one night stand.

We finish up our meals and are practically kicked out of our table so other patrons can eat and drink before the games starts. There is nothing like Wrigley Field. My dad used to bring Nicole, Trent, and me here all the time during the summer months. Every year we'd get excited about the season and every year we had been disappointed. Every. Single. Year. Always hoping the next one would be ours.

Walking out of the concourse and into the seating area, we are greeted with the most amazing view. The green grass is covered with players warming up for the game. This is my favorite part...seeing the players just hanging around makes them look almost like normal people and not the baseball gods they are.

Walker places his hand on the small of my back leading me towards our seats on the third base line, just a few rows above the Cubs' dugout. The warm August air makes it the perfect day to be outside.

"We are so close," I say, pulling my phone out to take a picture of one of my favorite players. "I just love this place. It's like a second home. Gorgeous."

"Yes, stunning," he agrees, but when I turn around he is looking at me, not the field.

I immediately blush. I can already feel myself falling for him. I can't. If a man like Robert could cheat on me what would a man who looks like and is as charismatic as Walker do? I should know better than to think they are all alike, but I can't help but be protective of myself and the possibility, especially since I have the baby to think about. I won't let myself get hurt again. I need to stay strong. But there is something different about Walker.

Breaking the tension, I suggest heading to the merchandise stand. I grab a new loose fitting pink Cubs shirt, which Walker insists on paying for, along with his new hat. After purchasing a bottle of water for me and another beer for himself, we get back to our seats just in time for the National Anthem.

I look around and notice how many Brewers fans are in attendance. Milwaukee is a short 2 hour drive and a lot of their fans come down whenever we play each other. When our team plays in Milwaukee, it's the same with the Cubs fans. They call Miller Park "Wrigley Field North" because we have been known to take up most of the seats in their stadium.

"These seats are fantastic! Thanks for

bringing me, Walker." Allowing him to put his arm around me I smile, suddenly overcome with how right this feels.

"No problem, baby. Like I said, I'm glad you agreed."

A tear falls down my cheek as his other hand finds my abdomen where our baby grows. I quickly wipe it away not wanting him to see.

The next two hours fly by and I am barely paying attention to the game. Walker's soft touches and caresses on my arms, my stomach, and hands are making it really hard to concentrate on anything else other than where they will land next. I know how they feel intimately and I'm craving that touch again.

Somewhere in the middle of the 5th inning he catches a foul ball in his hands that just barely misses the little 4 year old boy sitting in front of us. Without hesitation he hands it to the little man, earning himself a youthful cheesy grin.

"Thank you. He's been hoping to get a foul ball all summer and this is the first time it came near us. You are a saint," the father says to Walker, patting his son on the head.

"No problem," he says turning a sexy smile towards me. "Did you hear that, baby? I'm a saint."

I lower my eyes and lean into him.

Suddenly, I am hyper aware that I want him to want me too. He should be in as much misery as I am. "I'd much rather you are a sinner," I say, giving him a wicked half smile.

His eyes widen and I know it worked and the word "damn" slips from his mouth.

~~

It's the 8th inning and my body is angled towards him, tingling all over, while I eat popcorn and watch the Cubs lose.

"Erin?" I pretend to let Walker drag my eyes away from the action…or lack thereof.

"Yea?" I turn my face to find his inches from mine.

"I'm going to kiss you and lick all the salt off those plump lips," he states as a matter of fact, and I am certain that if I had been standing, I would have melted into a puddle at his feet.

Walker reaches over and grabs the back of my neck bringing us the few inches closer. I'm already breathless. His tongue darts out and runs along the top lip and my eyes shut awaiting the feel of them on mine. His knuckles brush across my cheek and I lean closer to him, silently begging him to fulfill his promise. His tongue nudges my lower lip and I open my mouth slightly allowing him more access. He takes advantage, pushing further in; I turn and place my palms on his chest, curling my fingers into his shirt. Unexpectedly he loses control. His tongue thoroughly ravishes my mouth. I'm so turned on I can't see straight.

Our heated passion is short lived as a freezing cold beer drenches us. Both gasping, we look up at the drunken man who looks oblivious to what he just did.

"What the fuck, man. You just poured beer all over me and my girl. You need to apologize," Walker half yells. The drunk is a short man. Even from the higher level seat he's in, he and Walker are still just eye level.

"I'm sorry bro." The drunken man stumbles on his words and I start to laugh.

"Are you seriously laughing at this?" Walker asks in disbelief, probably wondering why I'm not pissed that I took a beer shower.

"Yes! This is hilarious," I say, shaking the beer off of my hands.

"Come on, let's go clean up."

He drags me, still laughing, up the stairs back to the concourse. It's practically empty and now that the game is tied, no one wants to miss a thing. Finding the bathroom he guides me towards them.

"I'll meet you back here. I still have that

shirt I bought so I will just put that on," I say, heading towards the ladies room.

Once inside I take my time pulling off my jersey and trying to wipe off most of the sticky beer with a couple of wet paper towels. Tending to my face, I jump at the sound of the door.

"Walker! What the hell are you doing in here?"

He looks concerned, but halts when he finds me standing in a white lacey bra. His eyes grow wide.

"I was worried. It's been quite a few minutes. I'm sorry. I just didn't know if you got sick or you fell or some shit like that. You are carrying our child. I'm allowed to worry, right?"

His eyes are intently focused on my chest. I can see the tension building in his eyes. My skin is covered in goose bumps, under his gaze. My need has to be met. Relinquishing my restraint, I rush over to him and jump into his arms, circling my legs around his waist. His sturdy hands grip me by my thighs pushing me back towards the wall. I grab onto his shoulders and our lips collide. A small moan escapes me when I feel his massive length put pressure on the swollen apex of my thighs. I'm sure he can feel how wet I am even with clothes between us.

"What are you doing Erin?" He breathlessly asks between kisses.

"Being *adventurous* Walker. Those dreams have me so strung up. I need release, please," I beg. Walker makes me beg.

Someone walks in and he rushes me into the handicap stall covering my mouth. I still have my legs wrapped around his waist so I grind my hips into him, teasing him, and letting out a loud muffled moan. *This man will be my undoing.*

"Shh!" He tells me, as he takes his hand off my mouth, and moves it to the button of my jeans. It opens with a pop and my zipper slides down easily. Lowering one of my legs to the ground, he brushes my core on the way back up and pushes my pants down just a little bit. A toilet flushes and I start to giggle.

"This is so romantic," I joke against his chest, but who really cares about romance right now?

"I said to be quiet, Erin. I am going to make you come. That's what you asked for. I promise I'll always give you everything you ask for."

I open my mouth but he silences me with his, and slips his hand into my panties before I can realize what is happening. The air blowers go off in the background covering up my load moan. He reaches down further finally learning how soaking wet I am. With my face to his chest, I can feel his heartbeat quicken against my cheek.

"So fucking wet. You want this don't you?" He teases.

"Yes," I whimper, and he pushes his index finger inside me. I wriggle beneath his touch.

"You're so tight, Erin. Been a long time?" He asks bringing his thumb to my clit.

"You know how long, Walker. Please don't stop," I whisper.

"Pull your bra down, Erin."

I comply, his head taking a hard nipple into his mouth. "I missed these."

I can't speak; all I can do is feel. This man consumes me.

His middle finger joins the other and my insides clench them together. I'm so close I can taste it. He presses harder with his thumb and pumps his fingers in and out until every dream I've had of him comes to a head. He breaks the suction on my breast and looks at me as I come. Not able to hold my screaming in any longer I bite down on his shoulder to muffle my screams. My eyes roll into the back of my head as I ride the wave of ecstasy.

Coming down from my high he slides his fingers out of me and brings them to his mouth sucking the juices off. "Mmm, just as I remember. That was fucking hot."

Completely mortified I try to look anywhere but at him, ashamed that I let my hormones rule me. He grabs my chin forcing me to look at him.

"What's wrong, baby? Do you regret that? I'm so sorry."

"It felt amazing but I'm so embarrassed," I tell him honestly.

"I told you Erin. You need something I will give it to you. You asked for that and I was more than happy to oblige. You never need to be embarrassed with me, okay?"

"Okay." I can't help agreeing. Grabbing at the button on his jeans I announce that it's his turn.

"No, baby. This was for you. Although, if you want, you can return the favor later." He winks at me, bringing my hands to his mouth, kissing them. After I put my new shirt on we walk out of the stall and we wash our hands. As we exit the bathroom there is another obnoxious drunk man just outside.

"Looks like someone got a home run!" He yells so the whole damn stadium can hear, holding his hand up for a high five from

Walker, who ignores him.

"Nope! Just a triple," I say, without flinching, and high five him myself.

Walker stops at my words and turns around in the middle of the concourse, smiling at me and looking like he just won the lottery. Staring deep into my eyes, he says "Remember when I told you that you would be mine?" When I nod, he continues, "Well, you can be sure that Prescott will be tacked onto that pretty first name of yours in the near future. I'm going to marry you."

The day at the ball park was indescribable. I learned a lot about Walker, and besides that, I am hopelessly attracted to him. I also saw a sweet side to him. He attended to my every need, walked me to the bathroom every half hour, always had a bottle of water ready for me when I finished one, and made sure my sore feet and I had a seat on the El for the way back, after paying someone $10 to give up theirs.

It's dark by the time Walker escorts me up to my door. Noelle isn't home and although I shouldn't be, I'm nervous to ask him in not wanting this night to end.

"Let me stay tonight, Erin." His voice takes me by surprise.

"You want to come in you mean?" I ask

looking for clarification. There is no way. He is bold enough to ask to stay the night? I don't know what kind of girl he thinks I am, although I did just let him finger me in a bathroom stall...and I did have a one night stand with him. But, that doesn't mean I'd allow a sleepover. Okay, who am I kidding; he makes me want that, desperately.

"Yes, I want to come in but I also want to stay the night." Sensing what I may be thinking he adds, "Just to be with you. To hold you. After the first night we spent together you left the next morning. I have regretted letting you walk out that door ever since the minute it closed behind you. I want to erase that memory. Not the making our child part, but the walking away part. I want to wake up next to you, make breakfast, and go home knowing I will see you again. Just, please, let me do this."

I can't say anything to him. Here is this strong, demanding man, asking me, begging me, to let him stay over? It melts my heart to hear the plea in his voice. Not knowing how to respond, I open the door all the way allowing him to pass through. I don't say yes, but I didn't say no either. We just let things flow.

I called Joe's Pizza, the best non-deep dish pizza around, to fuel my ever hungry belly. While waiting, he picked out "21 Jump Street", one of my all-time favorite movies, to watch. After stuffing our faces with the roast beef and green pepper topped pie, he pulled my head down to his lap and I fell quickly asleep.

"What the hell is this?" Noelle's voice wakes me from a nice restful nap and startles Walker. My eyes find her pointing to the coffee table. "Get your feet off my furniture!"

Giggling at his shocked expression, I try to smooth things over. "Noelle, this is Walker. Walker, this is Noelle."

"THIS is Thunder Tongue?" She asks calling him by our secret name we gave him.

"Thunder Tongue?" Walker's interested eyebrows raise.

"Oh my God, Noelle." I shake my head hoping the earth will swallow me up.

"Yes," Noelle answers Walker. "So, Thunder Tongue, get your feet of my furniture."

He allows me to sit up and then takes his legs off the table and stands. Putting his hand out, he tries to shake Noelle's. "Nice to meet you Noelle. I'm, ahem, Walker. The baby's father."

I think I literally just swooned.

"Nice to officially meet you too, Walker. I remember seeing you at the bar, but you are much hotter than Erin screams out in her dreams." She extends her hand to his and they shake. "Also, if you want to make it to see the birth of your baby, you best not put your legs up on my coffee table again, or any other table in this house for that matter."

"NOELLE!" I yell, as Walker nods his head with a chuckle.

"I'm just dropping by to get some stuff. I'll leave you two love birds alone to get reacquainted. Though what you were doing looked very boring." She waves her hands walking towards her room.

"I can assure you that the day was VERY eventful, Noelle," Walker retorts. "I wore her out. Just giving her a break before round two."

Stopping dead in her tracks, halfway down the hall, she backs up giving him a megawatt smile. "I like him, Erin, but housetrain him or he is going back to the pound."

Noelle gives a cocky glare, throwing her blonde hair over her shoulder and walking back down the hallway.

"She's a trip," Walker states, standing up reaching down for my hand. "Let's go lay down baby."

My heartbeat rapidly picks up. My shaky hand grabs his and uncertainty washes over me not knowing if I really want him to stay or not.

"Uhm, I need to clean up the kitchen," I

stall, hoping he doesn't hear how breathless I am.

"That can wait until the morning," he says, pulling me up so I am and flush with his body and placing his hand on the side of my neck. Thank God, he's going to kiss me again!

"No it can't," Noelle's voice booms, sauntering back into the living room, killing our moment. "The dishes need to be cleaned up now. You want bugs crawling around this place?"

Walker smiles at Noelle's back leaving the house. "Go get ready for bed and I'll clean up," he says and turns towards the kitchen.

"But, it's my..."

"No 'buts' Erin," he says whipping back around and placing his hands on both sides of my face. His mouth is intimately close to mine. "I'm going to say this one time, and one time only. You are carrying my child. That means we will be in each other's lives for the rest of our lives, like it or not. And for the rest of our lives *I* want us to be a family. A couple. The mother and father of a beautiful baby boy or baby girl, raising them in the same household. So, please. I only have six very short months to show you how amazing that can be and I want to start right fucking now."

"You only want that with me because of

this baby." Not wanting to look at him any longer, I look down finally revealing my hidden fears to Walker. "One day you will realize that and leave me, or cheat on me, or...I don't know."

"Look at me Erin," he softly whispers, and I obey, lifting my eyes to his. "I am not him. I am not Robert. It's not fair to put me anywhere near the same category as that asshole. He was stupid. He didn't realize what he had when he had it. I realized it after only one night with you. Do you know what we could have? Love, a family, true happiness? I want all of those things with *you* and I want the chance to make you want it. So let me stay. I'll sleep on the floor if I have to but really, I just want to hold you. Please"

My voice couldn't form the word 'no' even if I wanted it to, so I nod my answer and am instantly rewarded with that one dimpled smile. He places a soft kiss on my forehead and turns to start cleaning up. "Go get ready for bed," he says. "I'll be there in a few minutes."

My feet somehow carry me to my bedroom and I'm hoping by the time he enters my room I will find my voice and thank him for taking care of the mess.

The thought that soon we will again be in a bed together sends my nerves into a tailspin. I hurriedly search through my drawers trying to find something sexy but not "do me". I have no plans to sleep with him, although, God knows I want to. But somehow I don't think sleeping in my comfortable sweat pants and t-shirt is a good idea either. I don't want to repulse him after all.

I hit the jackpot when I find soft pink cotton shorts and a white camisole. Thank goodness I shaved my legs this morning. After closing the bathroom door and stripping down, I curse myself when I notice my shirt must have fallen out of my hands. Slipping the shorts on I pull my pink Cubs shirt over the front of me to cover my breasts and peek out the door. Walker still hasn't made it in and my shirt is right next to the dresser.

Attempting to make a mad dash, I halt when my bedroom door opens and Walker's green irises meet mine.

"Well, well. Catching you like this kinda reminds me of the morning after we met." He winks, sending tingles throughout my whole body.

"I just, uhm, forgot my shirt. So, I'll just grab that and be right out." I race to snatch it up and run back into the bathroom as he chuckles.

Once properly dressed, I wash my face and brush my teeth. Taking a deep breath, I quietly unlock the door, which I have never locked before, and open it finding Walker laying flat on his back, legs hanging over the side of the bed, arms across his stomach. "Walker? You can use the bathroom now."

"Thanks, baby," his tired voice calls, as he pulls himself up and walks past me.

I pull down the comforter and turn the lights off, nervous about sleeping next to him. My exhausted body tells me I shouldn't care because I will most likely pass out in a short time. As I crawl under the covers light seeps into the room from under the bathroom door. When he finishes up he opens the door wearing nothing but boxer briefs. He flips off the light before I can see what color they are, but my hormones don't care. They are too busy running around like toddlers on sugar.

The bed dips and without hesitation he pulls me towards him, turning me so my back is against his warm chest. Kissing the spot just behind my ear he whispers, "Good night baby."

Clearing my throat I say, "Good night. Thanks for cleaning up, Walker."

"No problem."

His arms get tighter around me and his hand slides over my rib cage and down to my stomach stopping just above the waistband of my shorts.

"And good night little baby," he says lovingly, circling his fingers around my abdomen, and taking me by surprise.

When his breathing becomes steady I relax, not even realizing how tense I was. I roll over to my stomach and am startled when he speaks.

"Side or back, Erin."

"What?" I ask confused.

"The baby book says you can't sleep on your stomach. You can sleep on your back for the beginning of the pregnancy or your side the whole time but no stomach. Flip over." His tone tells me he is not playing around.

"Walker, you can't just..."

"I can. Flip over." His strong arms grab me and pull me back into him. "Much better. Don't move Erin, or I'll tie you down and make you do what I want."

I can't be certain if I want to obey or not, but one thing is for sure, that threat is going to make for some interesting dreams tonight, and I'm hoping he doesn't learn firsthand how hot he makes me, or how loudly I scream his name in them.

12

Oh God that feels so good. Walker's hands between my legs have me feeling brazen and grinding against them for more friction.

"Don't stop," I call out, almost to the brink.

"Not until you come, baby." His palm pushes down on my clit as his unrelenting fingers move faster. "You're almost there. I can feel your tight pussy squeezing me. Come, baby."

I'm within reach. "Oh, God. Please Walker!" I beg.

Frustration takes over as I sit straight up in bed sweating, with release just out of reach.

It was a dream. Damn it!

"Erin?" His sultry voice sounds in the darkness sending my pulse racing. I had almost forgotten he was here. His touch at my shoulder blade moves down to my lower back and up again. "Bad dream?"

I shouldn't do it. I shouldn't. *Screw it.*

"Walker," I say, slowly turning my body so my face is near his. "I need you."

"Oh." A light bulb goes off as his eye brows raise. "A good dream then?"

"I need you," I repeat, tossing my leg over his hips, straddling him. "Please. Don't make me beg again."

"Are you sure?" He growls, running his hands down my shirt and then pushing it back up baring my stomach. "This isn't why I stayed the night."

I answer him the only way I can. I climb on top of him my lips meeting his as I grind on his very solid erection. The friction easing some of my need, but it's not enough. I need more. I need it all.

"I don't want to take advantage of you baby," he says, drawing circles on my stomach.

Prying my lips away from his, I look into his eyes. "What part of me on top of you seems like you are taking advantage of me? If you want me to say it so you understand I will…

Fuck. Me. Now!"

A moment passes before I hear, "Your wish...", and I'm flipped over onto my back.

It takes mere seconds for him to frantically rip off all of our clothes. Then I feel his dick suddenly at my entrance, asking for permission. "Walker, I can't wait another second. In!"

"Erin, I just...I've never been with a woman without protection." He hesitates, while pushing my hair aside.

"That's...Uhm, cute... but it doesn't matter now, right? You can't knock me up twice." I lift my hips inviting him in.

He laughs but relaxes and slides in gently, inch by ever loving inch. It feels like heaven. It won't take long to cure this tension I have built up.

"Shit, Erin. So tight around me. And warm... shit! I'm not going to last." He glides in and out delicately, teasing. The strain of his muscles is evident as he holds himself above me.

My body bows off the bed and my hands reach back to grab the headboard, pushing my breasts up. He brings one into his warm mouth while his teasing pace has me bucking against him. "More," I pant.

"You want more, baby? Your wish." His body pushes up against mine, encouraging my legs to come up and wrap around his back. My insides stretch with the deeper position, taking him all in.

"That feels incredible. So much better than in my dream." Sweat breaks out as my body meets him thrust for thrust.

"A dream come true, Erin. I want to be your dreams come true." He pushes deeper than I've ever felt causing shockwaves through my body. "Come for me. Let it go."

His words catapult me over the edge and I'm calling his name and God's out so everyone in the vicinity can hear me. My eyes are tightly shut but I see white light behind the lids. His grunts become louder.

"I'm going to come inside you Erin," he says firmly. "And when I do you'll be mine. Do you understand?"

I open my eyes to look at him a second before another orgasm rips through me, unexpectedly, and I yell out "yes" more times than I can count. A few more thrusts and Walker claims me, filling me. His forehead against me, his eyes make contact with mine as he comes inside me. Breathlessly calling out, "Erin."

~~

The uncomfortable growling of my stomach wakes me from the best night's sleep I've had in a long time. The smell of bacon fills my bedroom and I roll over, hitting a rock hard wall of man. "Good morning, baby. Would you like breakfast?"

His green eyes have no hint of sleeplessness in them as he caresses my hair, placing a stray lock lovingly behind my ear. After our middle of the night romp you would think he would look exhausted. "Good morning. How long have you been up?"

"Well considering it's 10am, I've been up, showered, made breakfast, and been staring at you like a stalker while you sleep. God, you're beautiful." His smile brightens up the room more than the sun. I could lie in bed staring at the sexy vision before me all day, but this baby is calling out for some nourishment. And my bladder calls out for relief.

"If all stalkers looked like you I'm sure there would be no need for restraining orders, unless you keep me from that amazing smell. What is that?" My body aches a little as I sit up and stretch.

"Hickory smoked bacon and chocolate chip pancakes. The best in the burbs," he gloats, placing a kiss on my forehead.

"That's my favorite breakfast of all time!" I jump up excitedly thinking about the warm maple syrup covering the butter topped stack of goodness.

"I know, Noelle told me. Just think, if you move in with me you could have chocolate chip pancakes every morning." Cue one sided dimple grin.

Wait. What?

"When did you talk to Noelle? And move in with you? We just had one date, last night at that, and you want me to move in with you? Are you crazy?" I throw question after question to him as he stands up, dressed in different clothes than from yesterday. "And where did you get clothes?"

"Ok, let me answer those in order. Uhm. I asked Noelle when she ran back into the house last night after you went into the bedroom. Yes, move in with me. Yes, even after one date. And I am crazy...for you," he says, placing his hands on my shoulders. "Cheesy? Yes! And the best part: every time you have one of those dreams you can just wake up and I'll be right there to, ah, soothe you." He smirks, causing my jaw to drop and I shake my head in astonishment. "Well, it was worth a shot. Oh, and I had a bag packed and in the car yesterday."

Still shaking my head I mumble something along the lines of 'confident bastard' and close the bathroom door behind me. As frustrating and pushy as he is, I kind of like it. It feels amazing to have someone giving me so much affection and attention. I guess I never realized how much Robert didn't do for me. I can't remember the last time he had kissed my forehead or made me breakfast, for that matter. I don't think he ever did. I felt more adored than I ever did with Robert, especially during our heated passion last night. Trying to keep my heart guarded is going to be tough. I can already feel him starting to take up space in it.

Walker's deep voice catches my attention through the thin bathroom door. He is talking to someone. My nosiness gets the best of me and I step out to see my phone up to his ear.

What the hell is he doing?

His laughter booms off the walls as he tells the person on the phone that he is indeed standing in my bedroom. A sense of horror consumes me, and I have no clue who he is talking to until he says, "Sure, I'll come with her to dinner. What time?"

My mother. He answered my mother's phone call while I was in the bathroom! I'm going to throw a tantrum.

"Walker give me the phone!" I lunge at him trying to steal it away.

"Ok, six sounds good, " he says, ducking out of my grasp, and nodding as though he thinks my mom can see him.

"Walker!" My temper is flaring.

"No, she'll come, I promise." His eyes smiling, he looks at me. I shake my head and mouth "hell no."

"Alright, nice to talk to you too Eden. I look forward to having a face with a name as well. See you at six." He hits the end button, putting the phone back down on my nightstand, confirming what will undoubtedly be the worst dinner of my life.

"Eden? She let you call her Eden? Are you kidding me!?" I ask completely in shock, hands firmly on my hips and yes, tapping my foot.

"What? She said I could call her that. Something wrong?" His lips find mine but I don't kiss back. When he makes a second attempt I give in. It's useless to resist.

"She never let Rob…Uhm, my other boyfriends call her that." I fumble on my words regretting having brought up Robert, again.

"Well, two things." Both hands grip the nape of my neck and his mouth moves closer. "One, let's not ever talk about 'Rob…Uhm, your other boyfriends' because I can get insanely jealous. And two, glad to see you are finally admitting that I'm your boyfriend."

His grasp tightens and he aggressively

pushes his mouth to mine, persistently kissing me. My fingers come up and wrap around the belt loops of his jeans pulling him into my greedy, hungry body. Walker groans and I can feel myself getting worked up. I want to push him down on the bed and replay last night's events together. He gently frees my lips and looks down at me cutting my thoughts short. "You're so beautiful, Erin."

A blush runs through my cheeks as his thumbs run across them. "Thank you."

"Glad you agree," he comments, entwining our fingers and pulling me to the bedroom door, "On all accounts."

"What?" He says nothing and I continue to allow him to lead the way to the kitchen, the sweet chocolate aroma distracting me. "Wait. No. Not my boyfriend. You're not."

"I am Erin. Live it. Love it. Accept it." He lightly pushes my shoulders down to sit in the kitchen chair. "If you want it to be official…me asking and all that crap, it won't happen. It would give you the opportunity to say no. I'm not going to let the mother of my child date anyone else but me. No other man will be touching you or even come close ever again if I have anything to do with it."

Is he serious? Even if I wanted to date someone else, what man in their right mind would take on a woman who is pregnant with someone else's child? But, the thought of last night has me squirming in my chair.

Think clearly Erin. Don't let him push you around.

"I don't plan on dating anyone else, Walker. So, there is no need for all of that." My teeth bite down on a crispy piece of bacon as Walker pours syrup over my pancakes.

"So, if you plan on being with me only then it means we are exclusive, which in turn means that you are my girlfriend. And as my girlfriend and the woman pregnant with the heir to my throne," he pauses to wink at me and then continues, "you need to eat." Pointing to the syrupy soaked heaven in front of me, he smiles. My stomach decides to make the choice for me.

"We can label it. But if I am going to be your girlfriend you have to stop being so pushy. Stop assuming that I'm going to go along with your crazy shit." I moan a little as the first bite of chocolate hits my taste buds. *God this is so good.*

"Not gonna happen, I'm a 'push to get what I want' kind of guy. The last time I didn't go after what I wanted she ran out the door and out of my life for three months. Thankfully fate brought us back together so, no, I'm not relenting. Now eat." He shovels a huge pile of food into his mouth essentially putting an end to the conversation.

Looking at him, I lay my fears on the line. "I just don't want to get hurt again."

"Never. I treasure what is mine." His serious tone seeps into my body causing a shiver up my spine. "And you, Erin Decker, are mine."

His words are genuine and for the first time in almost four months I feel like there is hope for me yet. I just might be able to let myself trust someone and open up.

"Ok, then." I drop my fork down with a clang onto the plate. "Ask me."

His eyes look up from his plate. "You won't say no?"

I shake my head side to side.

His smooth fingers lift mine up and bring them to meet his other hand. "Erin. Will you be exclusive with me and give me the title of luckiest fucking boyfriend ever?"

Laughing I accept and seal it with a quick kiss.

"So, what are you doing next weekend?" He asks, taking a sip of orange juice.

"Relaxing. It's Labor Day weekend and I was just planning on hanging out around here." God these pancakes are good. He was right. Best in the burbs. "Why?"

"Go on a date with me, again. Friday night." It's not a question. It's a statement.

"Again with not giving me a chance to say no." I shake my head not sure if his persistence will ever get old. "What time?"

"Four. I'll give you more details later." He stands up kissing me on the forehead, takes his plate to the sink, rinses it off and tosses it in the dishwasher.

I savor every last bite before standing to help him clean up but he finishes before I get the chance. How amazing is this man? He got up early, made breakfast and now is done cleaning it up? I'm not sure he is real but the soreness between my legs is telling me there is absolutely nothing fake about him.

13

Five o'clock rolls around way too fast with the day spent lounging around, showering, stealing a few heated kisses, and getting ready for an evening of hell with my family. Once Noelle stopped laughing at Walker's conversation with my mother she said she wouldn't miss this dinner for anything.

I'm amazed at how comfortable I've become with Walker in such a short time and even though I was practically bullied into becoming officially exclusive with him, he has proven with each passing hour that I won't regret it. I've never felt so cherished or wanted as much as when he looks at me or kisses me. So loved. He has been nothing short of a doting father to be.

Looking at Walker as he sits next to me I

can't help but think about my daddy and what he would have thought of him. A college graduate, shaping the young minds of America, taking responsibility for an unplanned child with his daughter, and trying with all his might to make her an honest woman. He would love him, and if not for those reasons, for his love of football and baseball. Walker even played in high school just up the road from where I went at Glenbrook North High School.

I only hope Walker can be even half the dad that mine was. I never felt like a burden to him. Even after long hours at work he would come home and talk to me about my day, what I did and play with all three of us kids on the floor. He never missed a recital, game, or school event. Every significant memory I have in my life has my father in it. A hard working man that valued his family over anything else. I can see that in Walker.

I know that regardless of whether things work out between the two of us, our child will have memories of Walker and me cheering them on, supporting them with love , accepting them, pushing them to be the best they can be. Everything and anything I could want for them will be given to them.

The drive to my mom's house isn't long, though the arguing between Walker and Noelle about who gets to be in the birthing room makes it seem like forever.

"Do you really think Erin is going to let you in there over the child's own father?" Walker asks, completely astounded by her declaration that only she will be in the delivery room. "Or her *own* mother?"

"I do, actually. I mean, I did clean up her puke for like three months and we've known each other longer. Besides do you really want to see her shit on the delivery table?" Noelle blurts out, completely mortifying me.

"Noe! Stop!" I yell from the passenger side of Walker's black truck.

"So, that's true?" He glances at me in disbelief. "Women shit on the table?"

"Oh. My. God! Can we not talk about this? YES! They do. The baby is pushing on all of your intestines and so unintentional pooping can occur." Maybe no one should be in the room when the baby is born.

Walker and Noelle break out in a chorus of laughter inciting my anger.

"You know what? Screw the two of you! My mom can be in the room and you both can sit out in the waiting area." My arms cross over my chest like a toddler.

Apparently they find that even funnier because the laughing gets louder.

"Baby." Walker's hand reaches over uncrossing my arms and lays his hand on my thigh. "Don't be mad. We're just playing around. Isn't it nice to see your best friend and fiancé getting along?"

"What?" Noelle and I both yell out simultaneously.

"Fiancé? Are you insane?" I turn my head to look out the window stifling a giggle of my own. So damn pushy.

"Only when it comes to you Erin and whatever happens during the birth of our baby, I don't care, I just want to be there for their first breath…so I'm one of the first faces they see." He pulls me up and I feel his lips graze my knuckles as my guarded heart opens up a smidge more.

"Ok, you two are going to have to clean up my vomit with that fluffy shit. Knock it off and turn here, baby daddy." Noelle fake gags from the back seat while pointing Walker in the direction of my mom's street.

"One day Noelle," Walker states making the turn. "You are going to find the love of your life when you least expect it. You are going to be walking around minding your own business, just going on your merry way and SMACK! Love is going to knock you on your ass."

"It doesn't happen that fast Walker. You

need to work on love and trust before it can wrap you up so much you can't see straight," she counters.

    His double squeeze of my hand has me turning back to face his emerald eyes. "I'm proof that it does, indeed, happen that fucking fast."

    Speechless.

    I point out my mom's house and the truck pulls into the driveway. I spot Trent in the doorway just like last time. I'm getting used to seeing him in my father's place and it's helping me heal over his loss. The look on his face is anything but soothing though. His dark brown eyes zoned in on the driver side of the truck...Walker.

    "He looks pissed." Noelle states the obvious. "And hot! Erin, seriously, why don't you tell me how much hotter he gets each day? I can't believe that bitch dropped him and that cute ass baby of his."

    Walker looks at me for explanation and I give him a slight shrug hoping he drops it until I fill him in on my crazy family history.

    The walk up the steps is thick with tension, Walker's eyes not leaving Trent's. The screen door opens and Trent's eyes flash to Noelle's, changing his demeanor from hard ass to just not happy. To my surprise Trent's hand comes out to shake Walker's. "Trent Decker, Erin's brother."

"Walker Prescott, Erin's boyfriend." He shakes firmly and earns me a questioning look from Trent.

"Boyfriend?" My mother's voice carries over my brother's broad shoulders. "Well if you would return my phone calls, I would know that you two have brought your relationship to the next level."

"Well," Noelle says, pushing past us all and bringing my mother in for a quick hug. "In the car they were engaged, so I would say they brought it down a notch since." She winks at me and then shamelessly rubs her hand over Trent's shirt. "Wow! Fatherhood looks sexy on you."

My little brother's eyes follow Noelle's ass down the hallway as she makes herself at home. After my mom pokes Trent in his side, she introduces herself jokingly to Walker as his future mother in law. I'm shocked as she leaves me hugless, kissless and without a greeting. She puts her arm through his and pulls him the way Noelle went.

"You brought Noelle?" Trent's harsh whisper pulls me from the sight of my mother and my baby's father so cozy with each other. "You know how I feel about her."

"You really need to tell her Trent. Having a child won't determine if she dates you or not. She loves Jason. If you want to be with her, let her know before some other guy comes along and tries to sweep her off her perfectly pedicured feet." I pat his shoulder leaving him in the door.

Saying Trent has a crush on Noelle is a huge understatement. Last year when Alex left him with little Jason, he decided to really take a look at his life. The construction business he was starting with his friend Colin had just taken off and he was dealing with the unexpected load of being a single parent. I helped him out since I was off all summer, to Robert's dismay. Every time Trent came to pick up Jason, if Noelle was home, he seemed to fall more and more for her snarky attitude and love for his son.

She was his type. Beautiful, smart, and despite how anal retentive she is about certain things, when it comes to Jason, she treated him (and his messes) like her own. So, a year later Trent is still quietly admiring her from afar, even though he hasn't seen her in almost two months. He has sworn me to secrecy, but I am constantly telling him that he needs to get off his ass and tell her.

Loud giggling carries through the house leading me to the family room where I find the sexiest thing I have ever seen. Walker is in the middle of the area rug, laughing, with all five of my nieces and nephews while they use him as a wrestling buddy. Body slam after body slam he takes a serious beating from each of them. Two year old Nick delivering the below the belt blow that brings tears to Walker's eyes and an end to the fun.

"Alright kids," Nicole yells over the chaos. "Let Uncle Walker up so he can grab some frozen peas."

Uncle Walker? I leave him alone for two minutes and my *sister* is calling him their uncle?

The kids peel themselves off one by one and run down to the basement screaming of sword fights. Grunting, Walker stands up and limps to my side. Without thinking I wrap my arm around his waist. "Are you ok? That looked like it hurt."

"I'm fine." He mimics the hold I have on him and lowers his head to my ear so no one can hear. "Good thing you are pregnant because they might have just rendered me infertile. You can tend to it later if you want."

I want.

Placing a chaste kiss on my lips he swats my behind and walks to the kitchen. "Let's go baby." I obviously was too distracted to hear my mother call us for dinner.

The dinner is no less than crazy. Brad,

having to work at the hospital today, has Nicole taking care of the kiddos on her own again and they are in rare form, throwing things across the table and refusing to eat. I am a bit horrified, though Walker is amused by it all.

"I want at least three, but it looks like four would be a blast," he confesses and my stomach drops.

The look on my face must be priceless and he pushes my chin up to close my gaping mouth and laughs. I can't imagine four little Walkers running around.

After we're all done my mom decides a movie would keep the kids calm while the adults talk. Gathering in the family room, we sit for what I am sure is an interrogation for Walker.

"Walker," my mom starts. "Why don't you start by telling us about yourself?"

With his arm around my shoulders he pulls me closer and rubs my arms. "Well, I just graduated this past May from college and am lucky enough to be working at Hudson along with Erin. Most of my family lives here, in Northbrook, except my parents who moved out to Michigan."

"What did they say when you told them about the baby?" Trent's question has the calmness I was experiencing from Walker's touch quickly fading. I guess I should have asked him that too. How selfish of me not to think about him dealing with that.

"I haven't told them yet. I want to tell them face to face, and for them to meet my beautiful girl, so we're going to be doing that this weekend when we head up to visit." He must be a mind reader because his hold tightens just as I try to push him away.

"I don't recall the conversation where you asked me to go with you to visit." The harshness that comes from my mouth embarrasses me. I shouldn't react like this in front of my family but unless he asked when I was sleeping I don't remember ever agreeing.

"Our date. You said you were free all weekend for Labor Day. I figured it could just be a 60 hour date." He winks like it's supposed to cure the anger boiling beneath my skin and continues, essentially dropping the subject. "So, I have a sister Deliah, I'm 23, rent an apartment close to Erin and Noelle and am a huge Bears and Cubs fan."

"Ok, quit the bullshit Walker. Are you with my sister because she is a sure thing now that she is stuck with you? What happens when the baby is here? Are you going to just drop her like she is nothing and leave her vulnerable and dejected?" Gasps from everyone fill the room and my hold on his arm is like a vice, stunning me silent. If I was embarrassed before, this takes the cake.

"Trent!" Nicole scolds, as my mother demands for him to apologize.

"That was an asshole thing to say," Noelle chimes in.

"No, Ma! I'm not going to apologize. Answer!" Trent pushes and Walker complies.

"I have no problem with his questions. I have a sister and get being protective." He gently pushes me away from him and scoots to the edge of the love seat making sure Trent can see him clearly. "Erin has become everything to me. Yes, the way we met was unconventional and I would give everything I own to have been there for the first three months. It kills me that I wasn't. I thought of her night and day and when I found her, I knew that I would never let her go again. Ever. If she doesn't want me then I will spend every day for the rest of my life trying to change her mind. I will love her and our child more than my own life. I will give them everything they could want and more, and not just tangible things, but love. Protection. Affection. All the things that someone as amazing as your sister deserves, but it may never be enough. She deserves the moon, so I plan on trying to lasso it every single night until it is hers."

Tears fall down my cheek with his declaration. The walls around my heart that

Robert created come crashing to the ground shattering, as if they can never be rebuilt. Walker has officially taken over my heart. Wiping the wetness off my face with my fingers I stand up grabbing his hand.

"We have to go. I'm tired. I think Walker has had enough for one day." I turn to Noelle. "Ready?"

She agrees and starts to hug everyone good bye. I do the same and take a few minutes to love on my nieces and nephews before I go.

"I'm sorry Erin," Trent says walking us to the door. "I just needed to ask."

"I understand. I love you," I say leaving him in the doorway to shake Walker's hand and repeat his apology to him.

Walker accepts, giving my brother a break.

Noelle uses the bathroom before we leave, so I take Walker outside and show him how much his words affected me. We turn the corner out of sight and I shove him against the garage door and wrap my arms around his neck. "Walker that was the sweetest thing anyone has ever said about me. Thank you for that."

"I told you Erin. I'm not going anywhere and anyone who thinks so will be proved wrong and anyone standing in my way will be dealt with. Family included."

"Catch me," I say as I jump up. He does and my lips crash to his, relentless.

His mouth opens slightly and I push my tongue through, hoping to convey every emotion I am feeling. Lust, admiration, even something close to love, for this man.

His massive fingers grip my thighs so tight they start to throb, working me into a frenzy. He spins me so my back is now against the hard metal of the door. Our lips break apart but his move to the curve where my neck meets my chest. Uncontrollable moans escape my lips and I push my breasts so they are inches from his mouth. All he has to do is lower my tank top just a little...

"Seriously? Can you two wait until we get home?" Noelle interrupts, jumping into the truck, and I'm left wishing she would go the hell away so I can feel his lips everywhere on my body. "I'll make sure to wear ear plugs tonight."

"Don't make me go home, Erin. I'm staying the night." Walker's mouth covers every inch of my neck. There is no way I can say no.

"Ok," I agree as he drags my body down his, setting me on my feet.

14

It's been six days since our date to Wrigley and five since he met my family. He has practically been a staple at Noelle's and my house and I'm trying to keep anything below my belly button to myself. We know we have an amazing physical connection, lots of heavy petting since Sunday have proved that, but I'm trying to focus on the other aspects of our relationship. Waking up next to him has been nice and true to his word, he has taken care of me.

School has started and per my begging and pleading we are attempting to keep our relationship under wraps for the moment. I don't want to begin the new year with a scandal. Teachers at a middle school are worse at gossip than the students. I have yet to tell the Principal about my impending bundle of joy and have a meeting scheduled at the beginning of next week to inform him. In the meantime I'm trying to find clothes that hide my fifteen weeks and growing belly but don't make it obvious I'm hiding something.

The door opens before the first bell rings and I don't have to look up to see who it is. "Hey Walker. How are you?" I'm still trying to become comfortable calling him babe or baby.

His lack of response has me looking up from my grade book. I find him absently walking down the rows of desk towards mine, nose in a small book. "What is that?" I ask curiously.

His eyes find mine as he lifts the book up so I can see what has him preoccupied.

It's a small blue book with what looks like a pink egg in the center and little sperm figures trying to penetrate it. "My Boys Can Swim?" I laugh hysterically trying to catch my breath.

"What? It's helpful and hey I'm damn proud! My bad boys broke that condom open and got you with one shot!" His chest puffs up like a proud freaking peacock.

Ignoring his comment I continue writing down the grades for yesterday's homework knowing that he likes to sit until just before students file in. I'm sure the rumors have already started even though we maintain no physical contact. At school anyways.

I slam the book shut earning his attention once again eyeing the brown bag in his hand. "What's in the bag?"

The first bell rings notifying us that students will soon enter our rooms. He lifts the bag up shaking it as if to ask 'this bag?' and I nod. He reaches in teasingly, but doesn't pull the contents out.

"So besides that book you just saw I've been doing some research and I'm finding such interesting facts about our baby." His eyebrows rise goading me to question what he found.

"Like?" I ask impatiently. He can't know more than I do. I've been reading every damn baby book possible and even baby name books.

"Since you are officially fifteen weeks today, I read that the little one is the size of an apple." He says finally pulling a green apple out of the bag. Turning it this way and that he asks. "Can you believe they are already that big?"

Staring at the fruit in his hand, I can believe it. It's a long way from the bean I saw back in July. He takes the few steps necessary to stand at the front of my desk and places it down in front of me looking at me with seduction. "You look so fucking hot Erin. I'm having a really hard time keeping my hands off of you right now."

Turning around, he says goodbye and heads towards the door as the second bell rings. My classroom is still empty and my hormones are on high Walker alert.

"Why a green apple, Walker? Aren't apples for teachers typically red?" I call out before he hits the doorway.

Without missing a beat he spins around, arms braced on the doorframe, and I'm met with lust filled eyes. His black polo stretching as far as it will go across his heaving chest. "I've heard green makes you horny."

"You don't need anything green to get me horny, Walker. All you have to do is walk into a room," I state, and by his expression I can tell he wasn't expecting that to come out of my mouth.

Pushing off the frame he stalks towards me like a man on a mission. As soon as he is a breath away his palms wrap around my neck pulling his mouth to mine. This kiss is different than the atmosphere. It's gentle, fueled by passion, and sexy as hell. At any moment we could be caught but I don't care. My no touching below the belt rule is killing me and my dreams are getting more and more persistent. I want him and I want him here. Now.

Dragging himself away from me with a pained look he smiles and I realize he just doesn't want to stop. "You surprise me Erin. At every turn I am taken by surprise and I love it." He walks backwards and runs his hands through his hair. "I'm falling for you, baby. Hard. Real hard."

And he's gone before he can hear me whisper "me too."

The tips of my fingers run along my lower lip feeling the loss of his. Kids shuffle into the room but I barely notice. Taking their seats, one of the over achieving students yells my name but I'm a goner.

Walker's reading books, looking things up like an excited father to be. He's falling for me. Hard. I tried to protect my heart and after only a week it is now his to guard and I trust him to do it. I trust him.

"Ms. Decker, is something wrong?" My student breaks me out of my trance.

"Oh, no Sarah. No, everything is just perfect. Thank you," I reply, asking them all to take their seats and open their books.

A small chuckle comes from another girl, Liz, sitting directly next to Sarah. "Maybe Mr. Prescott's cute face has her distracted. He just left her room for like the 100th day in a row," she whispers.

Shaking my head, it has to be bright red. "Alright, girls. Quit talking and open up your books."

Yes, his cute face does have me distracted...as well as his smoking hot body.

With each passing period the level of necessity I have for Walker's touch increases exponentially. In between each class he enters my classroom with something green. Each time saying "I walked in the room hoping you were as hot for me as I am for you...but just in case I brought this..." laying down an object on my desk and skimming the tips of his fingers over my lower lip.

After first period it was a green pen. Confused by what he meant, I quickly figured it out when he brought in a green sticky note pad the next time. A green Gatorade, green sharpie and green sheet of construction paper that said "falling so hard" later, and I was ready for last bell so I could get him away from here and put my hands on him.

~~

Since it's Friday, school passes by at a snail's pace. It seems to do that when you are looking forward to the first weekend after the year starts and it's a three day one at that, not to mention Walker has me completely keyed up. I shouldn't complain. I love that we are keeping each other on our toes. I am nervous though. We leave for Michigan today and in just a few short hours I will be meeting his parents who have no clue I am pregnant.

The final bell rings and the students of the last class flee out of their seats and start to yell over each other. I pack my stuff and decide to finish grading during the car ride and shut the lights off in the room hoping to get into Walker's arms sooner than later.

"Erin!" Emma yells all the way down the hall.

What the hell does she want? I've had to deal with her constantly talking about Walker and double dating; even though he keeps telling her he has a girlfriend. She is getting on both of our nerves and I'm not even sure how much longer I can take her crush on him. I'm hoping she doesn't bring it up again because while I am patient and waiting to make our relationship public until next week, Walker is fed up from hearing Robert's name and that I haven't at least told Emma we've long been broken up.

"So, I was thinking...," she starts, students still milling around the hallways. "Since Walker seems to be hung up on that bitch of a girlfriend maybe we can all go out casually. You know, show him how amazing I am. What are you and Robert up to tonight?"

I cringe and a menacing baritone voice speaks before I have the chance to rip her throat out. "I don't know what Robert is doing tonight but Erin has plans, with me. And I don't want to hear you call her a bitch ever again." *Shit.*

"Walker..." I warn as students still hover around us. He's sure to get called in for the language.

"No, Erin this stops now! I'm sick of hearing his damn name." His voice rises just a bit before little giggles surround us.

Yup, definitely getting called in.

"What's going on?" Emma chimes into our discussion, which should be private. "My comments weren't directed at Erin, but I'm sorry you overheard. I mean, sorry I said it."

"What's going on is that Erin and my girlfriend are one in the same. She is no longer with that moron you keep pairing her up with on double dates. She won't be dating him and I won't be dating you." His words remorseless, Emma takes on the look of a hurt puppy.

"Walker, apologize," I scold. "That was mean."

"Emma, I'm sorry but please don't put the mother of my child's name in the same sentence with that douche. She is better than that." He snakes his arm around my waist at the same time as I tense up.

Gasps and then silence.

"WALKER!" I yell bringing his attention to the fact that he just told the entire school I am pregnant.

"What baby? You're mine." He seriously doesn't know what he said.

"You're pregnant, Erin?" Emma looks for clarification.

Looking down at my fingers that are wrapped around each other I give her the answer. Knowing it's nothing to be ashamed of I look up. "Yes."

"What is all this noise in my hallway?" Principal Callow interrupts. "Aren't you all supposed to be heading home?"

"Mr. Callow," Liz's ear to ear smile answers. "Ms. Decker is pregnant and Mr. Prescott is her boyfriend."

Emma awkwardly turns to walk away. Walker lets out a small breath that tells me what just happened doesn't bother him at all, and I pull my hands over my face while Principle Callow tries to clear the halls.

"Aren't you supposed to be married to have a baby?" Asks the small voice of a student I don't recognize. "That's what my mom told me. Are you and Ms. Decker married?"

"I'm working on it," Walker replies, as he's looking at the ground and bends down on one knee.

Oh. My. God.

"Walker get up! You are not proposing to me right now!" I command, completely mortified by his constant insistence of taking our relationship further every chance he gets. Girlfriend, fiancé, move in, marry him, and have four babies. My head is spinning.

"Baby, I'm tying my shoe." He laces up his brown Doc Marten and a feeling of utter humiliation and misunderstanding shoots through my body. He grabs my hand but doesn't get up. "But someday soon I will be down here, asking for your hand, with the most beautiful ring you have ever seen and promising to love you day in and day out until my last breath. Do you understand?"

"I understand. Today is not the day to do that and I need time. A lot of time." I tug on him but he doesn't stand. Most of the hallway has cleared at this point but the remaining audience doesn't deter him.

"I'm sorry everyone found out this way. You know me; I don't hold back what I want to say and it had to be said. She needed to back off." His hands grab my hips and his thumbs rub over my baby bump directing his words to my stomach. "I love you little one and one day soon I'm going to tell your mother how much I love her and how I can't see my future without her in it...but shhhh. Keep it our little secret." His eyes meet mine. "She isn't ready to hear it, yet."

"My office, now!" Mr. Callow's angry words bring me back to my surroundings.

~~

Principal Callow wasn't upset that we were a couple or the fact that I was pregnant and would most likely not be here for a portion of the second semester. He was, however, a bit pissed at the production that Walker caused in front of students. If we didn't want gossip, we would be sadly disappointed. As we sat in the office the principal fielded three calls. Parents were being more nosey than anything else, wanting to confirm the rumor that their child had told them.

Promising to keep our relationship professional and private at school we left in our separate cars, me still fuming from his lack of respect for my choice in waiting.

He more than made up for it when he arrived at my house an hour later, shoving me up against the door after I shut it, and releasing all the days tension away with his fingers, while whispering how I wouldn't be holding him back any longer. I was his to do with as he pleased, and in the middle of his pleasuring me, I would have agreed to anything.

So much for the rules.

"Say it Erin. Say you are mine to do with as I please," he commanded, holding my orgasm hostage.

"Yours," I whispered. His long fingers moved faster and I came apart.

15

Walker's fingers dance up my thigh as the sun is setting behind us sending me into complete submission. Since his demand to not hold back just hours before, I've let go. The past week was spent denying myself his touch. If my body longed to rub against his, I would deprive it. If he reached to intimately touch me anywhere besides my face, I would push him away. But not anymore. Something changed. As mad as I was for what he pulled at the school, I felt as though I was free. With the exception of his parents, everyone knew now and I didn't have to hide it anymore. Trying to keep it quiet felt wrong, but this baby deserves to feel like the blessing that it is. After tonight I would be fully able to immerse myself in this pregnancy and not stress. I can't wait.

I must have dozed off for a little while.

When I came to, Walker was pulling into the driveway of a beautiful brick home. Two stories with a red door that had what looked like a handmade wreath. The wraparound porch completed the entryway with a beautiful white swing built for two.

"This is beautiful." My gaze falling to the two car garage with a boat parked on one side of the driveway.

Parking the car, Walker grasps my chin bringing my face to his and lightly kissing my parted lips. "No, you're beautiful."

A blush creeps across my cheeks and out of my peripheral vision I spot two shadows on the porch. His mother and father are anxiously waiting for us to get out. I pull my overly large purse in front of my white maternity tank top and jean shorts as I step out of the car hoping to cover my stomach since my zip up is in the trunk. The shirt would give me away in a heartbeat, and I want Walker to tell them, not for them to guess.

When we are within his mother's reach she opens her arms and Walker embraces her while shaking his father's hand. Gesturing to me, he makes introductions. "Erin, these are my parents Jack and Savannah Prescott. Mom and dad this is Erin Decker, my girlfriend."

Gripping the purse tighter to me, we exchange greetings and I reach to shake hands with them, but true to Walker's form he doesn't hold back. "And this…" he pulls my bag away from me, lovingly gliding his fingers over my protruding belly, "is your soon to be grandchild."

∼∼

"Walker, they hate me!" I sob on the bed of our shared room. His parents had two separate bedrooms for us but after his announcement they figured he couldn't do any more damage.

His mother barely looked at me after hearing the news, and his father just stormed into the house. His promise that they would love me and be excited was bullshit. Dinner was silent except for some small talk about the weather and how the first week of school went. They didn't even ask how far along I was or how we met. I wish he would have eased them into it or at least warned me. I guess I should have known better.

"Baby, they don't hate you. They just need to get used to the idea." The bed dips as he sits and hands me a tissue, rubbing my back. "I guess I could have told them more gently."

"YOU THINK?" I yell, standing up and stalking to our bathroom to throw away the Kleenex I just snotted in. "God Walker. We're here for three nights! Three days! And you thought telling them like that would make it easy?"

Turning around, his boxer clad body now leans in the doorway with a sad look. "I'm sorry baby."

All at once I want to reassure him, smack him, and rip the last piece of clothing off of him. I go with reassurance.

"It's fine. You can't undo it. We can work on them tomorrow because I refuse to leave with them hating me." I walk into his embrace, wrapping my arms around his upper body. He puts his arms around my shoulders and places a soft kiss on my hair.

"Again, they don't hate you. We'll work on their excitement about it though. I promise by the end of the weekend you will have them as much wrapped around your finger as our little girl will have me wrapped around hers."

I smile into his bare chest. Usually we call the baby "bean" or say "them" or "their." This is the first time either one of us has said boy or girl. "You think it's a girl?"

His embrace gets tighter. "I don't care either way, but I want one at some point. Hopefully within the four we will be having." His hand slides down grabbing a large portion of my ass.

My body stiffens. "Let's just focus on this one."

"For now." He swats my behind and leads

me to the bed.

~~

I barely slept. Worry about seeing his parents in the morning consumed my thoughts as Walker's quiet snores echoed through the room. As the sun shined in through the large window adjacent to the bed, the snoring ceased and the wandering hands began.
"Walker. Stop." Swatting his hands away I pull the covers off and stand to stretch.

"How can you tell me to stop and then push your beautiful breasts out at me like that?" He points out my hard nipples pushing against the fabric of my sleep shirt.

I pull my arms down covering them and walk to the bathroom. "Get up! There is some quality family time to be had."

Splashing some water on my face, I am startled when Walker's hands grip my hips and his morning hardness presses into my backside. "You're carrying my baby, Erin." He pushes further into me squeezing out a moan from me. "Anytime I am with you…or inside you, is quality family time."

I look up in the mirror to see him staring at his hands around me, lust in his eyes. His statement makes me want to bring him back to the bed and show him how much it affected me. Up until right now I never even thought about us being a family. I've been so wrapped up in trying to figure out if I should let him in and trust him that I didn't realize that whether I do or not he *is* my family.

My nerves kick in after we get ready for the day and make our way to the kitchen. His parents are already sitting at the table with coffee in hand and his dad holding the newspaper. It reminds me a lot of my parents on any given morning. My dad read the newspaper from front to back each and every day.

"Good morning," Walker's mom greets us. "Would you two like some coffee?"

Her tone is loving and sweet and she has said more words just now than last night.

"I'd love some but Erin can't," he tells her then looks to me. "Want some juice, baby?"

With my nod he heads to the fridge and I take a seat at the table.

"Erin, listen. We got off on the wrong foot. My son can be…" She pretends to think about it but I know exactly what she is going to say. "He likes the shock value of things and has no brain to mouth filter. I'm so sorry I reacted that way."

She laughs along with me but the moment is short lived when Jack interrupts.

"How do you even know it's my son's child? According to our phone conversations about you, and that fact that you are what...sixteen weeks? And you had a boyfriend just before him. How do you know Erin? Did you even consider that he is only 23 years old?" His dad slams his hand down on the table, spilling coffee everywhere.

"Dad!" Walker's tone makes me jump higher than his dad's fist and he is in his father's face in a flash. "Don't you ever, and I mean ever, talk to her like that. Do you hear me? This baby is mine and I wholeheartedly accept that with open arms. She is my world and I won't allow you to treat her as anything other than that. She is carrying your grandchild and you get to choose right now if you want to be a part of his or her life or not!"

"Walker. Jack," his mother says, trying to cool the situation down. "Let's just calm down."

"I won't calm down mother. He needs to apologize to her." Walker's standoff with his father doesn't falter but in the end he loses. His dad stands up and stalks out of the room, leaving us all in an awkward silence.

"Erin, I will apologize for my husband. He doesn't take to these things as well as I do." Her sea green eyes look to me for forgiveness.

"It's okay Mrs. Prescott. I understand his concern. I hope you know that I am one hundred percent certain this little one is Walker's." My hands touch my belly protectively as I watch Walker stride out of the room.

She places her palm on top of mine and with an unshed tear in her eye she says, "I hope once he realizes his overreaction that you will be able to forgive him."

"There isn't anything to forgive...at least on my end." I watch the empty doorway Walker exited through and follow him.

The front door is open, leading outside, but Walker is nowhere in sight. I hear heated words across the yard, coming from the open garage. Curiosity gets the better of me and I tip toe towards what can only be Walker and his father.

"...and she is priority in my life now Dad. You have no right to question her." Walker's raised voice echoes out from the open side door.

"Son, I'm looking out for you. Don't you think I have your best interest at heart? I don't want some girl you barely know stringing you along like Tiffany did." His father's tone intensifies.

Walker loudly sighs. "She is NOTHING like her. Erin is kind and sweet and she would never lie to me."

"Maybe ask for a DNA test, Walker. That's all." His voice lowers.

"A DNA test Dad?" Walker yells. "Are you kidding me? Next you'll ask me to get her to sign a pre-nup."

"That would be wise but I hope you don't plan on asking her to marry you anytime soon."

"Actually I do. I'm in love with her and when that beautiful woman gives birth I hope for her and my child to have the Prescott name."

I run. Far. I know we're falling for each other. Two weeks is too soon to love someone. Isn't it?

~~

An hour later, Walker finds me resting in our bedroom, laying flat on the bed gazing out of the window towards Lake Michigan. I've only seen it from the Illinois side and it's seems calmer on the east side of it. He doesn't say a word to me.

The bed dips beside me and warm arms lay across my lower belly. His fingers tease my skin just above the waistband of my shorts. We lay there for what seems like hours but are probably only just a few short minutes. I relish in his touch. It feels amazing across my skin.

Goosebumps poke out of my flesh and escalate when light kisses glide over my exposed neck. His words repeat over and over in my head. I'm in love with her. I'm in love with her.

His pinky breaks the blockade of my waistband, lightly brushing back and forth. "Walker," I protest. As much as yesterday's school day foreplay has me ready to mount him, I still feel terrible. "We need to talk."

"Shh. Baby. Not now. I just need to touch you. Let me touch you," he pleads. Something he doesn't normally do.

I give in, letting him push my shorts down and give me release underneath his skilled fingers. Unlike last night, this time it feels gentler, and I quietly call out his name. Exhausted from the sleepless night and the orgasm he has given me, I try to muster the strength to return the favor. Despite Walker telling me it was all for me, he relents and I take off all his clothes. Placing my mouth on him, I drag my tongue down the bottom of his shaft dragging my finger nails over his thighs. His hands grip me at the nape of my neck and a deep moan escapes from the back of his throat.

"Baby, that feels amazing. So warm." He compliments me and I can feel he is getting harder and his balls tightening. I know he is close. I'm overcome with possession for him. I want to own him as much as he owns me. I take him deeper, hitting the back of my throat.

"Dammit. You are going to make me come too fast. I want to enjoy this."

I move faster, needier, circling his balls between my fingers. He's losing control. His hold on my hair is aggressive, his hips move as though he is fucking my mouth. It's hot, and I want him to spill into me.

"Fuck!" He yells a little too loudly, and comes into my mouth. Hot liquid slides down my throat.

Pulling away I wipe the little bit that has overflowed and is running down my chin. He quickly grabs me slamming our mouths together not caring that I taste of his seed.

"That was hot Erin. I've never had a girl swallow for me before." His thumb rubs along my lip.

"Well, maybe it's because I'm not a girl. I take it like a woman!" I joke, jumping up to straddle his lap.

"Have I told you how amazing you are?" He pulls on a loose strand of hair.

"Not today. You're slacking." I rub myself on his semi erect penis. Even though he just got me off, knowing I just made him come undone has me wanting more. I'm insatiable.

"If you'll let me, baby, I plan to tell you every single day for the rest of our lives."

16

The school week flies by and before I know it it's Friday and Walker stalks into my room with an avocado in his hand and places it on my desk.

"What's this?" I pick it up turning it back and forth thinking of the guacamole I could make with it. I'm always hungry. "You want Mexican after our appointment today?"

He laughs taking it from my hand. "No. You are sixteen weeks today and according to the baby book our little guy is the size of an avocado. Such a big change from the apple last week, and look; it's green!"

"Do you plan on doing this every week now?" I chuckle at his green comment.

"I do." He tosses it up in the air; catching it and placing it back down on my desk. "I can't wait until I have to go buy a watermelon. I adore you, Erin. Have a good day."

In a flash he is out of my classroom. After the blow up with his father Walker and I didn't stay much past Sunday. The tension was too high between his dad and him and instead of relaxing like he wanted to, the friction drove us away. Aside from a quick shopping trip with his mother, we spent the days avoiding his dad. I expressed how upset I was that Walker and his father were currently on bad terms. Having lost my own father, I'm constantly reminded that you just don't know when they will be gone. I was happy that my last words to my dad were "I love you" but I couldn't imagine if we had been fighting.

He assured me that eventually it would be fine between the two of them but I still couldn't help feeling like it was something that needed to be fixed immediately. Although, maybe if he would have broken the news to them a little lighter, then the reaction wouldn't have been so strong.

I also confessed that I eavesdropped on his conversation in the garage with Jack. On the drive back to Illinois I asked him about Tiffany. Jealously tore through me when he confessed she was his high school and college girlfriend. They dated for six years before she found out she was pregnant. He went through half the pregnancy before she confessed it was someone else's and she had been unfaithful for the previous two years. He was also the victim of a long term relationship that ended in infidelity. After he told me how she had lied to him, it reinforced how much he must trust me. If he could believe me, a woman he didn't know, that the child was his, then why couldn't I trust him just as much? I was getting there. I realized what I had and wanted to keep it.

He had said he was in love with me to his father, but guaranteed me that he wouldn't say the words to me until I was ready. So, in place of love he used "adore." Every chance he got he told me he "adored" me and every time he said it I "adored" him a little bit more, to the point that I had fallen so hard I smacked onto the floor. I love him and I hope that soon he will tell me so I can confess how much he has seeped into my skin. I feel him everywhere I go. If he isn't with me I wish he was. If he is right next to me I try to find a reason to get closer. I love Walker.

~~

Dr. Gale's office wasn't as intimidating this time with Walker by my side. I am nervous for him to be here but thrilled that he is going to get to hear the heartbeat. I had heard it at my 12 week appointment and was ecstatic to learn that baby was happy and healthy. I couldn't wait to see his face the first time he experienced it.

The nurses look at you different when you have sexy man meat walk around with you. They didn't stand a chance though. He was still in his work clothes. A light and dark blue stripped button up shirt spread across his chest showing every damn muscle. Casual Friday graced me with his ass hugging jeans that clung to him in a mouthwatering way. I may have been a little more affectionate around the office than I would normally have been. Walker noticed, commenting that I should just pee on him and mark my territory, but that his hand permanently attached to my belly should be enough. Tiffany had never let him go to an appointment with what he thought was his baby and he was overly excited.

After I change, and Walker takes the spot next to me, the nurse comes in with her magic heart beat wand, squeezing freezing gel over my belly and searching for a heartbeat. No sound came and after repeated searching she excuses herself and leaves the room.

"What's her problem?" He asks dumbfounded. Looking over at me he notices my body going rigid and tears threatening. "What's the matter baby? What did I miss?"

"I don't think she could hear the heartbeat Walker. Something is wrong. I can feel it." My hand squeezes his, looking for reassurance that I don't think he can give me.

I've been through this before. This time I have someone to comfort me, last time I was alone. A heartbeat wasn't found and a life was lost. That was a dark time in my life. I wanted that baby so much, and to think that I could lose this one too scares the shit out of me.

Thoughts run though my head about infertility. What if I can't carry children to term? My mother had a miscarriage between each child she had. One for me is frightening, but two is downright petrifying. Can I give Walker the four children he wants? I didn't recognize until this moment that I want to give them to him.

"Let's just wait and see. Let's not worry about something until they tell us to, ok?" His hand glides over mine trying to calm my nerves. It's not working.

Dr. Gale comes into the room and greets Walker and me, informing us that the nurse couldn't find the heartbeat, stating that they were going to get the external ultrasound machine out and check to see if everything is ok.

The whooshing of the machine gives little comfort. I can hear my erratic heart, beating in my ears. The black and white picture comes up on the monitor and Dr. Gale runs the transducer all around until after an hour, or just a really grueling minute, he reaches his target.

"There you are!" He exclaims. "You gave us a scare. See that?" He points to that familiar flickering on the screen. "That's the heartbeat. That monitor must be old. I'm sorry to have scared you."

My stomach drops with relief. It's amazing how a bleep on a screen can determine your life. This baby is my life and Walker is my life.

"We need to schedule you for a proper ultrasound for 20 weeks but I can tell you right now the sex of the baby if you want to know." He pulls me from my deep thoughts of love and life.

"Yes!" We both yell out making the doctor jump.

"Well ok. Let's see if we can get a good picture for you to put in a nice frame," he calls over our simultaneous giggling.

A few clicks of the machine and the doctor prints out three pictures, handing two of them to me and one to the nurse that I didn't realize was in the room. "Now, just get it confirmed in four weeks at your big ultrasound. Sometimes these ones can be mistaken. I'll have a printout for you of where to call and when to make the appointment. At that time they will be checking that all the organs, brain, heart, and such, look good."

With Walker looking over my shoulder we

see Dr. Gale has typed out "It's a beautiful baby girl."

Following the gender reveal I am hopelessly addicted to looking at the picture. My heart soars, thinking of holding my little girl. A daughter. I barely listen as Dr. Gale answers all of Walker's insane questions…one of the last ones having me mortified.

"Is it true that if you have sex before the six weeks after birth is up that she is more likely to get pregnant again? Because I wouldn't mind that, but I want to make sure I won't hurt her." He winks at me as my face turns fifty shades of red.

"I would highly recommend that you wait the six weeks and if you and Erin decide to have another child, you can try after that amount of time. If there are no other questions I'll let you two get a head start on your weekend." Dr. Gale shakes Walker's hand. "It was a pleasure to meet you Mr. Prescott. I can tell you care for Erin."

"I do. And I look forward to you bringing my little girl into the world. Thank you."

Dr. Gale leaves us alone in the room and I jump off the table to quickly change. When I am finished I pull the curtain back finding Walker staring at his ultrasound picture. He turns his gaze to me and I can see he is holding back his emotions. "You alright hun?"

It slips out. I'm not one for nicknames but it just felt right. Being with Walker feels right.

His eyes light up at my term of endearment and a smile breaks out on my face. I've made him happy.

"Erin." He takes the picture and carefully places it next to my purse on the counter. Taking the three steps needed to reach me, his hands grab my hips and he bends down onto both knees before me. He looks up to me, commanding, without words, not to dare look away. "Erin, you have no idea how happy these past couple of weeks has made me. I've dreamed about a little girl since the night you told me she was mine. She'll have your big beautiful brown eyes, thick brown hair and me, completely wrapped around her finger. She will be as adored and protected as her mother and will never go without. I promise."

"You're amazing Walker," I interrupt. I needed to tell him. "I'm so lucky to have you in my life. We are lucky."

"When I'm with you I feel amazing. You make my heart beat. You make my world turn and fill my lungs with air. I live and die by you Erin Decker." His grasp tightens. "I love our little girl so much and I love you Erin. So damn much it hurts."

My legs collapse beneath me bringing me to the ground with him. I gently place my palms over the top of his, still holding onto my hips. "I love you too, Walker. Not so much it hurts, because love shouldn't hurt, but so much that I give myself to you. My love. My all. Everything. It's yours."

17

Resolute in our newly declared love for one another and after leaving the OB office, I called my mother to let her know she would be having another granddaughter. After the high pitched screaming stopped and I was able to put the phone back to my ear, she asked what her name would be. Walker, overhearing my mom's question, announced that he gets to name her. Since I am getting used to his quirks I didn't push it further...we can compromise later.

On the way home I had to practically take a hold of the steering wheel so that he wouldn't follow through on his threats of pulling into a Babies R Us and buying, according to Walker, "every damn baby item she deserves." He was being cute but I wanted to wait until the 20 week ultrasound to confirm it's a girl.

Since that day Walker has been taking every opportunity to express his love for me now that it's out there in the open. If he isn't telling me he loves me he is expressing what he loves about me. Sometimes I feel like it's all too good to be true. A 23 year old man fresh out of college wanting to be completely tied down with someone he just recently got to know? I will admit we fit together perfectly, both mentally and physically. My body molds to his in such a way that you don't know where one ends and the other begins. And our personalities? When I was with Robert I felt old, but with Walker I feel my age. We can cuddle on the couch to watch a movie, sneak inappropriate touches when others aren't looking, and laugh so hard at how much he annoys Noelle, that I snort. Sexy, I know but I don't have to feel like I need to be someone I'm not when I am around him. I didn't realize I was doing that before.

"Erin, get your head out of Walker's ass!" Noelle snaps her fingers in front of my face getting my attention. "You're supposed to be spending time with me."

It's Sunday night and Noelle has been nagging me for a girl's night. We've barely had any alone time and I'm excited for some female bonding. Walker has been banished from the house until after school tomorrow and even though I miss him, I know that Noelle and I need some bestie time.

"I'm sorry. Just have a lot on my mind. It's been two days and Walker still won't call his parents and tell them about the appointment, or that they will be having a granddaughter. I don't want that for him or even this baby. They all deserve to be in each other's lives. Since losing my dad I feel even more strongly about it. I would give anything for him to be here for her, to hold her." Sitting with my back against the couch on the floor I rub my abdomen as I try holding back the tears.

Noelle moves closer, wrapping her arm around my shoulder, and pulling me into a comforting sideways hug. "I'm sorry Erin. I know how much he meant to you, to me too. He always treated me like his own daughter. Just know that he is always looking down on you. In fact, after getting to know Walker a little bit more, I know your dad sent him to you. He would be Walker's number one fan, you know that right? And he would be so proud of you."

"I know. I just miss him so much." Her arms squeeze me just a bit tighter.

"Ok." She pats me on the head and turns her body to face me. "So speaking of, how are things going with Thunder Tongue?"

I roll my eyes at her nickname. She sees him here all the time so she knows it's pretty serious.

"I was just thinking about how it just seems too good to be true. He is so excited about the baby and any other normal 23 year old would be running far away from such a huge responsibility." I sigh and stand up plopping right back down on the sofa.

"Erin." She jumps up walking to the kitchen to refill her glass of wine. "You should know by now that Walker is far from normal. Even though he gets on my last damn nerve with his gross feet all over my table, and I think he seriously moves things out of place in the fridge just to give me the shakes, I believe he truly wants to be there."

Sighing, I throw my head back against the cushion. "You're right. It just seems like the ball is going to drop. Like, the drama with his dad is just the tip of the iceberg on the Titanic of issues that are coming."

"I know I am the last person to say this to you," she says coming back from the kitchen, making me jealous of her wine glass full of beautiful Moscato. "But you shouldn't worry about anything until there is something to worry about. Don't think about all the bad things that could happen and focus on all the good. A month ago you were going to be a single parent and now you have the father of that beautiful niece of mine in both of your lives."

She's right. I hate when she is right. There

is no need to worry about something that may or may not happen, and at this point I don't see what could possibly go wrong.

"You have to give him props, Erin. I respect the fact that he is taking responsibility for both of your actions that night. Besides," she continues, "From what I hear at night he must be really into you to put that much effort in to making you scream his name like that."

My cheeks burn with redness as I throw a pillow at her legs, hoping she doesn't spill on the carpet. I'd never hear the end of it.

What she says reinforces that I am not the only one seeing how amazing he is. Not that what others think matters, but the fact that she can see how he is stepping up and how much he actually wants all of this, warms me a little bit.

After a few minutes we pop in a DVD and veg out on all the fried food we can get our hands on. When I jump up to put in the second movie, my text message alert goes off. Noelle snatches my phone before I get a chance to.

"Holy shit, Erin! Why the hell are you here with me when you could be gliding your hands down that bad boy. Where does that V end?" Her eyes bulge out at the screen of my smart phone as I seize it back.

"You are the one that prohibited him from

the house Noelle," I point out glancing down at my cell.

My jaw hits the floor when I see the picture Walker has sent me. He has a hat on that says "OBEY" and a white shirt pulled up gracing me with his amazing set of abs and a V that does indeed almost touch at the bottom. I have to squeeze my thighs together to keep my want at bay.

Walker: *IMAGE* Wish you were here

Me: So I can "obey"?

Walker: You're mine to do what I please with, but if you were here, you would be begging to obey me, baby.

Me: Oh, really? How would you get me to beg?

I know this is dangerous. I'm supposed to be spending time with Noelle, but that picture did amazing things to my body and now I want to do dirty things to his.

Noelle announces she is heading for bed and leaving me to my "sexting" with no chance to protest. I fall back into the couch opening up my phone again when the ping alerts me to a new message.

Walker: I would strip you of your clothes and spread those gorgeous legs

so wide to get a full view of what's mine.

Me: Walker...

I warn him to stop. I don't want to get worked up without him here to release me.

Walker: Then I'd nibble on your clit until your body bows off the bed and you are so close to coming.

Me: Oh my

Walker: Where's Noelle?

Me: Bed

After fanning my heated body for ten minutes with no response, I decide to calm down and get myself ready for bed since tomorrow is a work day. My nightly routine does nothing to ease me and as I'm about to crawl under the covers a light tap hits my window making me jump. I slowly walk to the other side of the bed to see what the noise was and am met with ravenous green eyes.

Opening the window so Walker can slip in, I step back allowing him the room he needs to climb in like we are teenagers. He immediately wraps his arms around my waist, pushing me into his body and licks my lower lip. An involuntary moan escapes and I bite at his tongue just as he pulls it away.

"I missed you," he whispers, gently placing

small kisses along an invisible line straight to my ear.

My hands come up around his neck pulling on the hair at the nape. "I just saw you six hours ago."

"I know." His pelvis grounds into my stomach and his erection, large and throbbing, shows me just how much he missed me. "My heart hurt thinking about not sleeping with you in my arms, Erin. I've become accustomed to you next to me."

I kiss him. Hard. All my anxieties from before have been forgotten. I love this amazing specimen.

Drawing back, I make sure our eyes meet. "I love you Walker Prescott. So much."

He freezes and my heart stops. I think I scared him, and the longer he is silent the longer time feels like it's standing still. We've said it a million times this weekend so I don't understand why this one would scare him. As I start to push away he flashes his one sided dimple smile releasing the worry from my body.

He brushes a stray piece of hair off my face letting out a rush of air. "My God Erin. Do you realize that is the first time you have said 'I love you' first? It sounds so beautiful coming from those lips."

His touch makes its way to my swollen belly caressing it with his thumbs. "I love both of you so much. I'd die before I'd let anything hurt either of you."

At the sound of those words my future flashes before me. Getting married, having children, growing old, sitting on the porch watching grandchildren; and in each vision I see Walker by my side with gray hair and still devastatingly handsome. I thought I knew what love was. I was wrong. This is love. I feel whole when I am with him and that doesn't scare me. Not anymore.

The sting of Robert's infidelity doesn't hurt as much any longer. If that never happened I wouldn't have met Walker and I wouldn't have the kind of love that I'm starting to realize I deserve. The kind of love I never had in the five wasted years with Robert. Walker deserves this kind of love, and trust. I know that he won't hurt me, that no matter what, I am where I'm supposed to be right now; in his arms, pregnant with his child, about to fully commit myself, honestly and truly.

"I need to say something to you and I need you to understand how important it is that you just listen." He nods and makes a zipping motion across his lips. "I'm serious Walker."

"Ok, baby." His lips connect to mine and quickly break away. "I'm all ears."

"I'm about to say words to you that I've never in my life been able to say and fully mean. They truly mean so much more than any 'I love yous' that I could say to you or anyone else."

I turn his body so his legs hit the bed and give a little shove so that he falls back. I lift one knee up onto the comforter and then the other to straddle his thighs and drape my arms around him. Looking deep into his eyes I make sure he will beyond a doubt hear what I am going to say. "I trust you Walker."

A flash of confusion washes over his face. "I trust you too Erin, but I don't think I understand."

Letting out a huff I try to stand up but his iron grip around my body keeps me in place. How do I explain this to him?

Taking a deep breath I try.

"I know that you don't like to hear about past relationships but just hear me out." He nods. "With every boyfriend, and there hasn't been many, I never fully trusted them. There was always something holding me back. I'm starting to realize that you cannot love someone and give your heart to them unless you can trust them with it, and I am giving my heart to you because I trust you. And I love you. Our little girl and I are so lucky to have you in our lives. I am so thankful for you."

In a heartbeat I am turned and laid gently down onto my back on what is now my side of the bed. Walker grabs the top of the blanket, nudging me to lift up my behind and bring it down and over me. As he stands, I notice he is already graced with his usual gym shorts and t-shirt pajamas. Walking to the door, he turns to me giving me the sweetest smile I have ever seen, and flips the lights off. A moment later the bed dips and his warmth envelops me, bringing me ever so close to his body. His soft breath tickles my ear and he whispers. "I trust you too, Erin, and I love you more than words can describe. I don't feel worthy of a gift as amazing as you and our daughter, but every day I am going to prove my worth to you. You deserve an extraordinary life. With me."

With tears rolling down my cheeks Walker and I fall asleep cradled in each other arms and with a prayer going up to my daddy and God for sending him to me.

18

It's been three weeks since I gave all of my love and trust to Walker and we are, yet again, walking into the school with all eyes on us. You would think that after the hallway display four weeks ago that the parents and students would stop making Walker and me the topic of their gossip. Walker can just let it roll off his back but he is getting increasingly annoyed with how much I'm letting it bother me. No one can seem to get over the fact that a teacher, who they all knew to be happily attached to a man named Robert, was now knocked up by a new, younger teacher, who just so happens to work in the same department.

My hands feel clammy wrapped inside of Walker's as we make our way into the brick building. I feel his fingers tightly grip mine and I look at his reassuring expression. "It's fine, baby. You really need to stop caring so much about what others think or say."

He tries to ease me a little bit, but I've heard what they are all saying behind our backs. Apparently, I was the one that hired Walker, and in order to get the job he had to sleep with me, and now his job won't be secure unless he sees the pregnancy through and sticks with me. Another story is that I cheated on Robert with him, though his infidelity is what led me to meeting Walker. I'm also faking the pregnancy, or so a few students who didn't hear me walk into the bathroom believe, from what their parents have told them.

Emma isn't helping my nerves either. Any chance she gets she touches him or laughs at something he says, pushing her most likely fake breasts into his line of vision. I'm starting to feel enormous and she looks skinnier than ever. He doesn't lead her on but I'm still pissed.

Every day we walk hand in hand to show a united front, but as soon as we enter my classroom I drop his hold and stomp my way to my desk, tossing my bag across it with a thud.

"My God that is so embarrassing," I huff out, turning to find a look of annoyance spread across his face.

"What's embarrassing, Erin?" He grinds out through his clenched teeth.

Looking at him in disbelief I motion to the door. "That. People staring at us and talking about us like we can't hear them! When is it going to stop?"

I don't have time to even see him coming but he is there, nose to nose with me, instantly.

"What are you embarrassed about, Erin? Me? The baby? What? Because me....I'm relieved that they all know that you are both MINE. Why can't you just let it go?" He seethes and then turns to leave.

"Because I can't, ok? I just want them all to stop!"

"I don't want to deal with this again. It's not going to stop and I'm starting to get frustrated so I'm just going to go."

Before I can get his name out of my mouth he is gone. Picking my bag back up, I start to unpack it. My students start to file in. I feel terrible, and know I have to make it up to him. I just don't know how.

Three classes later and I'm feeling pretty crappy about myself. I should have gone after him and apologized. I don't know how I would feel if Walker said he was embarrassed about people talking about or staring at us. I don't know if he realizes I didn't mean it how he thought, but either way I need to tell him I'm sorry.

Running to the teacher's lounge to grab a cup of decaf, I stop just inside the doorway, catching Emma with her gaudy claws on Walker's bicep. His back is to me and even though she is facing me, she is obviously distracted because she doesn't see me.

"Walker, I don't understand. I would never be mortified to have you on my arm even if you are way younger than me." Her aggravating voice filters through the air and all the blood rushes to my face.

As I quickly whirl around to leave I get dizzy and grab onto the door frame for support.

He told her what happened? Emma out of all people? She would use anything she can to get what she wants and I know, from the lady boner she walks around with when he is near, that she wants him. I don't know what I hate most...that he talked to her about it or that he didn't come back and talk to me.

Knowing I'm now going to be late for my fourth period class, I get my bearings and walk away seething with every step.

I manage to avoid Walker the rest of the day but since he is upset with me as well, I don't think he notices. I scurry out to my car thanking God I drove myself. Noelle is still complaining I spend too much time with Walker, and to soothe her a bit I'm having girl time dinner with her while he is meeting some friends. I leave before he does, grateful that I won't have to face him until later tonight.

~~

"Erin, seriously. I get that your hormones have you crazy but if I have to Lysol our couch one more time because you and Double T can't make it to the bedroom, I'm going to kick you out. Why can't you spread your love juice on his couch?" Noelle, not so discretely, asks me in the middle of our favorite Mexican restaurant.

When I met her at her office I kept what happened today pretty quiet. I'm not sure I'm ready for her to know. She hates Emma just as much as I do but I want to figure out what to do on my own without any outside influence. With that said, she decides that the topic of conversation should be my extremely active libido. For the past three weeks I can't get enough of him. We walk in the door and I have to have him then and there, but afterwards we always end up cuddled under my blanket in my room talking. We're still in the honeymoon stage where we are getting to know one another. That stage might be ending very soon after what occurred earlier in the day.

"Can you lower your voice Noe and what is Double T?" I ask before grabbing a salsa filled chip and shoving it into my mouth.

"Thunder Tongue." The nonchalant way she says it has my mouth gaping open.

"Seriously Erin. Close your mouth. I don't want to see where you store his cock."

"NOELLE!" I yell a little too loudly and giggle. I don't think her brain to mouth filter is working lately. Ok, well, ever. "Keep it down."

"Why should I when you don't? 'Oh Walker do me now. Our daughter wants you to poke her in the head with that huge dick of yours.'"

I am mortified. Looking around I see business men but no children. Thanking God I don't have to apologize to pissed off parents, I gaze farther across the restaurant and my heart starts racing as I see Anna sitting alone at a table.

"Oh my God, Noelle. Anna is here," I say while placing my hand over my eyebrows hoping she doesn't see me.

"That bitch that Robert cheated with? Where?" Noelle's voice reaches an octave higher than usual.

Trying to discreetly point over my shoulder in Anna's direction I realize that this won't go down quietly. Noelle won't stand back when the opportunity presents itself to confront the trash before us. She shoots straight up out of our booth with her eyes zeroed in on her target. I'm trying to figure out how much bail money I'll need to take out from my savings account, when she immediately sits back down with fear in her eyes.

"What?" I ask turning to see what has her in panic mode. Before I can make it all the way around her hand is on mine, causing me to whip back to face her.

"Erin. Uhm, before you look, I just want you to know that I can take them both. You don't need to be fighting while you're pregnant." Her wide eyes are scaring me.

Her hands tremble and my body starts to imitate them. Dread consumes me knowing that most likely when I turn around I will find Robert with her. My stomach is queasy and I just want to get the hell out of there. I'm not ready to face him and I surely don't want to see him with her again. The images of them the last time I saw him flash before me. The betrayal stings, but a quick caress of my belly and I know I wouldn't have my daughter or Walker if he didn't.

I motion for the waitress to bring our bill and tell Noelle that it's time to go. My curiosity gets the better of me and I stand up and face the windows where Anna sits, but I don't find her with Robert. No. It's much worse. What I find is Anna's hands on either side of Walker's face, smiling wide. His hands are lovingly holding her around her back. The nausea I felt minutes before returns and I have to sit.

"I'm so sorry Erin. I didn't want you to see

that. I was going to tell you..."

My hand flies up to stop her from finishing. I know she would have told me eventually, but her keeping it from me at the moment pales in comparison to what I just saw. Even Emma's touches and his divulging information to her is just a blip on the radar of my anger.

Screw this.

Practically mowing over the server, I barrel towards the woman who has caused me way too much heartache so I can rip her arms off her body. Thoughts of having my baby in jail run through my head as I imagine her blood sprayed all over the floor. And Walker? Well by the time I am done with him, he won't be able to have the three other children he so desires.

With Noelle flanking me we must come into their peripheral view because two sets of eyes come into contact with my livid ones. They separate from one another and I zero in on Anna.

"You fucking bitch!" I scream as loud as my voice will go, hoping there really aren't any kids around. "One wasn't enough? You had to go for two? Can't keep your fucking hands to yourself?"

"Erin!" Walker's deep voice radiates through my body as he tries to grab a hold of my arm.

"Don't touch her Walker." Noelle's warning comes from behind me.

"And you!" I shove my index finger into his chest. "You told me you were nothing like Robert and here I find you with your hands all over the same fucking woman! So much for going out with your friends, huh?"

"What are you talking about?" His tone is confused and he gestures over to a table of guys. "I am out with my friends, Erin."

I quickly glance at the two men staring at the show in front of them.

"What am I talking about? I'm talking about you screwing around on me." I direct my finger in a pointing gesture towards Anna. "First she fucks Robert and now you! Do you just go around collecting his sloppy seconds? Jesus, I thought you confiding in Emma was bad but this? This is bullshit."

His eyes go wide looking from me and then to Anna and then back to me.

"Shut up Erin," Anna finally chimes in. "You don't know what you're saying."

"Oh, I don't huh? I catch you in my boyfriend's apartment and in my boyfriend's bed taking it from behind and now I see you with your disgusting hands all over my new boyfriend. Who else have you fucked? Maybe I should give your husband a call. Let him know he should get tested, you skank!"

"No need," an unfamiliar voice speaks out from behind me. "I can hear it perfectly fine from right here."

"Oh shit," Noelle says griping me by my upper arm.

"Erin," Walker quietly calls my name. "This is my cousin Anna…and this is her husband Bruce. I was here drinking beers with the boys and saw Anna. I haven't seen her in a while."

"Cousin?" I ask making sure I heard him right.

He nods. "Yes, cousin."

The entire restaurant is silent as the soap opera unfolds before them. A furious pregnant woman accusing her boyfriend of sleeping with his cousin? Yea, we'll be on Springer in no time.

Reality sets in as I put pieces together. I just caused a scene in one of my favorite restaurants, used foul language, accused Walker of something he didn't do, and called Anna out in front of her husband. The last part doesn't bother me as much as the rest, but the situation kinda sucks.

"Let's go Erin." Noelle tries to pull me towards the exit.

"Cousin?" I ask again hoping it's still true but feeling so fucking stupid.

"Yes, Erin! My cousin...," Walker says.

"And her soon to be ex husband," Bruce calmly proclaims before turning to leave the group.

Anna calls out, running to keep up with him.

"Oh my God. I'm so sorry," I say, allowing Noelle to take me this time, leaving Walker staring after us, not bothering to follow.

The car ride is silent and Noelle takes me straight home instead of returning to her office to retrieve my car.

I blew it. Walker is going to hate me. I didn't trust him and to top it off I may have set off divorce proceedings. Bruce deserved to know, but it still saddens me that I'm the one who told him in a not so discreet way. I'm a terrible person.

I can't believe Anna is his cousin.

I sit straight up in my seat. "Fuck!" I yell.

Noelle slams on the brakes. "What?"

AMY MARIE

"If Anna is Walker's cousin that means she will be this baby's second cousin."

19

The next morning I feel like I drank a whole bottle of tequila despite going to bed early from exhaustion. My head is pounding and every time I woke up last night to use the bathroom I would feel as though I spun in a circle for five continuous minutes. Deciding that I not only needed a mental health day, but also a "don't want to face Walker" day, I call in and arrange for a substitute for my classes.

My body feels heavy as I head to the bathroom for the tenth time in as many hours but stop halfway as my mother's ringtone screams from the nightstand.

"Good morning, Erin." Her singsong voice carries through the phone. "I wanted to catch you before work."

"I'm not going to work mom. I feel awful." I sigh just a bit too loudly. "I have a headache and I'm dizzy and I just feel like I need to rest. Did you need something?"

"I was calling to see if you and Walker want to join us again on Sunday? I'd love to see the two and a half of you then, but sounds like you might need some motherly love today, huh?"

"That actually sounds kind of nice. I think I screwed up last night." I drag my hand down my face in frustration.

After she tells me she would head right over I shut my phone off, upset that I haven't heard from Walker, and not wanting to spend the rest of my day wondering if he will call. Not that I blame him. I made an ass out of myself, embarrassed him in front of his friends, and ran out like an immature little girl. A grown up would have stayed to talk but I just couldn't stay a minute longer in Anna's presence and let's face it...I was mortified.

My mother lets herself in with the key I gave her just as I finish up my shower. She has Dunkin Donuts and a Starbucks hot chocolate. I waste no time letting all my tears fall, telling her about the previous night.

"Erin." Her hands glide over my back as we laze around on the couch. "Just give him time. I know you are shocked and feel humiliated at how things happened but think about what he went through. He just found out that his pregnant girlfriend's ex-boyfriend's mistress is his cousin."

She looks up to the ceiling while she is going over what she just said and continues. "Well doesn't that sound like a Jerry Springer show?"

"That's what I said!"

We both laugh and then curl up on the couch, settling in to watch some daytime television. My headache is now dull due to some help from Tylenol and my mom's suggestion that I drink more water to help ease the discomforts I'm having.

"In all seriousness, my daughter, you and Walker are strong. You will get through this. I can see it in your eyes, you care so much for him, more than you ever did for Robert."
"I do mom. So much. Walker and our daughter mean the universe to me. I've felt so lost the last twenty four hours not having him by my side. I feel like I'm missing half of me. I think Robert was immature love. What Walker and I have is the real thing. I can't see my future without him in it."

"I know baby," my mother says, pulling my head down to her shoulder, combing her hands through my hair.

Saliva seeps from between my lips as I wake up to another pounding headache. I sit straight up looking around for my mother and some water, only to realize the pounding is coming from the door. Slowly I get up and tip toe my way towards it. Glancing at the clock, I see it's already 4:30 and I have a pretty good idea of who it could be.

Three more loud knocks cause me to jump, and after confirmation through the side window that it's Walker I open the door to mean green eyes. He doesn't come in but just stares at me. The silence is killing me but I don't know what to say.

Ok, maybe I do.

"I'm sorry, Walker. So sorry." I lower my head in shame.

"Erin, look at me."

I can't. Last time I saw him I accused him of cheating.

"Erin, I won't say it again."

I look up and my body ignites. His commanding tone and fierce eyes have me fidgety and wanting to touch him.

A knowing smile spreads across his face as his thumb and pointer finger trap my chin, bringing my lips closer to his, and he wraps an arm around me, tugging me closer. The heat coming off his body has my mind running in circles. I can't think straight when he is this close.

"I was so angry about last night that I didn't know how I was going to react when I saw you this morning. Then after I realized you subbed out I tried to call you to make sure you were ok. I was so worried about you and I couldn't leave school. You didn't return my phone calls, or text me, and I started to worry that something happened to you or the baby. But now that I see you are ok I'm going to tell you how the rest of the night is going to go. Are you ready?"

I nod. That's as much as he is going to get out of me with him just a breath away.

"You and I are going to talk about what the hell happened yesterday, but there is something you need to do for me first." He moves his lips closer and brings his hands up my shirt, sending goosebumps everywhere. "Go into your room, and strip down completely naked, because I have the urge to ravish every single part of you. I plan on making you scream Erin…multiple times, and then after I feel I've exhausted you physically, we'll get to that talk."

His grip on my chin tightens as he pulls me to him. Instantaneously I grab him around his neck using my tongue to silently tell him that I want to do exactly as he planned.

Just as Walker picks me up under the back of my thighs, our moment is interrupted by the sound of my mother coughing from behind us.

Our lips disconnect.

"Erin?" He whispers.

"Yes?" I whisper back.

"Is your mother here?"

"I guess so. I thought she left."

"I didn't." My mom laughs from behind me, and Walker spins me a quarter turn so that we can both see her.

"Mrs. Decker. Nice to see you." Walker's voice is shaky, nervous. Something I've never heard before. "I'm sorry if you heard anything."

"Oh, honey." She grabs her purse off the table and lightly slaps Walker, who has yet to set me down, on the shoulder. "I know how my beautiful granddaughter was made and I've heard my fair share of dirty talk from Erin's dad."

"MOM!" I yell, wiggling so Walker finally releases me.

"What? Your daddy was very alpha Erin." Shaking her head, she lets out a breath. "Sexy as hell."

And with that she opens the door and

leaves.

"Well that wasn't awkward," Walker laughs, slapping me on my ass.

"Not at all."

~~

My mother's presence during Walker's schedule of the night's events didn't deter him one bit. At the moment I am completely spent, lying diagonally across my bed.

Walker asks if I need anything from the kitchen while walking around completely nude. My lady parts hurt as the tingly feeling resurfaces watching his ass muscles flex. I ask for some water and will myself to get up and put my clothes back on.

When he returns he slides his cargo khakis on, going commando, and sinks down onto the mattress next to me, handing over the bottle of water. How he expects me to have a deep conversation with him when I know he is sans boxers is beyond me.

I don't know how I could possibly want more. I feel like one of those people who you give an inch and they want a mile....or just another 8 or 9 inches.

"What?" He asks as I giggle, taking a sip of water.

"It's nothing. So, let's talk then," I say twisting the cap back on and rolling over to my side of the bed.

He mirrors me from his side, grabbing a hold of my hip and rubbing his thumb along the side of my bump.

"Well, for starters let's get something out of the way. I, in no way, want to talk about Anna or the fact that she is the one who your ex cheated with. I will say that I am sorry though. I had no idea she was like that and apparently Bruce didn't either. However, this conversation is about us. So, with that said, let me ask some questions that I need answers to."

He scoots a bit closer so that we are within a foot of each other. I could get lost in the green eyes that bore into mine.

"What did you mean about me confiding in Emma?" He questions.

I take a deep breath. This is probably going to be the easy part of the conversation and I'm finding it hard to confront him about this. Out of everything that happened this is the one thing that he was in the wrong for.

"After our little argument yesterday morning I was trying to figure out a way to apologize. I know that I need to let it all go and shouldn't care what everyone thinks but they are all talking about me and the things that they think I did wrong. So maybe that's why it doesn't bother you as much. So anyways, in between classes I headed to the break room and overheard Emma and you talking about how I was embarrassed. It hurt. How would you feel if I confided in another guy, who was constantly trying to get into my pants, about an issue between the two of us?" I look down towards his hand still caressing our daughter inside me.

He stops momentarily to bring my chin back up so that I am looking at him again and then continues his touching.

"Erin?" He glances up as if he is praying to God that I understand. "I didn't say anything to her. She was standing outside your classroom when I walked out. She must have heard us talking because when she came in to the lounge she started talking about what she heard. I put her in her place though. Told her that it's our business and it will never be hers. You must not have heard that part."

I feel stupid but there is just one other thing. "You were letting her touch you Walker. Your arms, your face, your chest…I want to be the only one touching them."

"I'm sorry, baby. I was just so dumbfounded by the load of crap coming out her mouth that I didn't notice it until just before I told her to knock it off."

His hand wraps around mine bringing it to his bare and ripped chest. When it comes in contact just above where his heart lies he kisses my forehead.

"As long as you have this..." He pushes my touch further into his body so I can feel his heartbeat. "This right here. Then you have all of me. My heart, my mind, my soul...anything you want Erin...it's yours. Do you understand?"

I'm a well-educated woman with a Bachelor's degree in math from a respectable Illinois school. I teach in front of hundreds of kids each day. But at the moment I can't speak. I do what I normally do when I am around him...I nod, and then I start to cry.

Typical hormonal pregnant woman.

"No crying unless you are happy," he says, wiping a renegade tear from my cheek.

"I'm happy, I promise," I say, finally getting my voice back.

"Are you sure? Because that leads me to the biggest part of our little chat." He sits up, adjusting himself so that his back is against the headboard.

Following his lead I gently pull myself up to sit so my feet are by the headboard and my arms are propping me up. "I am, but go ahead. Let's get all this out of the way."

"Ok, well I didn't like what happened at the restaurant. To be honest the whole day pissed me off. I get that I was hugging the woman who helped him betray you but I truly believe a relationship is about trust and if you trusted me, then you wouldn't have reacted that way. A few weeks ago you told me that you trusted me and that it was a first for you. Are you still trying to get over all of the crap that Robert did to you?" His arms cross over one another on top of his chest.

I have to think about it for a minute so I don't say something that will be taken the wrong way.

"I don't know if this is going to come out the way I hope it does, but I'm going to try." My lungs fill with a deep breath before I start. "On top of these pregnancy hormones I also have these insecurities that arise from this rapidly changing body."

"I love your body, Erin," he interrupts, dropping his arms back down, grabbing onto my right foot and massaging it.

It feels like heaven.

"I know you do, but this is about how I feel and how I think about myself. I had these issues and then throw in what I thought was going on with Emma. All of the sudden I'm happily having dinner with Noelle and I spot Anna and I could only hope she wasn't with

Robert. The images of them flashed before me and then what I saw was worse. Her with her hands on you, and all I saw was red. I wasn't thinking. All I know is that it hurt, bad. Even more than what I saw with her and Robert. But, to get to your question, yes."

"Yes? To what question?" He asks, switching from one of my feet to the next.

"All of them. I trust you Walker. So much more than anyone I have ever been with, but I do have some trust issues that I am working on and they definitely come from trying to get over all of that. I think that because I trust you so much is why I reacted the way I did."

I pull my legs in underneath me and use my knees to make my way to him. Throwing one thigh over his legs, I straddle Walker, and place my hands on each shoulder. Shimmying just so that our naughty parts only have fabric between them, I can feel him growing underneath me. His touch finds the top of my thighs and squeezes.

"I want you to know..." I continue, "That I am so sorry for everything yesterday. I also want to make clear that I do in fact trust you." I kiss his nose. "And I love you." I kiss the dimple on the side of his mouth. "And I adore you." I kiss his parted lips. "And I want you. Again. Right. Now."

I don't have to repeat myself. In just a few

swift movements his pants are unzipped and my shorts, along with my panties, are moved aside, relieving the ache that I have for him...for the third time today.

~~

After my legs were strong enough to stand, and with Walker in the shower, I head to the kitchen to fuel us up for another round later.

I almost drop the chicken I was pulling out to thaw when someone starts banging loudly on the door. I know Noelle was going to happy hour with some coworkers so she is most likely drunk and can't find her keys.

I don't bother to see who it is as I swing the door open. "You drunk ass. Can't find your..."

My chest tightens at the site before me. Standing just a few short feet away is Robert with bruises covering his cheeks and a black left eye, which is currently zeroed in, along with the right, on my stomach.

Looking up, his calm voice doesn't match his expression. "We need to talk."

20

"Oh my God. What the hell happened to you?" I ask and then slap my hand over my mouth. I think I have a pretty good idea what happened.

Robert throws his hands in the air and pushes his way past me. "What the fuck do you think happened Erin? You told an entire restaurant that Anna and I are fucking and her husband was there! How could you do that?"

I'm stunned into silence. He uses it to his advantage and looks around before heading to the fridge and grabbing some water. Leaning against the counter he rolls it up and down over his eye.

"Her husband came to the office today during a meeting and started a fight in front of a prospective client. So, you cost me money too!" He yells.

Finding that my feet and voice do in fact work, I leave the door open and walk over to him, snatching the bottle out of his hand. "Get the hell out, Robert. Now! I never want to see your face ever again."

I twist the top off of the bottle as I find the Tylenol for the headache that has started to hurt my eyes again.

"And another thing," I whip around pointing a finger in his direction, "Sounds like you are still currently screwing her, so in my opinion you deserved to get your ass kicked. Made an improvement on your face from what I can see. She has children Robert. Doesn't that mean anything to you?"

"Not really." He shrugs pissing me off even more.

I can feel the headache pound with each heartbeat and I'm starting to sway a little bit.

"Erin, baby. You almost broke my dick off riding me like that. Next time let's just keep it to me pumping you from behind." Walker's voice carries from the hallway.

I almost forgot he was here.

His one sided dimple smile appears when he sees me and I notice all he has on is a towel.

Droplets of water cascade down his body and I become a thirsty woman, wanting to lick them down.

"Who the fuck is that?" Robert's question pulls me out of my lust induced fantasy and fear takes over, imagining what could happen here.

Walker and Robert in one room. Not. Good.

"Who the fuck am I?" Walker moves closer to us and takes a stance next to me. "I'm her fucking boyfriend. Who the fuck are you?"

He turns his head to look at me and winks. What. The. Hell?

"Her boyfriend? Wow. Picking up where I left off huh?" Robert points to my stomach. "At least it won't be my problem this time."

My heart starts racing faster as Walker steps up chest to chest with Robert. It would be almost comical having Walker in a towel if I wasn't scared that he was about to kill Robert.

"What's that supposed to mean douche bag?" Walker seethes. I can almost see the smoke coming from his body. "The only problem I see is you."

Robert seems unaffected by Walker as he turns back to the fridge attempting to get another water bottle. Walker slams the door, smashing Robert's hand before he can pull it out.

"Fuck!" Robert yells, shaking his hand.

"I'll ask only one more time. What fucking problem?"

"That problem," he says, pointing to my belly that I am now protectively covering. "Good thing she found you because I have no intention of taking care of that. I was happy the first one didn't stick because I'm too young for that shit."

I hear it before I see it: The loud cracking sound of Walker's fist coming into contact with Robert's face. Robert falls to the floor and it's immediately followed by the loudest roar of Walker's voice that I have ever heard.

"Don't you fucking talk about my baby like that. I will fucking kill you. Do you hear me asshole?"

Walker bends down and his towel drops, showing me the boxers he has on underneath. Now I know he knew Robert was here before he found us in the kitchen.

When Robert doesn't answer, Walker grabs him by the shirt and pulls him up. Robert scrambles to hold himself up by the counter.

"Your baby? She looks well into the pregnancy. No way that is yours." Robert confidently states. "You're just the patsy who is taking the responsibility I hear."

"Oh no. After Erin thanked God in Heaven for you not getting her pregnant she came and jumped right on my train. I heard you said she wasn't adventurous. I'm assuming she saved it all up for me because I've never had so much amazing fucking sex in my life. That baby is most definitely mine, so you can take your pussy ass, and get the fuck out before you physically can't," Walker threatens with veins popping out of his neck.

A wave of dizziness overtakes me and I whimper, causing Walker to center his concentration on me. Robert uses the distraction to pull his hand back and swing.

"Walker!" I scream, warning him just before it comes in contact with his stomach.

He hunches over for a brief moment before he swings his leg around knocking Robert back to the ground.

"GET THE FUCK OUT, OR I CALL THE FUCKING POLICE!" Walker kicks him in the ribs as he lays there.

Groaning, Robert stands up and runs to the door as fast as his weak body will carry him. I walk to the edge of the table and bend at the waist hoping the nausea subsides, but it doesn't. Walker's strong arms pick me up taking me to the couch and placing me down gingerly.

"You ok, baby? I'm so sorry about that. He deserved it though." He glides his hand up and down the cheek not pressed to the couch cushion.

"I'm dizzy and my head has been killing me for days. I don't feel well," I say while basking in his soft touch.

"I'm sure all of that didn't help. Let me go get dressed and I'll lie with you. We can watch a movie."

He stands and walks out of the living room. A few minutes later he is back by my side with a granola bar and orange juice.

"You should eat something. It's already 8 o'clock." He pushes the wrapper of the bar down and hands it to me.

I slowly sit up and take the glass from him as well. The coldness feels great going down my throat, but it's not helping with the headache or the reason I feel like I went on a Tilt-A-Whirl.

"Better?" He asks when I finish both.

I shake my head side to side. "Do you think we should call the doctor?"

"I don't know baby. Do you think it's that serious?"

The door flies open and I jump to my feet thinking Robert has come back.

It's a very tipsy Noelle.

"Hey love birds! Did I interrupt a good old shagging on the couch again?" Her blonde hair is pulled into a messy bun on the side of her head, telling me how far gone she is.

She needs to look perfect at all times. Hair and makeup need to look like perfection.

"Uhm, no," I answer as Walker tries to sit me back down. "I need to go to the bathroom."

"You just missed Robert, Noelle," Walker tells her while holding my arm up, guiding me to the hallway.

"Are you kidding me? Oh my God I totally would have punched him in the face, but then I wouldn't want to get blood on the carpet." She looks down at the floor lovingly.

I roll my eyes and push Walker's hand off me. "I got it."

"I did get a few in for you, Noe," he proudly admits. "And look, no blood."

They both laugh and I join in, but something starts to not feel right.

"Walker?"

"Yea, baby?" He is back at my side.

UNEXPECTED

The last thing I remember is falling and Noelle screaming.

~~

A beeping sound gently coaxes me out of a peaceful nights rest. With my eyes still closed I try to feel around for my cell phone but I can barely move my fingers.

"Are you ok Walker?" An unfamiliar female voice can be heard.

Who the hell is that and why is she in my bedroom?

"No Deliah. I'm not." Walker's strained words come out just above a whisper.

His sister is here?

"I'm so sorry to the both of you for your loss," Noelle cries from my left side.

Why are they all in here? What loss?

Oh God.

My baby.

I try to scramble to get up but I feel weighed down and my arms and feet won't budge. I will my eyes to open just a sliver and find Walker on the right side of the bed with his head on my hands, and a beautiful brunette, who I know from pictures is his sister Deliah, stands above him rubbing over his back.

"Her eyes are opening up," Deliah says halting her comforting touch on Walker.

"Erin. Want me to get your mom? She is in the cafeteria getting coffee." Noelle's face is close to mine but I'm looking at Walker whose eyes are blood shot red.

"Walker," I call out still trying to reach for him. "Walker."

"How do you feel baby? Are you ok?" His grip tightens on my fingers to the point where they begin to tingle. Tears fall down his face. My fears are confirmed.

"Oh no. Walker, tell me it's not true. What happened?" I do what I can to make the words louder.

More of his tears fall and his body is taken over with loud sobs.

I'm so sorry to the both of you for your loss.

"Noelle. Tell me! Tell me I didn't lose her! What happened?" I can finally raise my voice and Walker's eyes meet mine.

He stands up, wiping his tears on his sleeve and sits on the edge of the bed.

Deliah speaks up but her eyes are as glazed

over as Walker's. "You got dizzy at home. You fell and hit your head before Walker could get to you. They did some tests and they think you might have gestational hypertension. It can lead to preeclampsia, but nothing to worry about just yet. They are running a few other tests just to be sure it's nothing else."

"But the baby is ok?" My voice is shaking with the hope that she is fine.

"Yes." Walker finally speaks.

I look to Noelle again. "But you said you were sorry for our loss. I heard that. Or didn't I?"

I scrunch my face trying to remember if I did.

Noelle clears her throat looking to Walker and shaking her head.

"My mom," Walker starts. "She was in a car accident this morning. She didn't make it. Noelle was talking to Deliah and me."

My body shakes as my emotions take over. "Walker I am so sorry. Oh my God."

It was his mother and I feel selfish for being glad it wasn't the baby. I feel terrible that he is here with me and he should be on his way to Michigan.

"You need to go. You need to be with your

Dad." I start to sit up but he keeps me still.

"Don't worry yourself right now, baby. We need to get you and the little one healthy first and then I can see about heading up there," he says.

"Walker, I can take care of her. You won't have to worry about her. You can go," Noelle tries to suggest.

"No!" He yells.

"Calm down," Deliah says, coming up next to the bed. "We don't need to put more stress on her."

"I'm sorry Noelle, but no. I need to be by her side. I won't leave this hospital without them. They are my life." His eyes plead with Noelle as if he thinks she could make him leave.

"I understand." She looks at me and walks towards the doorway. "I'll go get your mom."

Deliah steps forward offering her hand out to me. It feels frail, lifting it up, but I manage to make contact with a quick shake. "I'm Deliah. It's nice to finally meet you, though the circumstances kinda suck."

"Nice to meet you too. My condolences about your mother. I am thankful to have met her," I say, saddened, as I realize that she will never meet her granddaughter.

The nurse comes in checking my vitals and telling me she will go to let the doctor know I'm up. Deliah says her goodbye and leaves Walker and me alone.

"You scared me," he says kissing my forehead before sitting down in the chair he pushed up against my bed. Tears stained on his face.

"So, I hit my head?" I ask, rubbing the tender spot just above my ear.

"You did and I was cursing myself the entire time in the ambulance for not catching you. I'm supposed to be there when you fall." He shakes his head in disappointment.

"Well you're always there when I need you and you were there when I fell in love. That's what matters. And now, with what has happened with your mom...it's my turn to be there for you." My hands glide through his longer than usual brown hair.

His head falls down to the side of my belly and he starts crying again. I continue to rub his head, neck and back until it seems he has fallen asleep.

A few minutes later the doctor comes in with the nurse and my mother not far behind. After my mom's crying stops the doctor tells me that all my tests came out okay and I should start to feel better soon. He states that I'm showing a few symptoms of preeclampsia including headache and dizziness. He will be sending my hospital visit information to Dr. Gale and to follow up with him in a week.

My mom and nurse leave to get my discharge papers and a wheelchair as Walker collects my belongings.

"What was your mom's middle name?" I ask, attempting to sit up on my own.

Curious he stops what he is doing and says, "Grace. Why?"

"Savannah Grace? That's a beautiful name Walker. What do you think about giving the baby her name?"

My palms are sweaty. I don't know if he is going to be upset with the suggestion.

"Erin. Besides my daughter, that is the greatest gift you could give me."

21

My heart is breaking for Walker. In our short time together I have never seen him this way. Sullen and quiet is far from normal for him. He is, next to Noelle, one of the most outgoing people I know. Sitting in the car with him for the last two hours as we drive towards Michigan feels awkward, with barely any words spoken between us.

As I stare out the window, watching the landscape roll by, I think about how I had to fight both my mother and Walker to be able to go with him. They felt that I needed to rest, but I was adamant about being there for support. The doctor even reassured them that I was just fine to travel. My mother, resting in the backseat, was our compromise to ensure that if Walker needs to be somewhere I will always have someone watching me and Savannah.

I loved the name and my mom was thrilled. Her eyes started to water a tiny bit when she returned to the hospital room and we told her.

The silence in the car made the drive up here seem to take forever, and when we arrived, Walker's dad was sitting on the porch with his head in his hands, not bothering to look up. Walker sat next to him and joined in his silence. Mom and I thought it was best to go into the house giving them some time alone.

A short while later Deliah's husband, Derek, walked in with their two young boys who immediately sprinted into the backyard. My mother and I were in the kitchen packaging the abundance of casseroles that had arrived at the house so we could freeze them. Derek began helping us silently, as if his hands needed something to keep them busy.

As we placed the last bag into the freezer Walker, Jack and Deliah joined us in the kitchen. Deliah hugged me first, then, surprisingly, his dad followed. It was a short embrace, and seemed forced, but I accepted it. I introduced Jack to my mom and she expressed her condolences. I'm sure they were getting tired of hearing it but what else can you say? A few moments later, Deliah and Jack left the kitchen to pick out his wife's clothes for the funeral home.

The days seem to blend in with one

another. People were coming and going from the house, bringing flowers and more casseroles. I try to keep myself occupied by heating up lunches and dinners for everyone and cleaning up after them. I noticed that Jack seems to be warming up to me. I've seen his quiet smile more often than expected and noticed how he touches my shoulder when I bring him a plate or refill his glass.

Walker, Jack, Deliah and Derek have been busy at the funeral home today. My mother and I have been getting the house ready for the luncheon the Prescott's will be hosting and keeping up with Derek and Deliah's kids.

The morning of the wake friends started dropping by occasionally but no other family has shown up yet. I overheard Deliah saying some of them were upset they had to drive so far for the funeral when, according to them, it should have been in Illinois where Savannah was born and raised. His dad's only response was that "if they didn't want to come they could keep their happy asses home."

Seems that might be the case.

A few hours later as I was cleaning up from yet another hasty meal, Walker steps into the kitchen, wraps his arms around me from the back, and lays his head down into the curve of my neck.

"Hey," I say softly, reaching behind me to

stroke his hair.

He doesn't respond except to turn me around and pull me out of the kitchen. My mom gives a sympathetic nod as we pass her. He leads me upstairs to our room and closes the door behind us before laying me on my side and crawling behind me. His chest to my back. The silence fills the room.

"Walker?"

"Shh. Erin, I just want to hold you and our daughter right now. I need to physically know you are with me. I don't want to talk," he says, rubbing his hands over our little Savannah.

I let him caress every inch of my body that he can reach as I lay there with my eyes closed. I want to be there for him and if this is what he needs, then I'm giving it to him.

A bit later I wake up sensing his absence. The sun is still shining so I know I must not have dozed off for very long. I roll over and see the darkened bathroom knowing that he must have gone downstairs.

When my feet hit the bottom step I am frozen by the sight of Anna in the living room with a beautiful blonde woman about the same age. Anna's eyes catch mine and I can see they are red and puffy. As much as I want to give her the middle finger and walk away, I can't. Savannah was her aunt.

Entering the living room I find Walker on the other couch just out of my previous view. His eyes light up for the first time since the hospital and I can't help but smile back at him. Getting further into the room, I can physically see him become nervous.

Standing, he crosses the room to meet me, whispering in my ear.

"I was just about to come up and get you. I'm so sorry. I didn't know either of them were coming."

I give him a confused look and he kisses my nose.

"Hey baby!" He says, loud enough for them to hear. "I didn't want to wake you. I know how my girls love their sleep."

I'm so baffled by his immediate change in behavior. Happy to nervous to happy again.

"Girls?" The blonde asks throwing me a glare then looking at Anna, who doesn't dare glance my way.

What was that about?

"Yes, girls." Walker's voice, which was so sweet moments before, now becomes irritated. "Erin is my girlfriend and she is carrying my daughter."

His arm comes around my waist

protectively but I move out of his grip, extending my hand to her, not understanding why he is being so rude and not introducing me properly to his family.

"I'm Erin. Nice to meet you."

She looks at my hand like it will give her rabies and tells me exactly what the change in mood and impoliteness is for.

"I'm Tiffany. Walker's fiancé."

Hmm. Not family. My shoulders tense up and I immediately stand up straighter.

"I'm sorry." The bitch laughs. "I meant ex-fiancé."

Without missing a beat I retort, holding my hand over my heart for dramatic effect. "Oh, good! For a minute there I was nervous I was a home-wrecking, cheating whore like the other two women in this room!"

I shouldn't have said that. It was mean, and besides, Anna is grieving. But I don't care. I know she brought her here.

Anna and Tiffany gasp while Walker's laugh bellows from behind me. As I turn to walk away and look for my mother, the laughing becomes contagious because I can't help but start giggling myself.

I stop when I spot my mom standing just

outside in the hallway. She smirks at me lifting her hand to give me a high five. I raise my hand to hers, relishing the sweet sting of contact. Walker comes up behind me, still chuckling and pulls me into the half bathroom. He is so imposing that there is no extra room for anything beside the two of us. He lifts me up, sitting me on the sink, and dives into my mouth like he needs to kiss me more than he needs his next breath.

"That was amazing baby. Did you see her face?" He asks in between the strokes of his tongue. "I'm so sorry I couldn't tell you before you saw her."

"Why is she here?" I ask, pushing on his chest.

I'm not being selfish. I know that he dated her for a while and she knew his mother, but trying to start a war with me, especially at his mother's funeral, makes me think she might just be here to cause trouble.

"I don't have an explanation except that Anna and Tiffany are best friends and maybe Anna needed support. I know that Bruce didn't want to come with her."

His hands run down my arms and squeeze my thighs.

"Ok," I say casually. I just wonder how great of friends they are if Anna didn't tell her I was pregnant. I wonder if Tiffany even knows that Anna fucked my ex.

"Ok?" He asks, shocked.

"Yes. There is no jealousy here Walker. This is not the time or the place and knowing what I know and seeing her just shows me I have nothing to worry about. I love you. She doesn't bother me." I kiss him chastely and push on his chest letting him know I want to get down. The hard sink is hurting my ass.

"I adore you, Erin."

"I adore you too, Walker. Hard."

I open the door and am met with Tiffany's crystal blue eyes. I narrow my eyes at her in a silent warning to stay away from me and what's mine.

"I'm sorry about your loss Tiffany," I say, looking back at Walker, and then to her again, meaning it in more than one way.

She huffs and stalks away.

The wake and funeral were both beautiful despite the evil glares from Walker's ex. Even though it was close to winter the temperature was in the 70s with the sun shining. A sign that Walker's mother was looking down on us, smiling. Tiffany and Anna didn't even so much as look my way the rest of the time they were here. Not that I cared. I was here for Walker.

Most of the family from Illinois showed up finally, just before the wake. But, they left hastily after the luncheon, leaving my mother and me to clean up as everyone said their goodbyes. Walker has a ton of family, and I was exhausted and wiping my forehead while lying on the couch when he found me.

"Baby, you need to go lay down. You are doing too much." His large hand wrapped around my arm attempting to lift me up.

"I'm fine. I just needed to rest for a minute," I say pulling him down to join me.

"I don't want you to exhaust yourself. I told you...you and Savannah are my life now." His green eyes, that have a bit more life in them now, look into mine.

"Savannah?" A rough voice calls from the doorway.

It's his dad.

He steps closer to us looking down at Walker and me.

I nod before Walker speaks up. "Yes, Savannah. We found out Erin and I are having a girl and decided to give her mom's name."

Walker is finally able to draw me up off the couch.

For the first time I see tears come from

Jack's eyes. It dawns on me that I haven't seen one tear from him, not as they said goodbye at the funeral home, not as they carried her out, not as they lowered her to the ground.

"A girl?" He looks directly at me.

"Yes. Savannah Grace," I answer in barely a whisper.

I don't know what to expect. I really don't know Jack that well. What if he doesn't want that?

My mother told me that she and Jack had a heart to heart yesterday and a come to Jesus talk. She wasn't sure she got through but made it a point to let him know he needed to count his blessings and accept Walker's decisions.

"It's perfect," he states, reaching out to my rounded belly, silently asking permission to touch it.

I nod, watching his hands make contact with my stomach for the first time.

"Savannah Grace I hope you know what a wonderful angel you have looking down on you."

A lone tear rolls down my cheek. His dad wipes it away and quietly apologizes to me before leaving the room. I'm speechless. I hope this can finally rid all the tension and unite us all as a family.

~~

It's Friday and we are planning to leave tomorrow so we can rest up before going back to work on Monday. It was tough to get two subs for the week for our classes but Mr. Callow was very understanding and it was all worked out.

After Jack heard we were naming the baby after his wife he warmed up to me a lot more. We even held a conversation for more than a few sentences and he promised to visit for Thanksgiving. My mom jumped at the opportunity to invite herself and the rest of the family over to my house for the holiday. Noelle will be less than thrilled.

After my nightly routine I throw myself down on the bed ready to call it a night when Walker loudly enters the room with a banana in his hand. His mood has been improving daily and I believe the change in his dad's attitude towards me has helped him, in addition to being surrounded by everyone he loves.

"What cha got there stud muffin?" I jokingly ask as I try to sit back up.

"A banana. For you." He points the fruit at me just out of reach.

"I can't eat that Walker. For one I'm not hungry and two it's green. I don't like the rock hard ones."

He raises an eyebrow at me as I catch my mistake. Walker can turn anything into something dirty. He reaches the bed and slowly pushes me back, my lack of ab muscles make it difficult to do gracefully.

"For one, Erin," he says with a low growl. "Today you are 20 weeks and our little one is the size of a banana. I got you a green one because you know what green does," his eyebrows raise, "and I know for a fact you love it rock hard."

He pushes himself between my legs brushing his rock hardness against me. An embarrassing moan escapes my lips when he does it a second time.

"You like that baby?"

A third time has me panting. In pregnancy hormone days it's felt like years since I've had him inside me. I don't think now is the time nor the place.

"Walker, don't you think this is wrong considering what we are here for?" I try to argue but it's useless. If he continues I'm not going to stop him.

"If I've learned anything this week Erin, it's that I don't want to take any minute for granted. I want to love you. Every inch of you." His lips reach my ear and chills shoot through my body.

His name comes out in a breathless moan just before he brings his mouth to mine, grinding into me one more time. My body is on fire. I can't control my hands as they scratch down his biceps. A few more thrusts and I'm going to go over the edge.

"I need you to stop. I'm going to come with all my clothes on."

"Well let's rectify the situation."

I instantly regret saying anything when he pulls himself off me. I want him to finish what he started and from the look in his fierce green eyes I know that's what he intends to do.

Sitting back on his haunches he gently slides his hands under the long t-shirt I wear to bed, and up my thighs, connecting with the outer edges of my green cotton boy shorts. The soft materiel sends goose bumps down my legs as he pulls them over my knees and tosses them to the side.

"I love you Erin," Walker quietly declares, crawling back up my body until his mouth reaches his destination between my legs. My eyes involuntarily shut as pure bliss washes over my body and almost as quickly as he started I am sent over the edge releasing the week's tension.

When I've come down from the high that only Walker can give me, I feel the soft brush of his lips making their way up my stomach, pushing my shirt up. They finally nip at my right breast as his fingers pinch the left one between them. My yearning for him intensifies once again, causing me to rip my shirt off in one swift move.

"Greedy are we?" Walker chuckles, giving the left breast the same attention.

My fingers grip his longer than usual hair and aggressively bring his mouth to mine. With our tongues busy we use our hands to break Walker free from his clothes. It takes my breath away every time I see his glorious body on display and ready for me. Only me.

Positioning himself back on top of me, but careful not to put all his weight on my stomach, he takes his cock and glides it up and down between my clit and entrance. My need builds for him again.

"I need you in me Walker. Stop teasing me," I plead.

He chuckles again and turns our bodies so that we are lying on our sides with him behind me. I can feel his erection pressing into me easily.

"So wet, baby, and so damn tight. You feel amazing." He pushes all the way in and kisses the curve of my neck.

His hand slides over my hip and grips it

gently for leverage and he begins to move inside me. It feels incredible from this position and I know it won't be long until he gives me my release again.

"Faster. I need it faster," I beg, reaching my arms up and pulling on his hair.

"I can't baby. Not today," he says, slowing down. "I need to make love to you. Please."

There is no way to argue with that. I would give him whatever he asks.

He sets the slow pace and with each thrust I can feel every inch of him slide in and out of me. Each one pushing me further and further to the brink. When he can no longer take the exquisite torture anymore he steadily drives into me reaching around to flick the bundle of nerves between my legs.

"Come with me Erin. I want us to come together."

His fingers let loose an assault on my body and our orgasms merge as one. I feel it from my curled toes to my beating heart. It's the most intense release he has ever given me. With him nipping at my shoulder we repeat our love to each other over and over.

Minutes pass before our sated bodies allow us to move. As Walker saunters to the bathroom I turn, finding the banana on the nightstand, and pick it up.

"My teacher in health used these to show us how to put on condoms." I giggle remembering that day and how immature the class had been.

"Well that banana having a condom on it is apparently about as effective as one on me." He winks and closes the bathroom door.

22

Unfortunately my birthday lands on the same day as Thanksgiving. Spending the day cleaning, cooking and getting fatter than I already am is not something I really enjoy doing on my twenty-eighth birthday, but I am thrilled that all of our families will be together. Except that Noelle's parents decided to head to the Bahamas for the holiday. I'm a tad jealous of them, seeing as I didn't really enjoy my last vacation like I should have. If I would've known that things would work out months later I might have had a better time.

"This looks like shit!" Noelle screams as she sets down the last piece of silverware on the beautifully decorated table.

"You're insane Noe. It looks amazing." I roll my eyes at her type A personality.

Looking at all the hard work she has put into it, I'm surprised at an extra place setting. My sister's husband has to work yet again but he still has a spot.

"You put one too many," I say pointing the knife in my hand towards the table.

"No. I invited a friend." She smirks, turning a shade of red.

"Must be the good kind of friend if you are blushing, Noe." I laugh, turning my back to her to finish up halving the sweet potatoes. I don't dare ask about him. I know he will most likely be gone in a week anyways. I wish that she could find someone to settle down with. She is bound to get hurt the way she is going.

An hour later Walker arrives to help us out with last minute things. I find him at the door singing happy birthday, with a bouquet of flowers in a crystal vase. Noelle takes them from me and places them in the middle of the long table she rented for the occasion.

We move swiftly in the kitchen and I try ducking Walker's constant advances. He can't seem to keep his hands off me.

Losing his mother has taken a toll on Walker. He is more attentive than usual, which is saying something since he is always paying special attention to me.

A while later everyone starts to arrive and

my house fills to the brim with all of the people I love. Deliah, Derek, Jack and the kids arrive first. He and his dad have spoken on the phone at least once a week and Jack even made an effort by emailing me on one occasion to see how the baby is progressing. I know Walker tells him everything but it's nice to know that he is trying. I do my part as well, jumping on the phone when he speaks to Walker and I am around. I know he is lonely but his work keeps him busy.

My mom, Nicole, her kids and lastly Trent with little Jason, who also decides to greet me with a happy birthday song, are the last to arrive.

It takes a lot of coaxing to get everyone seated with their drinks for our buffet style meal. It's funny to watch Nicole and Trent swat at the kiddos as they try to stand on their chairs and reach for the food. Noelle looks to be physically in pain when she sees they still have their shoes on. I pity her future children.

The doorbell rings just before we all start to dig in and Noelle jumps up like a giddy school girl on prom night. Opening the door we all stare at a man who is just as tall as Walker but not near as muscular. His blonde hair looks like it needs to be combed and you can tell how blue his eyes are from across the room. He places a quick kiss on Noelle's waiting lips and glances back at us, giving a nervous wave.

"Who the fuck is that?" Trent's harsh whisper in my ear demands to know.

"A friend she said." I shrug looking into his saddened brown eyes. "Trent, you need to stop dicking around and tell her. Stop acting like a teenager and man up."

A swift shake of his head and I know the subject is closed. I don't know why he tortures himself. I'm sure Noelle has feelings for Trent. I just think that she doesn't know what to do with them.

Noelle introduces us to Chase, seating him next to her and Trent offers to do the prayer.

"Heavenly Father we thank you for the food which we are about to receive. Today I am thankful for having all my family in one place, a house to call my own and thriving business. I pray that you are looking out for my father in Heaven as well as Walker's and Deliah's mother. I pray that you bless each and every one of us in our everyday lives and help lead the blind to finally see what's right in front of them."

My eyes fly open and catch Trent looking at a wide eyed Noelle.

"In Jesus name, Amen." He closes his eyes and finishes his prayer.

"Amen," we all say in unison before picking up our utensils and eating.

From beside me Walker squeezes my thigh, and I look at his questioning glare.

"I told you. Don't ask." I softly laugh.

"Oh, I don't think anyone needs to," he says kissing me on the cheek and turning his attention to his meal.

The dinner is amazing and the conversation easy. The entire time Trent and Noelle sneak glances at each other but never at the same time. At some point all this has to stop.

After we've cleaned up all the dishes, the kids bundle up and head outside in the backyard to play together. I smile, looking out the kitchen window and knowing that soon Savannah will be surrounded by all those cousins.

My mom and Deliah set out all the desserts as well as a birthday cake. I snicker seeing that it says "Happy Birthday 'Sally'" and know immediately that Walker picked it out.

"Who is Sally?" My mom asks Walker.

"Just some smoking hot woman that changed my life." He smirks with his arm draped over the top of the couch.

My mom slowly slips next to me. "Erin, don't you think that's rude of him?"

Walker and I burst out laughing and I assure her that it's our little joke.

When the kids come in we all gather in the dining room as they sing to me and I blow out all 28 candles with the help from my nieces and nephews. Blowing out the candles I don't make a wish. What do you wish for when your reality seems to be better than your dreams?

My family knows that I don't like them spending money on gifts, but Walker apparently doesn't listen. As a large, beautifully wrapped box is placed on the coffee table in front of my now resting feet, I narrow my eyes at him.

"I told you not to get me anything!" I softly slap his chest but rush to open the paper.

He laughs and assures me it's a gift to him as well. I blush thinking about what he could possibly get me that would benefit him, but realize he wouldn't have me open it in front of everyone if it was dirty.

I move around my ever growing stomach and start pulling items out one by one. The first is a gift certificate for a spa day including a manicure, pedicure and pre-natal massage. The second is a bottle of sun screen. I look at him confused, but he nods his head towards the box urging me to continue. The next is a pair of sunglasses followed by a black maternity bathing suit.

I'm confused as I look into the box that is now empty. What good is a maternity suit when by the time summer gets here I will have already given birth? Walker laughs and hands over a long envelope and I quickly open it anxious to know what's inside. I have an idea but I want to make sure I don't jump to conclusions.

What I find is my passport, that I'm positive Noelle snuck out of my safe, and tickets for Walker and I to go to Cozumel for New Years.

"This is fantastic Walker!" I screech, flinging myself into his waiting arms.

I'll get to enjoy Cozumel this time around and the one on one time doesn't hurt either.

"I just want to experience the beautiful place where you found out you were having my child. I know that it was a scary and unsure time for you, so I want to go back and make it amazing for you." His mouth meets mine and following a long drawn out kiss I hear Trent clear his throat.

"There are kids around," he says sternly, but I can tell he thinks it's funny.

Embarrassed, I pull myself away and tuck every item back into the box, taking it to my bedroom.

The rest of the night is spent relaxing with

our bellies completely full. The boys watch football and the girls chit chat at the table. Noelle and Chase are practically sitting on top of each other as Trent seethes where he sits. Once their lips touch he jumps up, throwing the empty water bottle in his hand across the room, causing everyone to jump.

He silently bundles Jason back up and takes him out the door, slamming it and leaving us all completely silent. Everyone's eyes search out one another's.

"What the hell was that about?" Noelle's shocked eyes meet mine.

I know what it was about but it's not my place to tell her. "No idea." I shrug my shoulders hoping she will drop it. Noelle can spot one of my lies a mile away. I'm sure the discussion is far from over.

"He has a lot on his mind." My sister Nicole chimes in looking annoyed. "We all do."

She has been very quiet today and I can tell she is stressed out. While the kids are content with my mom, Deliah and Derek, coloring at the table together I take the opportunity to get in some one on one time with her and motion for her to meet me in my room.

Closing my bedroom door behind me I encounter a sobbing mess sitting on my bed. I rush to her side wrapping her in my arms telling her it will be ok. I don't know how much that can be true since I haven't a clue what is going on.

When she finally catches her breath she seems to vent all her frustrations out.

"Brad and I are getting a divorce." She breathes out so quickly I'm not sure I hear her right.

"What?" I turn my body to face her, stunned. "Oh, Nic. I'm so sorry. What happened?"

"I don't know. We just drifted apart. We haven't slept in the same bed since Nick was born. My whole life is my kids and I think I just have let my husband's needs fall to the wayside. He says it's not me, but I can't help but think my deteriorating body is the issue. I feel like a gross slob."

She gestures towards her body like I am supposed to agree with that statement.

"Nicole! Don't ever say that. First of all your kids should be your life. They depend on you. You are an amazing mother and if he is upset that you are taking care of their needs over his then he isn't worth being married to the most amazing, loving and beautiful woman." My thumb brushes a tear off her cheek.

"He never said that. It's all my thinking. I

just don't know what his reasons are. He says that we've grown apart." She throws her hands up as her voice gets louder. "What does that even mean?"

I pull her back into my arms and her head drops onto my shoulder. "I don't know. I wish I knew. I'm sorry. Does mom know?"

She nods a 'yes' and we just sit in silence for a little while.

She sniffles, wiping her last remaining tears and smirks at me. "So what about Trent and Noelle, huh?"

"I know. Talk about a soap opera. I'm not getting in the middle of it." I giggle. "The two of them have been in love with each other forever but neither of them wants to make the first move. They are both so head strong that it probably will never happen. Or if it does it will be the undoing of both of them."

"I can totally see that." She sniffles. "Let's get back in there."

After she cleans herself up we head back into the living room to try and enjoy the rest of the night. With Trent gone the tension seems to have left as well.

Everyone, except Walker and Chase, leaves with hugs and kisses. All three of us watch as Noelle breaks out the Resolve and immediately begins scrubbing and bitching about each stain on the carpet. I'm going to hear about this for days.

Walker sits with me on the couch. It's been a long day. Pulling my feet up onto his lap he starts to massage them, telling me how much he can't wait for our vacation. Once Noelle is done scrubbing the carpet and putting everything back just how she likes it, she leads Chase to her bedroom. It's going to be a long night.

The walls in Noelle's room begin to rattle and I almost feel bad for all the times she has had to listen to Walker and me when we were intimate. With the TV turned up to block out her moans, I barely hear the doorbell when it rings. Walker gently places my legs down heading to the door. He opens it and finds Trent.

"I forgot my phone. I waited until I dropped Jason off at Alex's parent's house before I came back." He brushes past Walker retrieving it from the entertainment stand and turns to me. "Listen. I'm really sorry."

Just then a thumping noise intrudes on our conversation as Noelle's screams of pleasure radiate outward towards the living room. I watch Trent's eyes dilate. He's instantly furious. His fists are balled up so tightly I can see the whites of his knuckles. This time he throws his phone across the room shattering it against the wall.

"FUCK!" He screams so loud that the banging comes to a halt.

He storms out of the house slamming the door so hard that my picture of Jason falls off the wall, glass shattering.

Pissed I run to the door, flinging it open and yell out to him. "Unless you tell her and she doesn't reciprocate then quit acting like an asshole!"

I can slam doors too!

Walker chuckles behind me and I spin around giving him a glare. His deep sexy voice replaces his laughing and I can't help but smile.

"Feel like showing me how thankful you are for me in the bedroom." His eyebrows wiggle up and down suggestively.

I reach my hand out to his and lead him to my room. As I hit the entrance to my room Noelle's door flies open. She stands there looking like a sexed up Greek goddess with a sheet draped around her body.

"What the fuck was that?" She asks.

"Oh, just the blind trying to lead the blind," I say aggressively dragging Walker into my room. "Hey Noe, Trent left some glass for you to clean up."

~~

The next morning Walker's side of the bed is empty. I know he promised to help Derek with some home improvement project this morning but I was hoping he would wake me. He never does making sure I get my baby sleep. There is a Tupperware container on his nightstand, and a white note with my name in his handwriting on top of it. Opening the letter quickly, I read what he has written.

My adoring Erin. I didn't want to wake you. Today is Friday and you know what that means? Yup. Inside you will find your weekly reminder of how big Savannah is currently. The 26th week is not as sexy as the banana but I could use them as tie ups if you like. I will see you tonight. Have a great day. I love and adore you.

Walker

I pop open the sealed container finding uncut scallions. I pick them up turning them around in my hands and laugh.

God I love this crazy man.

23

"Oh my God, that feels amazing," Noelle moans. "Yes, oh god yes, right there. Don't stop! Deeper."

"Noe, seriously. We're in public." I laugh at her. I don't know why I bother. She doesn't care who hears what she has to say, inappropriate or not.

"But this feels so damn good, Erin. I want to take her home with me." She winks at the short and cute little woman who joins in my laughter while continuing to give Noelle's feet a deep massage.

Walker not only bought me a visit to the salon but has Noelle's hands and feet getting polished as well. I don't know where he gets all this money from. He pays more each month for his apartment than I do and has a lower salary than me since he is a first year teacher. When I ask how he can afford the vacation, all the dinner dates, maternity clothes, and baby items he has been stock piling he just tells me that he was born to spoil his girls. I drop it. It's not any of my business...at least not right now.

"So," Noelle drags me from my thoughts lightly slapping my shoulder. "Have you and Walker talked about the future?"

Her blue eyes sparkle when she talks about Walker and me. She is constantly saying how much she loves the two of us together because he makes me happy. I am happy. We've had so many road blocks and right now it seems that the highway is clear.

The only issue currently is that he hasn't been around as much lately. We still usually meet up at one or the other's house at night but we aren't attached at the hip as much as before. He's been taking calls in the other room and having to run errands almost every day. I try not to think the worst. I'm really working on proving I trust him. He just isn't making it easy.

"What do you mean?" I pick up my decaf hot tea from the cup holder glancing at her.

"You know what I am talking about Erin. You two are doing great and you are going to have his baby in three months. You must have talked about living arrangements with him or marriage even. I don't know. Just something more than what you are doing now."

"We haven't really. I think he is just trying not to push too much. In the beginning it seemed like he didn't want to leave me with any choices and now he is giving me space," I say shrugging my shoulders like it's not a big deal.

"Is that what you want?"

"No." I answer too quickly but this actually has been on my mind. I know I need to fight for what I want but I'm too shy to tell him I want to move in together and I don't know how Noelle would react. We both own our house. "I want to move further in our relationship."

"How far, Erin? Marriage?"

She grabs my hand when I don't answer. I am too stunned to form a response. I was with Robert for four years before I even considered marrying him. Four months with Walker and I would marry him in a heartbeat. How is that possible?

"Erin?" She raises her voice a bit, pulling her feet out of the foot tub and turning to me. "Erin. It's ok to want to marry him. I know that feeling must be scary but anyone can see the two of you belong with each other."

"It's only been a few months, Noelle. How can I love him so much already that I would drop everything if he asked me to fly to Vegas?" A tear falls down my cheek and I catch it before it hits my leg feeling completely stupid.

"Because he is the one!" She squeezes my hand getting me to look at her. "Don't let your feelings for him scare you. I know he feels the same. I see it every time he watches you across the room or when you fall asleep watching TV. Just talk to him. You can't tell me you don't think he wants the same things as you?"

"What about you? What if we want to move in together?" My palms get sweaty just thinking about not living with her anymore. We've spent the better part of nine years being roommates. She has been the only constant in my life in a world of so many changes. Good and bad.

"Then do it," she nonchalantly declares placing her feet back into the warm water.

"Just like that you would want me to leave you?"

"Are you kidding? I don't want you to leave. I need you too." My narrowed eyes must show her how upsetting that statement is because she decides to clarify. "Listen. Over the past decade I have watched you date some pretty shitty men. Robert was just the crappy icing on the shit cake. I saw you devastated over your dad, your lost baby with Robert, his cheating and this past summer when you thought it was you against the world. Your life has been full of loss and now when I see you with Walker I know that you are done with all of that nonsense. It's time for you to start living and it starts with Walker. He is so good for you Erin. You need to move in with him because you need to be happy."

"I love you Noelle." I drag my newly painted toes away from my pedicurist, Jasmine, and stand up to embrace her.

"Ok, now enough with the girly shit. Sit down," she laughs looking down at my toes. "And now she is going to have to fix your polish."

I look at my toes and see turquoise smeared all over my toes. "Shit."

"Damn it!" Jasmine yells causing Noelle and I to hysterically laugh.

~~

Our day of pampering came to an end and I had to tip Jasmine extra due to the mess I created. We had lunch at Lou Malnati's before we went home.

As Noelle pulled into the driveway the car jolted forward when she slammed on the breaks.

"What the hell!" I yell grasping at my belly. I'm 30 weeks now and I don't think stopping short is the best for me or Savannah.

"That stupid mother fucking ASSHOLE!" She screeches out throwing the car into park and jumping out.

I look up and spot the object of her rage. Robert is standing on our porch.

I jump out as quickly as my big belly will allow and try to diffuse the situation. I'm too late. By the time I reach them Noelle has successfully slapped him across the face and is on her way to doing it again. Robert stops her hand mid swing but she recovers by kneeing him in the groin.

"Leave asshole! You thought Walker hit hard wait until you feel what I have for you." She yells at his curled up form on the ground. "You low life piece of shit. She deserved so much better and it took you being a cheating bastard for her to get that. Get the fuck off my property."

"Noe, stop! I think he's had enough." I almost laugh at the fetal position he is in. What a little wuss.

"A little bitch slappin' does a cheater good, Erin." Noelle kicks him one more time before stepping over his body and opening our front door.

Robert groans in pain at my feet and this time I laugh, duplicating Noelle by stepping over him and into the house.

"I just want to talk to you Erin. Please."

"Come on in when you can walk," I say without a backwards glance.

I waddle in to find Noelle holding a bottle of tequila in her hands. "Drinking already?" I ask amused.

"Oh, no. This is for me to throw at dickweed out there." Her face is dead serious so I walk over taking the bottle out of her hand.

"He said he wants to talk. Didn't you say you needed to take a shower?" I'm not sure having them both in the room for an extended period of time is a good idea.

"Nope. I'm staying here until he leaves. Anything that prick has to say to you he can say in front of me."

I leave it alone. I wouldn't win the argument anyways. She knows everything and she is right. Anything he has to say I will just tell her when he leaves.

A few minutes later Robert walks in eyeing Noelle to make sure she doesn't attack him again.

"I won't touch you anymore. I've had my fill of nastiness for the day. But I swear if you make her cry or touch her I will murder you. Blood all over my floor or not." The seething anger radiates off of her skin. She snatches the tequila back, taking a shot straight from the bottle, and sits at the kitchen table.

I don't think she is kidding.

I can't fathom why I want to hear what he has to say. The last time he was here I ended up in the hospital. It wasn't his fault but I'm sure the stress of him being here and the mean things he said contributed to my anxiety. I'm hoping he is here only to apologize.

Pouring myself a glass of lemonade I sit on the recliner, far away from Robert, who sat on the couch. Silence fills the air and Noelle's heavy breathing is the only thing I can hear. She must be irate. I feel bad. Maybe I shouldn't have let him in here.

"I'm so sorry." Robert finally breaks into the quiet looking at where Savannah is happily moving around.

A quick "psh" comes from behind me and Noelle is now busily tapping away on her phone.

"Sorry? For what? The cheating? The terrible comments you made the last time you were here?" My eye brows rise in anticipation of what he will say next.

"Shit Erin." His hands run through his slightly longer hair. "Everything. Every damn thing. But what I'm the sorriest about is what I said to you about our baby."

"THAT IS NOT YOUR BABY!" Noelle shrieks making me jump.

"No. I know this one isn't mine but what I said about the baby we lost. I didn't mean it." His head drops into his hands and he lets out a loud sigh.

"Why are you apologizing?" I sip my lemonade casually letting him know that it means nothing to me. He hurt me and I can forgive but I will never forget. What he did lead me to the greatest things in my life but I will not thank him or forget the hurt I experienced because of it.

"Anna left me." His brown eyes look sad. I don't give a shit.

"So what? You want me back now?" I snort. "Not happening. I have a real man now. One that I know would never hurt me the way you did. One who I put my faith and trust into and know, for a fact, would never betray that. He knows what he has. You never did."

"No. It's not that. I just…she wanted to work things out with her husband. She never was going to leave him for me. Not that I blame her. What good can come from a relationship of two cheaters? A lot of mistrust. I can't even tell you how sorry I am for what I did. I should have talked to you when I thought things were going downhill. Maybe we could have fixed it, or maybe we could have gone our separate ways and still been friends. I don't know. I just know that I will never forgive myself for what I did to you." He stands looking towards Noelle and then the door. "I should go."

"Oh, don't leave on my account Robert. Feel free to stay about five more minutes." A devious smile crosses her lips and I know she had to have been texting Walker.

He looks at me confused but I'm not wasting any time. "You should probably go. I can guarantee in five minutes you won't be happy you stuck around."

I'm pushing on Robert's back while Noelle cackles and just as he reaches for the door knob it swings open to over six feet of sexy anger. If looks could kill Robert would be dead on the floor right now. Walker immediately grabs a hold of Robert's jacket and lifts.

"Walker, stop! He was just leaving," I yell out.

At the same time Noelle yells, "Kick his ass."

"No!" I say and Walker gently places Robert back down. Like a cockroach he scurries out of the house and to his car.

"What the hell was he doing here Erin? Are you ok?" Strong arms wrap around me careful not to squeeze me too tight. His soft gentle kisses are placed on top of my head.

"She's fine. Asshat just wanted to apologize and say that Anna left his sorry ass," Noelle's fading voice calls from down the hall. "I'm going to shower now that the show is over. What a letdown."

"Seriously, I'm fine. I promise. You can go home now. I don't want you to be too tired for our flight tomorrow." I look up and kiss the bottom of his chin.

"My stuff is already packed up. I'm staying here tonight. Now go shower so I can get you dirty again." He turns me around and pushes me gently forward with a slap on my ass.

"Hey!" I try to sound offended.

"Now woman!" And with that he turns to head back outside. I just hope Robert is gone.

~~

The shower felt fantastic. The oil they used on my back during the massage was starting to stick. Towel drying my hair I walk into my bedroom with only one of Walker's Chicago Bears shirts on.

"I don't think you've looked sexier. Come here." His arm reaches out for me and like a magnet I am drawn to him.

He lovingly pulls the shirt up exposing my bare chest and pink lacey thong. Since I've gotten bigger I have been wearing cuter underwear. I feel huge and they make me feel pretty.

"These are sexy," he says rubbing his hands behind me to caress my ass.

A whimper escapes me with how good that feels.

He pushes himself back so he is sitting in the middle of the bed. "Grab that bag on your nightstand and come sit in front of me," he softly commands.

I grab the white bag and peek inside. It's a bottle of coconut lotion. "What's this for?" I ask, sliding across the bed so that my back is to his front.

"Well," he says, taking the bottle from me. "You are thirty one weeks and I thought I would do something different. My book says that Savannah is the size of a coconut. Knowing you don't like the taste, I decided to get some lotion and massage it into you. Now, I know you had one today but I hope they didn't give you the kind I plan on."

Small, soft kisses run up and down the back of my neck causing my heart beat to quicken. My masseuse today was amazing but not nearly as amazing as when Walker touches me.

The sound of lotion coming out of the bottle has me giggling but once he places his hands on my shoulder all humor is gone. His touch is gentle and precise, hitting every single erotic zone on my body.

Ok, maybe every zone on my body is erotic when he is around.

"I love you Erin," he whispers against the skin between my shoulder blades.

His hands find their way to my breasts and the attention has me wanting to move his hands much lower.

"I love you too, Walker." I cry out when his hands reach my stomach and my head falls back giving him easier access to my neck.

"I love this. I love that my hands are just inches from our daughter. I love her so much and I haven't even seen her. Erin, thank you so much for this. For giving me a chance. I am going to make you so happy." He promises.

"God Walker, you're turning me on." I push his hands lower hoping to connect them with where I need them most.

"What was that?!" His hands jump and find their way back to my belly.

"Oh my God, Walker. Don't tease me damn it." My frustrated tone takes even me by surprise.

"I felt a bump."

Oh my God. I'm used to it. Day in and day out I feel Savannah moving around and don't think twice about it anymore. Every time Walker is around she chooses to stay still. At thirty one weeks he has yet to feel her move. Time to put my hormones aside.

"Here, sit against the head board." I point and he quickly complies.

I follow him leaning back and place both of his hand over her favorite spot on my right side. Savannah moves an elbow underneath his touch causing him to pull away.

"Holy shit! That felt like a snake in your stomach. What was that?" I'm sure his smile could light up the night sky right now.

"Her knee or her elbow. Kinda freaky huh?" I laugh and he brings his palms back over my belly.

She moves again and I can feel his smile on the back of my head. "Hi Savannah. It's Daddy."

Tears prick the sides of my eyes as he talks to her. Telling her how much he loves her and even singing to her. I've never heard him sing and it's beautiful. She continues to kick the crap out of me. I start to become uncomfortable but decide that his happiness is worth the constant kicks to the ribs.

He continues to talk to her and rub his hands along my

body. My arms, legs and shoulders have never had so much attention. My blinks become longer and soon I am fast asleep dreaming of a little five year old girl with brown hair and green eyes being pushed on a swing by her daddy.

24

After hours of turning down Walker's offers to join the mile high club we arrive in Cozumel. The island is just as beautiful as I remember it, except it seems ten times better since we left fifteen degree weather to come to here where it's a balmy seventy-five. The trip from the airport is familiar as we pull up to the same hotel Noelle and I stayed in. The Occidental. What's even wilder is the room we are staying in is the same one I was in back in July with Noe.

The room looks exactly the same but this time I have my man with me.

"Did you know this is the exact room I stayed in with Noelle?" I ask placing my beach hat down onto the side table.

"I did. I planned it that way," he says eyeing me. Probably to be sure I'm not upset.

"Why?"

"You'll see." His gaze looks out the window and towards the beach.

Ignoring his mysterious answer I look around the room that brings scary memories of uncertainty. The last time I was here I was petrified of things to come. I'm so thankful for the way things are turning out. I love this man.

"I got you a gift." Walker says bringing me back to the present. I find him unzipping his garment bag.

"No more gifts Walker!" I yell, twirling the diamond letter "S", for Savannah, pendant that he gave me for Christmas.

It was yet another crazy holiday. Noelle refused to have it at our house so my mom graciously hosted. It almost seemed like an impromptu baby shower with all the gifts for little Savannah. My sister seemed to be doing better with the divorce, Noelle's parents joined us, and Trent refused to glance her way even once. On top of the necklace, Walker got me a new Kindle, a gift card to add to my eBook collection, a framed picture of the two of us, another framed picture of Savannah's twenty week ultrasound and at least fifteen movies. All I got him was tickets to see the Bears play their last home game, which I made him take Trent to so I didn't have to sit in the cold.

"Just one, baby." Finding what he was looking for he pulls out the most beautiful dress. It's a knee length orchid color one shoulder maternity dress with a purple tie just above the belly. Even the one side that has a sleeve has the dark purple outlining it. It's gorgeous.

"Walker," I gasp, bringing my hand up to my chest. "It's beautiful!"

He brings it towards me and I run my fingers along the soft silky fabric.

"No. You're beautiful. This pales in comparison." A gentle touch of his fingers along my cheek has me shivering.

"What is this for?" I take the hanger from him, walking towards the full length mirror and holding it up to me. I can't wait to see how it fits.

"Go take a bath and relax. When you are done, get ready for dinner and ringing in the New Year with me inside you." I didn't even hear him come up behind me. His body molds to mine making me want to skip dinner and jump on top of him.

~~

An hour and a half later I am scrubbed,

shaved, polished, and made up. I slip on the stunning dress and clasp on my necklace. It's perfect. Walking out of the bathroom I spot Walker on the patio looking out towards the ocean, the breeze blowing through his hair. His body is graced with black dress pants, a white button up dress shirt and a purple tie that matches the belt of my dress exactly.

"Hey there sexy," I call out just as I reach the patio. His green eyes look lost in thought. "Are you ok?"

He takes the few steps needed to reach me. "I'm perfect. You look amazing Erin." Looking past me into the room his eyes look as though they are searching for something. "Where did you find out you were pregnant?"

"Here. In this room." I turn my body, pointing to the table that holds my beach hat. "Right there is when I realized I was late and where I sat when the first pregnancy test showed up positive."

"The first?" His right eyebrow raises in question.

I bring my attention back to him. "Yes, we took *a lot*." I laugh at how insane I was, buying all those tests.

"Let's go. I don't want to be late for dinner." His hands reach for mine spinning us back into the room and out the door.

UNEXPECTED

~~

I'm so tired. Dinner was amazing. I don't think I have eaten that much ever. Our private dinner on the beach, listening to the waves, was beautiful and my company was damn hot. I have had confirmation that Noelle spilled every single detail of our trip to Walker because he insisted on taking me to the club where the old man and I danced.

I'm not even sure I want sex at this point. Between the traveling, dancing, and all the food I just want to crash onto the bed before midnight strikes. When we reach the top of the steps closest to our room Walker gently pushes me back against the door, his lips inches from my face.

"Do you love me Erin?" His tongue darts out licking my bottom lip.

Ok, maybe a quickie.

"Yes," I breathe out. "So much."

I reach up on my tip toes to make the kiss deeper but he pulls away. "I love you too. With everything that I am."

He swipes the key card and the door flies open, taking me back to our first night together. I stumble in as he catches me. Rotating me around another night flashes before me bringing back one of the worst memories of my life. Candles are lit everywhere and music is softly playing. It's a scene too familiar from when I caught Robert cheating. A bottle of sparkling apple cider is sitting on the table chilling with two glasses. I step back, retreating, and bump into a massive chest.

"What's wrong baby?" Walker's voice breaks through the terrible memory, reminding me that part of my life is gone.

Shaking it off I reach my arms back, grabbing a hold of his hand and given a reminder how different this time is from that horrible night. "Nothing. Nothing at all. This is amazing."

"This is nothing compared to what you deserve." He kisses my neck and I turn around to give him more access. He continues a trail down the shoulder the dress doesn't cover, moving me back towards the bed. My fingers find their way to his shirt and I pull up, trying to un-tuck it. My knees hit the back of the bed and his hands stop mine from pulling it up any further. "Right now is not about sex, Erin."

His eyes are glazed over as if he has unshed tears in them. I look around the room again to find that I didn't make contact with the bed but instead one of the chairs at the table. "Walker?"

"I love you Erin." A lone tear falls and my own start to flow. "Please sit."

I do and in seconds he lowers himself onto one knee. "Oh my God Walker."

"No talking Erin. Hear me out. I know we've only had the past four months to get to know each other but they have been the most incredible in my life. If I am not near you I am thinking about you and our daughter. I want what is best for all of us and what's best for me is to never live a day without you. I want to wake up to you every morning and be the last voice you hear at night. I want to make dinner with you, fight with you and make up with you. I want you to be happy and I know you will be happy with me because I will spend every day of the rest of my life making sure you smile. I adore you. I love you. I trust you with my heart. In this exact spot your life changed forever when you found out you were having Savannah. Now, I want it to represent another life change...one that will connect us all permanently. I know I'm pushy and I tell you the way things are, so that you don't have the opportunity to say no, but right now I'm asking. Please, Erin Melissa Decker, would you do me the honor of not only being the mother of my child and future children but becoming my wife and making me the luckiest man on earth?" His green eyes look vulnerable like I could make or break him with just one word.

My chest is swelling with love and adoration. My heart about to explode. This beautiful, loving caring man wants me to be his wife and I want nothing more than to make that possible. Tears fill my eyes and I can barely see anymore. I grab a tissue from the table and wipe my eyes wanting to be able to look into his with my answer.

"Walker Henry Prescott, the last time I was here I left scared to death, not knowing what my future held or how I was going to get through it but this time...this time I'm leaving one hundred percent sure that my future is safe and secure. There isn't a minute that goes by that you aren't on my mind. I feel loved and cherished. So, yes! I would love to marry you and make us both some of the luckiest people on this earth." My sobs fill the room as I watch him take out a blue box from beside him.

He opens the case and I find the most stunning Tiffany Soleste engagement ring. The round diamond is surrounded by double rows of bead set diamonds. More diamonds run along the sides of the ring and it sparkles underneath the brilliant moonlight filtering into our room.

He pulls it out of the box and grabs my left hand, placing it gently onto my ring finger. "Thank you. A year ago I wouldn't have thought this is where I would be but I've learned to embrace the unexpected because it can bring some of the greatest things into your life. I love you Erin."

His words are sweet but I can't stop staring

at the rock he has placed on my swollen finger. "Walker this is too much. Are you on a 30 year payment plan for this? It's gorgeous. My God."

He lifts my chin up so that my attention is on him. "Erin. I want you to know that you never have to worry. Not about me hurting you and not about us financially. I can provide for us if you don't want to go back to work. I can give everything you and our family need as long as we aren't foolish."

"I love my job Walker and I like to earn my own way. Plus, on your salary alone we can't afford to keep me from working." I shake my head side to side.

He grabs my hand and pulls me to the bed. As he sits, he sets me down on his lap sideways so I can wrap my right arm around his shoulder and admire my ring at the same time.

"I understand you love it, but that might change after Savannah arrives and I'm ok with that. But I do understand. I can afford not to work but I love the feeling of accomplishment and helping kids." He pushes my hair off my neck and kisses his favorite spot just below my ear.

"Did you win the lottery?" I joke but his hands sliding between my legs show me his is serious.

"I did but only with you." He caresses my

thighs and my legs involuntarily open.

After that touch the conversation was over for the next two hours. When we were satisfied and exhausted we lie naked on the bed caressing each other's bodies.

As soon as I could form a coherent sentence I asked him about the money situation. Not that I would want to stay home but if I was going to marry him I would need to know where the extra money was coming from.

"My paternal Grandmother left Deliah and me her inheritance. We were the only grandchildren on that side so we got it all minus what she gave to my mother and father. Everything was sold and we both get a large sum of money each month for the rest of our lives. She didn't want young kids acquiring such a huge payday so she stipulated that we receive a portion of it every month."

I told him I was happy he wanted to share that with me but I hoped to continue working. Having the option though made me feel better. When she gets here I might not want to work right away. He said to think about taking the rest of the school year off and maybe start up again next year.

"So, Noelle brought something up the other day." I want to have this conversation but my eyes are slowly starting to close.

"Mmm hmm." He softly says most likely falling asleep as well.

"Moving in together. Where are we going to live?" I question and fall asleep just after I hear him mumble "I've got it taken care of."

~~

I didn't want to take my ring off. I was getting used to the weight of it and the glare it creates when met with the sun. But I had to lock it in the safe when we ventured out, clad in our swimming attire, for some snorkeling and relaxing on the beach.

After a light lunch, Walker coaxes me into the water promising that if he sees a jelly fish he will jump in front of me taking the sting. Laughing, I promise to pee on him if he does.

The cool water feels marvelous after being in the sun for the past hour and Walker starts to get frisky.

"Knock it off. Anyone looking can tell you are trying to molest me." I laugh trying to stop his advances but he is too strong and I am definitely weak when it comes to him.

He looks around and whispers "No one is paying attention to us baby. Let me just get a quick feel and I'll stop."

"You promise?" I ask, wrapping my arms around his neck while simultaneously bringing my legs around his waist.

He reaches under my thighs pushing my bathing suit bottoms to the side and shoves one finger inside of me. A quiet cry leaves my body.

"I'm not making you a promise I can't keep." And with that his pushes a second finger deep into me. "Put your head on my shoulder baby. I don't want anyone else to watch you come. That's for my eyes only."

I can't do anything else but submit to him. Everything he does to me is magic and with just a few thrusts of his fingers inside me I forget where I am and who is around. The waves of the ocean roll over my body as I ride his fingers shamelessly.

"Feels good doesn't it baby?" Walker shifts just a little and suddenly his tip is at my entrance before slamming into me. "But that feels better."

"Oh God yes." His thrusts are slow and torturous but I know it's only because he doesn't want others to know what we're doing.

I try to move faster but his grip on my thighs control the pace. "You want to come Erin?" His other hand reaches up pushing down on my clit and I immediately explode. A few more pushes and he is groaning in my ear.

"My life would be void without you Erin. You are everything to me. I can't wait until you're my wife." He whispers just as he is pulling out of me.

"I can't wait either."

"So, let's not wait. We can get married right now." His serious tenor pulls me out of my Gulf of Mexico bliss.

"Are you serious?"

25

Pulling into the driveway after the most amazing and romantic trip I have ever been on, I notice my car is gone.

"Where's my car?" I ask jumping out of Walker's truck looking around the driveway like it might just appear out of nowhere.

"No clue baby. Maybe Noelle took it out. Call her." He shrugs and I climb back into the truck to retrieve my phone.

I'm going to give her an earful. My touch screen suffers the wrath as I pull up her number but disappears when I see she is now calling me.

"Noelle! Where the hell is my car?" I yell into the phone.

"Calm down, Erin. I took it to get detailed...you know a little last minute Christmas gift. Your car needed it. You're welcome." I can feel her smirk over the phone.

She does this on occasion. My car isn't that dirty but in her eyes it could always use a cleaning.

"I do have a problem though. I drove over to Chase's house and when I went to leave it wouldn't start. Do you think Walker can come take a look at it? Chase hasn't a freaking clue when it comes to cars." She sighs into the phone.

I haven't heard Chase's name since Thanksgiving. She must be making her rounds again.

I confirm with Walker he has nowhere to be and tell her to text me the address. I type it into the GPS and it shows we are fifteen minutes away.

~~

I don't know what Chase does but this house is stunning. It's white with light blue shutters and is two stories with a wraparound porch. A two car garage is attached.

My car sits in the driveway and we both get out, walking up the few steps to the door and ringing the bell. Noelle answers looking amazing in a long sleeve white sweater dress, brown tights and cowboy boots.

"Hey! Come on in. I just need to grab my coat and then Walker can take a look," she says turning so fast I get whiplash.

Walker's hand presses me forward by the small of my back and into the large foyer. We stand for a minute waiting for her to return but she beckons us from down the hallway.

"Come on Noe. I'm exhausted," I complain, but remember some big news I have to share and follow her. "And I have something to share with you! You'll know before my own mother!"

I find her in the living room staring at me. When I get closer to her I notice pink is everywhere and I'm startled by dozens of people yelling "SURPRISE!"

I step back and Walker's hands circle my belly. "Surprise, baby." He kisses the back of my head and urges me forward again. I'm in complete shock. I had no idea.

My mother is one of the first people I notice. She embraces me and pulls my left hand up to look at my ring. "It's beautiful. Congratulations." She drops my hand and takes Walker into a big hug.

I spend ten minutes greeting everyone who is there and having my new ring pawed at. Rosie tears up when she sees me.

"I'm so happy for you Erin. Looks like everything is working out the way it should be." She says wiping a tear from her face.

The entire house is full of my female friends and family...and Walker. He wanted to stay. The massive kitchen, with dark cabinets and beautiful marble counter tops are jam-packed with all kinds of food. Over the next few hours Savannah is spoiled with a tremendous amount of gifts and we won't have to buy diapers for the first year of her life. Noelle, Nicole, Deliah and my mom planned a bunch of crazy games including one where we sniff a diaper filled with melted chocolate and try to guess which candy bar it is. I lost.

As soon as our bellies are full, everyone starts to leave. My mom and Noelle clean everything up and I notice all the gifts are gone. I grab Walker's hips and place a kiss on his chin. "Thanks for taking the presents to the car, hun."

He pulls back looking down at me and his lips meet mine. Gently at first, and after I grant his tongue permission to enter it becomes more aggressive. I pull back not wanting an audience.

"They aren't in the car." He pushes my hair back behind my ears.

"Where are they?" I furrow my brows at his one sided dimple smirk.

"In her room," he answers and I hear Noelle and my mom laugh. "I have one more present for you Erin."

"Walker, seriously. No more presents. I'm not accepting it. I won't even look at it. You spoil me way too much." I reach up giving him another quick kiss and turn away.

"You've already seen it," I hear him say from behind me. "As a matter of fact you're standing in it."

I stop looking around. My mom catches my eyes and she is grinning from ear to ear. I whip around stalking back to him. "You bought me a house?"

He grabs my hand, pulling me to the oversized rocking recliner, sitting down and dragging me onto his lap. "No. I built us a house. Actually, I was building it for myself but after we found each other again I decided to make it bigger and add all the things you love. There isn't a ton of furniture because I wanted you to pick it out with me and we will decorate the walls with pictures of our wedding and all of our children."

"I already own a house Walker." I'm not saying I don't want this one, I do. It's stunning. From what I have seen of the downstairs I'm in love. It's an open floor plan and the living room ceilings are two stories high. The back wall is lined with sliding glass doors and windows leading onto a deck that has a big gas grill on it.

"I can handle the mortgage Erin," Noelle interjects. "All you have to do is let me buy your half out."

Not looking her way I keep my focus on him. "Are you serious?"

He nods and I push him back, straddling him, raining kisses on him all over every inch I can hit from his neck and above.

"Erin Melissa! Get off him right now!" My mother scolds with a hint of humor. "At least wait until I am gone."

I lean my forehead onto his whispering how much I love him and he whispers back the same.

This man is amazing.

"When can we move my stuff in?" I giddily jump up looking at Noe.

"Already done," she says pointing upstairs.

"Want me to show you around?" Walker asks and I shake my head yes so fast I get dizzy.

"Let us leave first. I'm not sure if you go upstairs with Double T that you will come back down." Noelle winks at us.

"Double T?" My mom questions her. I'm sure my face turns an intense shade of red.

"I'll explain in the car Mama Eden." Noelle pats my mom on the shoulder and walks towards the door.

"Don't you DARE!" I yell marching towards the front door as they get there.

My mom and Noelle place kisses on my cheek and give me hugs as I thank them for everything, giving Noelle and look of warning. She just laughs.

Turning back around I realize that we may not be coming back down tonight. This house is amazing and I've only seen half of it. He promised to take care of me, and even though I've tried to live an independent life, it's nice to have someone who wants to do things for me and who I would do the same for.

The tour of the house takes a while. Every time he brings me into a new room I feel the need to kiss and caress him. I almost fall over when I walk into Savannah's room. It's a light shade of pink. Over the white crib are white letters that spell out her name. Each letter with a little butterfly placed in the middle. In the corner is a rocking chair with an ottoman next to a nightstand and changing table. The room is decorated with light purple elephants and on the wall are the words "Embrace the Unexpected".

"It's beautiful Walker. Is this why you were so busy the past few months?"

"Yes. I'm surprised you didn't question me." He turns around shutting the soft light off.

"I trust you." I grab his outstretched hand letting him lead me down the hallway.

There are five bedrooms total: the master, Savannah's room, an office and two guest suites. It also has three and a half baths and sits on half an acre with a swing set already up in the backyard.

Savannah's room is great but the master bedroom is amazing. It spans the whole length of the house and faces the back yard. More floor to ceiling windows and a sliding glass door take up the whole wall. The bathroom has a huge Jacuzzi tub and separate shower with his and her sinks. It seems to be bigger than my room at my house. Well, Noelle's house now.

We each have our own walk in closet and along the side wall is a reading nook with silver, red and black throw pillows lining it. The bed is king size and has the most stunning black comforter with silver inlay. It has the same color pillows as my reading nook.

Walking towards it, I shed my clothes one by one and turn around meeting his hungry eyes. "Wanna break it in?" I quirk my eyebrow and he hungrily attacks.

~~

The sun shines bright into my new room. Even though the temperatures are in the teens I am currently cozy and warm in my new bed. Turning over I find I'm alone. My body aches as I sit up to stretch, glancing at the striking ring that graces my left hand. I'm startled when the door flies open.

"I'm sorry baby. I wanted to be back up here before you woke up." He places a tray down onto the bed. The smell is amazing and I find chocolate chip pancakes, bacon and orange juice lay on top of it. "Breakfast in bed. We only have a few more days before school starts back up and I don't want you to waste foolish time doing anything but staying right where you are."

He wiggles his eyebrows up and down and that yearn for him starts to build up again. "But first you must eat. I slaved over this all morning."

"You really do spoil me Walker. Please never forget how much I appreciate it." I kiss his cheek and dig in to the pancakes.

So freaking good.

"Anything for my wife." He smirks.

"Walker. That wasn't official. That was the two of us declaring our love for one another in the middle of the ocean." I shake my head.

He was pushy, as usual. He nagged me for

ten minutes begging to go and elope. I know my mom would be devastated and Noelle would hang me by my toenails.

"So when *do* you want to get married?"

I knew this conversation would come up sooner rather than later. I sigh, knowing he isn't going to like my answer.

"I'd like to wait until after the baby is here...maybe summertime so I can get my body back and not have a big bump in our wedding pictures. This gives me time to plan my dream wedding." I hope that satisfies him. It doesn't.

"Erin! Can we just go to the courthouse and then we can plan a big one later. I want us all to have the same last name when she arrives." He kisses my neck licking up to just below my ear. I'm so distracted and he is not playing fair.

Time to have some fun.

"About that." I reluctantly push him away. "I was thinking since we won't be married that I can just give her my last name. I mean maybe we can change it later."

"What?!" He abruptly stands up almost knocking the entire tray off the bed.

"Yea." I continue hoping I don't start laughing. "I mean, doesn't the baby take the mother's name if the parents aren't married?"

He's pissed, pacing back and forth. He stops mid stride and pierces me with angry eyes. "You listen here! I can understand if you want to wait to plan a big wedding but ONE of you is going to have my last name when that baby arrives and she most certainly will have it. I'll give you until summer, but she gets MY name! Do you understand?"

I let out a giggle and shake my head yes. "I'm glad you see it my way. A summer wedding it is."

The bite I'm about to take is ripped out of my hand and a heated body hovers above mine. "Was that you trying to get your way about the wedding Erin?"

All humor is gone. His hot breath reaches my mouth and I barely nod. I'm not scared. I'm turned the hell on.

"That was messed up Erin." His free hand is pushing up my nightgown between my thighs. "You're going to pay for your little game by making a little wager."

"What kind of wager?" I ask as his fingers creep higher making my skin pebble.

His free hand pulls the tray away from our bodies and onto the floor.

"First one to come wins. You come first you will have my last name by the time she is here. I come first I'll give you until the summer time.

But make no mistake...she will be Savannah Prescott. No compromise on that." And with that he rips my panties right off of me.

I'm so going to lose.

~~

It took everything I had in me but in the end...I won...by three thrusts.

26

School has been chaotic. It's hard to get the students back on track when they have been off for a few weeks traveling and being spoiled by their parents and grandparents.

Who am I kidding? I'm one of them.

I've lived in what I call my dream home for the past six weeks and I am still buzzing with excitement. I find something new that I love about it every day and we have been picking out furniture daily. That night he hadn't shown me the basement but it was finished with two separate areas: one that is Walker's man cave and one that we are currently making into a playroom for all the nieces and nephews as well as Savannah when she is older.

Things at school, besides the students,

seem to be pretty calm. Emma started dating another teacher so she has laid off paying so much attention to Walker. I could tell from the look on her face when I showed her my ring that she finally realized nothing was going to happen between her and Walker. I don't know why she didn't see that before. I've also arranged with Principal Callow a sub for the remainder of the school year and she should be coming in to go over classroom stuff next week. I'm excited to find out who she is.

I'm starting to feel very uncomfortable and regardless of how the doctor says I am doing I am still concerned. My blood pressure has been high but not to the point he thinks I need to be induced. I have an appointment every week now and today is one of them. At 37 weeks I barely fit behind my desk and my chair hits the chalkboard behind me. The students are careless, constantly bumping into me, and I'm thinking that maybe after next week I will start my maternity leave. That's only six weeks but Walker keeps reassuring me that we are financially stable enough if I want to take the rest of the school year off. So I decided that is what is best all around.

The school day ended an hour ago and I've got another thirty minutes before we need to leave for our appointment. Walker strolls into the room with his bag in hand dropping it at the door before locking it. I raise my eyebrow in question but I can tell from the look in his eyes he has plans for the next thirty minutes.

"Erin. Did you know that since the moment I saw you in this room that I wanted to take you on top of your desk? I mean it's every man's fantasy to have sex with his teacher. I'm a man Erin. A man with a fantasy." He stalks down the row of desks towards me.

My nipples harden and I know he sees them through my silk shirt. Pushing as far back as I can in the chair I get up walking around to the other side of the desk spreading my legs open enough so my flowing skirt rides up as I sit.

"What did you have in mind?" I pull my skirt up higher until it reaches the bottom of my massive belly.

Any other time I would be self-conscious about this but Walker always makes me feel beautiful, large ballooned belly and all.

Both hands grip mine when he reaches me and he tugs me off the desk aggressively, turning me around. A gently push between my shoulder blades and I am bent over awaiting his next move. I feel my skirt lift and both of his hands reach underneath and grab my hips. My satin lace boy shorts exposed.

"I'm thinking this is a great view." His hands reach into my hair and tug just as his other one yanks down my panties.

I have no time to decide whether this is wrong or not. I just want it. I always want him.

My insides tingle with anticipation of when I will be filled with him. I don't have to wait long.

"You're so wet. Always ready for me Erin." He pushes in deeper and a moan escapes.

"Shh, baby. We don't want anyone to catch us now do we?" He whispers.

I've never been so filled...this position is still new to me, and it feels amazing.

"Call me Ms. Decker," I command. It's his fantasy. I'm just playing along.

"Yes, Ms. Decker." He thrusts harder into me and I cry out. "Did I hurt you Ms. Decker? Do I need to stay after school?" He groans into my ear and a fire ignites.

"Yes! Oh God yes. Harder, Walker. I need it harder," I whisper. I can't take much more. One hand pulling on my hair and the other splayed over my ass and all I want is for him to make me come.

I love when Walker is gentle and loving but this is aggressive and my body is becoming electrified.

He plunges into me even harder and I brace myself on the desk careful not to lie on my stomach.

"I love nothing between us Erin. You feel fucking amazing," he pants out; making me wetter if that is even possible.

"Jesus Walker...so do you!" I shout just as he reaches around and presses his thumb between my swollen folds.

"Come for me Erin. Come all over me." His pounding becomes relentless.

I'm so close but when he grips my hair tighter I explode. It spreads throughout my body and stops in my throat, keeping me from screaming out.

His pace slows as he rides out his own orgasm and gently pulls out of me.

Circling around I adjust my skirt and manage to shimmy my way up onto the desk as I watch him zip up his khaki pants and tuck in his white polo shirt.

He looks up from tightening his belt smiling.

"What's so funny?" I pull him closer to me kissing him on the mouth.

"Nothing. It's a happy smile. I've wanted to do that for 5 months now."

"Well glad I could help make your fantasy

come true." This time I pull him flush between my legs and kiss him like I want to go for round two.

He stops abruptly but doesn't pull away speaking against my lips. "Uhm, Erin."

"Yea?" I ask as he looks down and I suddenly feel it.

"Did your water just break?" He steps back and a small puddle pools just in front of the desk. A shooting pain hits my belly and I step down slipping before Walker catches me.

"Yes! Oh my God. She's coming!"

~~

"I didn't break her water with my DICK!" Walker yells into the phone on the way to the hospital. "Just get to the hospital Noelle. Her mom will most likely beat you there so call her when you arrive."

Walker hangs up, passing me my cell phone. "She is crazy you know that?"

"So are you but I love you despite it." I laugh.

"How can you be so calm?" He asks tugging at his hair. He is going to go bald. He hasn't stopped doing that since we left the school.

"Uhm, because you, Noelle and my mom will be crazy enough for me, and stop pulling on your hair, that's my job." I grab the hand that has a firm grasp on his hair and bring it to my lips. "I can't believe she is coming."

"Me either." His eyes go back to focusing on the road ahead.

The ride to the hospital is short. We called Dr. Gale on the way to let him know I wouldn't be making my appointment. He gave instructions on what to do and said he would be by in a little while. We get checked in and are given a room before the nurse, who introduced herself as Ivy and could be Noelle's twin, comes in to do my vitals. She looks at Walker like she is starving and he is a piece of meat.

"My name is Ivy and I'll be taking care of you today." She says looking at Walker just as my first hard hitting contraction comes along.

"Excuse me, Ivy. When you're done eye fucking my fiancé," I lift my left hand, flashing her my stunning engagement ring. "Can you get my vitals and get out?"

Walker's body is shaking with silent laughter and I stare him down, cutting him short. Nurse Ivy, whose pale skin is a lovely shade of red, hurriedly takes my blood pressure.

"You're blood pressure is pretty high," she states before walking over grabbing my more swollen than usual hands. A curious look crosses her face before she lifts the blanket off my feet and takes a peek there as well. "I'll be right back."

She scatters out of the room leaving me with a man who looks overly concerned. "What just happened?"

"I don't know. Maybe it has something to do with the gestational hypertension but I've been pretty stable since October." I shrug, not sure. I know when Dr. Gale gets here we will have more info.

Less than fifteen minutes after I'm admitted Noelle and my mother can be heard down the hall. I shake my head at Walker, who is resting in a chair directly beside me holding my hand.

"Erin!" My mother and Noelle gush at the same time.

"How are you feeling? Any pain? Isn't 37 weeks too early? How did it break?" My mom puts out questions at rapid fire speed but the last one has Noelle in a full blown giggle fit. "What did I miss?"

"Nothing!" Walker and I both yell and my mom jumps back, her hand going to her chest.

Ivy walks back in and I notice Noelle giving her the stare down. Noe looks my way giving me the "who does this chick think she is" and I answer in best friend code that she is trouble. It's great to have a best friend who you don't even need words to communicate.

"I just spoke to Dr. Gale. He should be here soon but he wanted me to get a urine sample and check for protein. I saw in your chart you have gestational hypertension and that can lead to preeclampsia. With the swollen hands and feet we just want to be sure everything is ok. After we do that we can set you up on an IV and go from there. Any questions?" She smiles and flashes perfect white teeth but doesn't look Walker's way again.

I raise my hand to stop whatever was about to come out of Noelle's mouth and tell her no.

Minutes later I come out of the bathroom, urine in hand, when a contraction hits me so hard that I stumble. It's like slow motion...the cup goes flying right at Ivy who is patiently waiting for me. Thankfully the cup is sealed and she catches it but a little part of me would have been ok with it opening and spilling...just a little.

Ok, that was mean.

Dr. Gale arrives when I'm dressed in the standard puke green hospital gown after being poked three times for an IV by a different nurse. I told them to just put it in my hand seeing as I have no good veins in my arms, but like all the rest they try it first and end up putting it where I told them.

"Erin. Walker." Dr. Gale shakes Walkers hand and then turns to my mom. "Eden."

She smiles at him and introduces Noelle.

"Well. I have bad news and good news." He sits on the edge of my bed squeezing my ankle. "The bad news is that your blood pressure is high and your urine has protein in it so that baby needs to come out sooner rather than later. The good news is that you are going to have the baby today…we're just going to give her a little push."

Noelle and my mom clear out of the room so Dr. Gale can check how dilated I am. I was 4 cm.

Washing his hands he turns to me smiling. "So, I'm going to order some Pitocin and get your little one out as soon as possible."

Thankfully they hook it up through my IV. Four hours and an epidural later, I am nine centimeters dilated and listening to Walker and Noelle bicker.

"He said only two people. We've known her longer." Noelle motions between my mom, who stays quiet, and herself, trying to argue her point.

"I put that baby in there! I'm going to watch her come out. So, YOU'RE leaving," Walker argues back.

"The hell I..."

"Noelle, let's just leave them." My mom's calm voice breaks through. "Let them experience this by themselves. We can come in after she arrives."

"But I..."

"Noelle. Let's go." My mom stands essentially ending the conversation.

They both kiss me on the head and leave to go to the waiting room. Walker makes his way over to me sitting beside my hip.

"Erin, baby? If you want them in here..." He takes a deep breath. "I can go. I don't want to but I can if that's what you want."

I lift my free hand to his neck pulling him close to me. "I want you in here. I wouldn't have it any other way."

I draw him down to my lips kissing him feeling Savannah kick between us.

"Alright, Ms. Decker let's see if you are ready to go, shall we?" Dr. Gale interrupts our family moment but I know we will have plenty more in the very near future.

Walker's deep green eyes look into mine. "That name WILL change by the end of the summer," he states kissing my forehead lovingly.

Dr. Gale, with Ivy standing next to him, lifts up my sheet and checks me. An epidural is a wonderful thing. I can't feel anything, just a bit of pressure.

"Ten centimeters. Looks like you're ready to push." He looks up from the blanket. "Are you two ready?"

27

My life is complete. Never in my wildest dreams did I think I could love someone so much. Especially someone that came into my life less than an hour ago and yet there she lies swaddled up in the love of my life's arms, across the room. Savannah Grace Prescott. My head is spinning from my heart growing twice its size.

She blazed into this world after an hour and a half of pushing. Walker was a trooper, staying at my side through it all and giving words of encouragement when I begged the doctor to just cut her out of me. I had been too tired to push anymore. A bit later my promises to God that I would never drink wine again if he just got her out of me were answered. I hope he understands that what women say during child birth cannot be held against them.

At 2:22am on February 18th, weighing in at 6 pounds, 10 ounces and 19 inches long, Savannah was born. My body relaxed and Walker's tensed up. After cutting the cord and diligently following her around while she got checked out he snapped a picture from every angle.

Dr. Gale handed her to me first. Her soft dark blue eyes looked into mine and I was instantly under her spell. From the looks Walker was giving her I knew she had him wrapped around her very tiny and precious fingers. Her facial features matched mine but when she cried I could see Walker's intense look all over her.

Singing a song I can't hear from the bed in my new room, Walker rubs the top of her dark brown hair, kissing her every so often. His green eyes meet mine and the smile is one I know well. Happiness and excitement. The look he gets when nothing else in the world could compare to that moment…and it never will.

"I love you Savannah," he says, kissing her again. "And I love your mama too. You are such a lucky little lady to have the most beautiful, strong and smart woman to be your role model."

"Awe, Walker," Noelle's voice filters through the room. "I appreciate the compliments but you're going to make Erin jealous."

"Noelle, if I wasn't holding one of the most precious girls on the planet I would tell you to go…"

"Walker!" I hiss. "Language."

My mom laughs from next to me, coming in just after Noelle entered. She just stares at the little bundle but doesn't approach.

"You can hold her, Mom." I tap her hip pushing her along.

"I know baby." She lovingly flattens my hair down. "I just want to take this in. Your dad would be so proud of you and he would love Walker."

Tears fall down her face and mine shortly follow. I miss my dad everyday but I know he is looking down on us and I hope he truly is proud of where I'm at.

My mom walks over, reaching out, asking permission to take Savannah into her arms. Walker obliges, giving her his seat, before placing her in my mother's care. Not moving, he stares down towards them and leans in, kissing my mom on the cheek.

"I'm so thankful for you," he says placing a second kiss on her cheek. She grins from ear to ear. Reluctantly he walks away from Savannah and over to me.

I know not having his mom here is hurting

him but I am glad mine seems to be helping him heal.

"Hi Daddy." I smile at him.

"Hi Mama." He smiles back.

"I call next," Noelle tells my mother.

~~

I'm exhausted mentally and physically. So much so that I don't remember falling asleep but the conversation I wake up to needs to be halted.

"So, she shit on the table didn't she?" A hushed question from Noelle to who I assume is Walker.

"Noelle!" The quiet reprimand of my mother makes her laugh.

"I'm just curious Ma!" She tries to defend herself. "So did she?"

"She definitely did." Walker states and gives me a deer caught in headlights look when he notices my eyes are open. "NOT I mean. Did NOT."

"I'm never having kids. Not only will I shit but they will shit and it will just be a shitty mess." Noelle waves her hands around like she couldn't be bothered.

"I bet your next Noe. I told you some guy is

going to come in and tame that crazy ass of yours and then knock you up." Walker affectionately pats her on the head.

"Watch your mouth around the baby!" My mom shushes them.

I ask to hold her and my mom doesn't hesitate. Bringing her to me and placing her in my arms I feel whole, complete. I look into her eyes and I feel strong like I can take on the world. I love her so much.

A soft knock at the door drags my attention from Savannah. Jack, Walker's father, is standing at the door. A few warm hugs from everyone else and he is now trying to take her from me. I just got her back for the first time in a few hours but I don't even waver. He came all this way to surprise us and he deserves a smile after losing his wife a few months ago. Not to mention Savannah is her namesake.

"She is beautiful. Stunning. The best of both of you. Hi Savannah Grace." He cries, urging the flood gates of my tear ducts to open along with everyone else's.

This is a joyous but bittersweet moment. I wish Walker's mom could be here but know she lives on through our daughter.

Visitors come in and out including my sister who left her kids with my soon to be ex brother in law. The divorce proceedings have started but she seems to be in high spirits.

After work, Trent joins us, bringing dinner after Noelle left to go home and shower. A full day of hospital food and I welcome the site of a greasy cheeseburger. I've noticed he is taking a different approach with Noelle and is laying low. I don't think that can go on for too much longer.

When visiting hours are over and everyone is cleared out just Walker, Savannah and I are left. The whole maternity floor is quiet. The nurse came to take her to the nursery but Walker refused, not wanting her to leave his sight. Seeing how much he loves and cares for her makes me want to marry him tomorrow and make our family whole.

"Walker. Will you marry me?" I ask breaking him out of his daughter's spell.

He doesn't look up but I can see the one sided dimple pop in. "I already asked you baby."

"I mean when we get discharged. Go to the courthouse and just do it. I mean we live together and have a baby now. We might as well make it official." I shrug but he can't see. His eyes still trained on Savannah.

"No."

"No?" I ask, confused.

"No." He finally looks up giving me a serious look. "I want you to have your dream wedding. I want to take the time to give you what you want. For you to pick out the dress you always dreamed of and to have everyone there that you want. I want to see you walk down the aisle and I want our friends and family to witness how much we love each other. I want to give you the world Erin, since you have given me mine."

He glances back down at our daughter, tapping her nose, and starts to sing, putting us both into a peaceful slumber.

~~

A soft cry wakes me up and I find that Walker has set her down into the portable crib. Picking her up I pull my shirt up allowing her to get the nourishment she needs. Walker is fast asleep on the guest couch in the corner with one of the blankets he bought for her nestled under his head. When I look down I'm reminded how different my life is compared to last year.

I was planning a future with a man who was, unbeknownst to me, betraying me.

I never would have imagined I would be where I am today. I thought Robert was it for me. I went day in and day out accepting a man who just thought of me as mediocre. He may never have said so but knowing how Walker treats me shows how blind I was to what was really going on.

Savannah falls asleep still attached to me so I pry her off and place her back into her crib. Walker stirs a bit, moaning, and I can't help but walk over to him and place a quick kiss on his lips. His eyes flash open and all I see is lust.

"Do I really have to wait six weeks to get back into this smoking hot body? You should hear about the dream I was just having." His hands find my hips and try to pull me down onto his lap.

"Are you serious Walker? I just had a baby who, I might add, is right over there." I motion towards her quiet snores.

"I can't help it if my fiancé is hot...even after giving birth." He tugs a bit harder and I relent, sitting down on him.

"Six weeks. You have to wait six weeks." I kiss him on the nose and wiggle a bit in his lap.

"Then we can try for more babies?" One of his eyebrows quirks up.

"Let's worry about the one we have right now and talk about more after the wedding." This time I give him a slow sensual kiss.

"Get off me woman. You're teasing me." He lifts me up, turning me around to give me a swat on my ass.

"I adore you Walker." I blow a kiss to him when I rest my sore body back down on the bed.

"I adore you too Erin. And in six weeks I'm going to show you how much."

That night at the club I never expected to go home with anyone. I never expected to get pregnant or to ever find him again. I never expected to be able to trust anyone after what Robert did to me and I never expected to fall in love with a strong minded, pushy, and sexy man like Walker Prescott. But life taught me to expect the unexpected and embrace it, because if you don't you could miss out on some pretty amazing things.

Epilogue

Walker

One Year Later

My house is filled to the brim with pink shit. It's like the past year, everywhere I turn something pink, or a shade of pink, pops up. Right now it looks like a bottle of Pepto Bismol threw up in the living area of our house, and I wouldn't have it any other way. My favorite little girl is turning one.

Sitting on my recliner, the only manly thing in this room, I watch as Savannah toddles over to me in her "I'm ONE" t-shirt and pink (would you assume it was any other color) tutu.

"Come here sweet girl!" Her grin, which only consists of four teeth, widens and her pace quickens. I jump up; meeting her halfway making sure she doesn't fall in her attempt to get to me faster. "Where's your mama?"

I scoop her up heading towards the kitchen, spotting my beautiful wife of four months, whose body is clad in the tightest of jeans and a teal sweater that unfortunately covers her ass.

"Hey baby! Do you need help?"

"No," she answers not looking my way. "I'm almost done. I just need to get Savannah's gifts and bring them to the table and everyone should arrive at any moment."

She finally turns and smiles brightly when she sees me holding Savannah. Reaching for her Savannah refuses with a harsh "dada." My heart swells as Erin's face falls.

"You never want mama." Erin fakes a pout and Savannah laughs. Throwing her hand on her sexy hips, Erin acts hurt. "It's not funny baby."

"Just let me know if you need anything. I'll be over here with my number one girl." I laugh bringing Savannah back to the living room to play with a few toys.

"Hey! I used to be number one."

"You're like number one and a half now." I joke and get a rolled up paper towel thrown at me.

Don't let her fool you. She loves how much I love Savannah. How the two of them are my entire world. Two years ago that world consisted of drinking and partying. I had my mind set on taking things seriously when I graduated, but I didn't realize how serious it would get when I went to the bar that night.

I watched Erin most of that night. She pushed every guy away that approached her. I could see in her eyes she had been hurt, but she was so damn sexy. I just wanted to take her pain away. I never expected to be so instantly connected to someone. When she left the next morning I wanted to go after her, beg her to stay, but I was too macho to do something so girlish. I should have. I might have been there when she found out she was pregnant. I could have at least helped her though the first couple of months.

I have no regrets though. Every moment that lead up to that night and every event that has occurred since has brought me to where I am today. Playing with my daughter, in a house

I built for my gorgeous wife, with a job I love. I couldn't be happier.   That's a lie. I will be over the fucking moon tonight when all the party guests are gone and Savannah is asleep and I can be balls deep inside of Erin again.

"What are you thinking about over there Walker? That look is scary." Erin's eyebrow rises.

"Well you should be scared of what I'm going to do to you tonight. You're lucky she's in the room because I have the urge to come over there and rub my face between those..."

"Stop it!" She laughs, making Savannah stir around. "Not in front of the baby."

"How does she think she got here?" I wave, walking over and squeezing her tit anyways.

The doorbell rings. Let the chaos begin.

~~

Our daughter is spoiled. Not only with the insane amount of gifts she received but by the love of our friends and family. We're so lucky to have everyone so close. My dad moved here a month ago and is living with Deliah until he can move into his new condo down the street from me. He and Erin's mom have become close since she knows what he is going through.

My mom has been gone over a year but he is still not the same. I don't know what I would do if I lost Erin.

After all the gifts, cake and games, the house starts to clear leaving just close friends and family hanging around in the living room. Savannah passed out an hour ago and is now starting to stir. I get up to my feet but Erin beats me to it.

"I'll get her. I need to give her one more gift," she says before racing out of the room.

"Erin! You are worse with gifts than I am," I yell towards her back, making everyone in the room laugh.

"It's technically a gift for all of us." She yells back.

A few minutes later she carries a still sleepy looking Savannah in, a huge smile adoring her face.

"What did you get her?" I ask reaching my hands out for my baby girl.

"A shirt." She points to Savannah and sets her down.

When she turns to toddle over to me my heart stops and tears instantly sting my eyes.

Gasps erupt and I look at Erin whose face is nodding confirmation.

My beautiful, dark haired, green eyed little girl is sporting a purple shirt with the words "Big Sister" prominently displayed over the front.

My feet move faster than my mind and I wrap Erin up into my arms swinging her around.

"Are you serious? Tell me it's true."

I've wanted another child since Savannah was born. She told me she wanted to wait. Nothing would make me happier than to have a houseful of kids running around stealing my heart the way their mama did.

"Insanely serious." She kisses my lips and I take it deeper.

I pull away when Savannah wraps her arms around my leg. I pick her up kissing her on the cheek. "You're going to be a big sister!"

"We're going to be preggo buddies," Erin states looking over my shoulder.

When I find who she is looking at my mouth drops, but I knew it would happen sooner or later.

UNEXPECTED

"See Noe," I say. "I told you someone would sweep you off your feet and knock you up."

AMY MARIE

Find me on Facebook
www.facebook.com/AuthorAmyMarie

Or E-mail me at AuthorAmyMarie@yahoo.com

For now...

Please enjoy the first chapter of Noelle's story "Undone" due to be released Fall of 2014.

Chapter One: Noelle

I really hate this song. I mean really and truly hate this damn song. Why do they play this kind of crap in a coffee house? Ugh! Come on Starbucks lady. I'm all about you wiping that counter clean but I want to order my damn coffee!

Like a Virgin. Hey! Touched for the very first time, Like a VIIIIIIR...ok, that's enough. COFFEE LADY! I really need my caffeine fix after that brutal cycling class. My ass feels numb.

"Welcome to Starbucks. What can I get for you?" Shyanne, according to her nametag, asks looking bored out of her mind.

"Can I please have a Grande White Mocha?" I try to hide the annoyance in my voice and silently pray she doesn't spit in my drink.

"Name?" She barely looks at me as she places the tip of the marker on their trademark white cup.

"Noelle."

After getting my total, I pay for my coffee and shake my head irritated with the fact that she probably sharpie scribbled my name wrong. Tension immediately leaves my body when I turn and am graced with a vision greater than the Ryan Reynolds naked scene in The Proposal. A hot piece of man candy is at my 3 o'clock and I'm looking for a sugar rush...or a diabetic coma.

Yummy.

Wow! It just isn't fair to look that amazing. I bet he rolled his toned ass out of bed, ruffled his short blonde hair, skipped the razor, and threw on the first thing that he spotted. He has on dark wash jeans and a grey t-shirt that clings to his chiseled chest and bulging, wrap-me-up-tight, biceps. Not a wrinkle in the fabric. He looks like the kind of guy any woman would like to ride into the sunset...literally. I mean I'm restraining myself from doing it right now.

The Starbucks god catches me gawking. I can't help it. You shouldn't expect to walk around like that and not be undressed by my eyes. He flashes me his perfect white teeth and his smile brightens up his face giving me a glimpse at his irises. He has some seriously sexy, smoldering green eyes.

Look away! Look away! He will trap you in his vortex of emeralds!

I pull out my phone trying to look

anywhere but at him and shoot off a text to my best friend Erin.

> **Me: Holy crap! Major hottie at Starbucks!**
>
> **Erin: Did you take a pic?**
>
> **Me: Uhm, no way! For my eyes only.**
>
> **Erin: SHARE NOE!...never mind, you're too chicken anyways.**

Bitch! She knows I hate to be called chicken.

I can do this. It can't be that hard.

I move my fingers across the screen giving off the vibe that I'm just texting with my BFF. I hit the button to turn the phone to vibrate so the sound of the shutter doesn't give me away. Getting the perfect angle, I slightly point my cell his way and *FLASH!*

OH SHIT! Rule one of hottie picture taking: TURN OFF THE FLASH!

"Did you just take my picture?" Hottie McCoffee asks, directing his whole body towards me. He leans one of his elbows on the counter and clasps both calloused hands together.

I'd love to know what those rough hands can do to my body.

"Uh, no. I don't think so." I try to compose myself, my face crimson like the color of the top I have on today.

Would it look weird to fan myself right now?

"Hmm." He raises an eyebrow at me pointing at the offending cell phone in my hand. "Because I could have sworn I just saw a flash coming from your phone."

"Well it does that when I get a text," I lie, or try to.

Really Noelle? There is no way he is buying that.

"Oh, well I just thought that you wanted something to remember me by since you were just eye humping me," he says with a wink, reaching into his pocket.

"First of all, I was not eye humping you, and second of all…"

FLASH! Did he just take my picture?

"Did you just take *my* picture?" Anger blazes through me. I didn't even get to smile for it!

"Nope! I got a text," he says laughing, and then directs a smile at me that seriously incinerates my panties.

We stare at each other, neither of us speaking, and I can feel every cell in my body being turned on.

"JACE!" Shyanne, if that is her real name, yells interrupting our foreplay.

"That's me. Gotta go," Jace says as he casually strolls over, blasts Ms. Wait-10MinutesToTakeYourOrder with *MY* panty melting smile, and walks towards the door.

Oh hell no!

"Wait! Delete that picture." I mean how rude is he for not asking for permission? At least let me see if my hair looks ok.

He turns his back to push open the door and the light hits just right. He looks like an angel which contradicts me going to Hell for the thoughts running through my dirty mind.

"No thanks." And he walks out.

That just fucking happened? Ok, well at least I got a good picture of him to send to Erin. I plop down into the chair next to the window and send it to her.

Me: (Image) Here he is..enjoy because this was the most embarrassing experience of my life!

Erin: Damn!! Almost as hot as Walker. What happened? Forget to turn

the flash off?

Me: SHUT IT!.. But yes ☹ But he took one of me too when I wasn't looking.

Erin: Maybe for his spank bank?

Me: LOL. Probably! You know men spank it to this body on a daily basis.

I put my phone in my back pocket. I'm waiting to post the pic on Facebook with the status update, "Meet the new man of my wet dreams!" I'm sure all my aunts, uncles, cousins and, oh yeah, parents, would love that. I mean who accepts their parents' friend requests? Dumb asses like me, that's who.

"Janelle?"

"Noelle, and I'm right here. Listen, Shyanne, is it?" I pull a napkin from the dispenser and wipe down the counter. "How can you not be drooling over all the hot guys that come in here?"

"Jace is pretty gorgeous isn't he? He is in here all the time. Same time every day, even on weekends."

Well I guess she *can* be useful.

"Gorgeous doesn't even come close. I may have to come back tomorrow." I smile to myself. "Maybe he'll come in here shirtless and I can really get a good pic."

She giggles, but quickly quiets when she looks past me. Knowing the luck I'm having today he must be behind me.

"Why wait when I can just take my shirt off for you now? You just have to ask nicely." Man candy whispers in my ear sending sexy chills down my body, and then I feel his hand on my ass. *What the hell?* "Here's my number. You can use the picture you took as my contact photo," he says, slipping what I assume is his number into my back pocket.

"That was a text! You are so full of yourself. I don't want your number and stop touching my ass," I state as firmly as I can, but it comes out weak. His hands leave my body and I'm left breathless.

Shyanne starts giggling once again and I turn to see he's gone. I catch a glimpse of him getting into a sexy black sports car, a pretty blonde in the passenger seat scowling at him. She must be his girlfriend.

What an ass! Why would he give me his number if he has a girlfriend? Well player, your number is going in the trash, but that picture…that picture will stay safe on my phone.

~~

Ok, so that wasn't the most embarrassing moment in my 28 years of existence. There was this time when I was bowling with my ex-boyfriend and walked up behind him after arriving late. I slid my hands around his body and started to grope him only to find out it was another guy. His wife looked like she wanted to murder me but I was happy. The man had an 8 pack and I reached down far enough that I almost found the end of the V. That should have been my first clue. My boyfriend had a keg. I mean full on beer belly. You would think that being on the college's football team would've kept him in better shape. Apparently beer trumped working out. But I digress.

Deciding to get my red face and coffee out of there I step out into the Midwest sun.

Just as I get to my car my cell starts singing Sexyback by JT, my future baby daddy.

"I hate you!" I answer.

"That's not nice. You know you love me." Erin counters.

I adore Erin. She is the best friend any girl could ask for, but was handed a shitty deal last year when her ex cheated on her. Then she met Walker, one of the sexiest and sweetest men on the planet, and they just recently had a baby girl, Savannah. I get to be the maid of honor in their wedding this October and I'm truly happy that she has found someone who treats her like a queen.

"I do but that was so embarrassing! I can't believe you called me chicken. You know how I get." Turning on the car I blast the A/C.

"I know," she laughs. "What's funny is that I knew what was going to happen. Either that or the shutter would click. As organized as you are, you can be a total mess."

"Is there something you needed? I'm busy looking for a new best friend."

I would never replace Erin. She and I have been friends since freshman year in college when we were paired up as roommates. We continued to live together throughout college and bought a house together in the suburbs of Chicago after we graduated. We just couldn't stay away from each other. This past December she moved into a dream home with her dream guy, and now the house is all mine. It's nice not to have someone else there messing it up, but every so often I miss her being there.

"Yes, actually. First things first; did you give him your number?" She asks.

"Nope. He gave me his though...groped my ass while he was at it. I know it's a fine ass, but at least ask for permission first. I tossed it though. It seems the hottie has a girlfriend. Her name is Bitch, and she's blonde. I shall call her Blonde Bitch," I state firmly.

"You're a blonde!" She laughs. "Well the

girlfriend thing sucks. Anyway, besides that, the second reason I called is to ask if you wanna go to a party at Trent's tonight. Jason is visiting Alex's parents for the night and mom is watching Savannah so Walker and I can get a night out."

Trent is Erin's brother. Saying he is hot is like saying the sun is just a flame. The man is a walking lady hard on. His short brown hair and brown eyes set my body on fire anytime he is in a room but he is just so temperamental whenever I am around. We've barely spoken since Thanksgiving. Jason is his two year old son whose mom, Alex, took off just after he was born. It's heartbreaking because Jason is the cutest little boy ever. She is missing out.

"Uhm, Erin. Last time I went to one of Trent's parties I ended up in his roommate's bed." I roll my eyes remembering that horrid night as I turn out of the parking lot.

"Come on Noe! Mike moved out months ago and it's not like you had sex. He just wishes you did." She laughs. "And Trent wasn't there. I know for a fact if he was that wouldn't have happened. Come on! I need this night out."

"Ok. But you're DD. If your brother is going to act like a total douche to me again then I'm going to need lots of alcohol."

"Deal! We'll pick you up at seven."

~~

"I'm so excited you agreed to come tonight but why are you dressed like a hooker? My brother is going to go crazy!" Erin says, taking in my outfit. I'm dressed in a skimpy black halter top with a jean skirt and fuck me boots.

"I do NOT look like a hooker. I look like I need a man. Which I do! And anyways, I'd rather look like a hooker than a nun. Where do you get your clothes again? Amish Country?" I snap back. Walker chuckles from the driver's seat.

"This is Old Navy thank you very much!" She looks at her pink ruffle tank top and jeans. I notice how awesome her new cowboy boots look but don't comment just to irritate her.

"And I ordered these boots from Country Outfitter," she continues. "So shut your damn mouth. I look hot."

"Ok, Erin. Sure," I say as Walker speeds down Lake Street.

"You always look hot baby." Walker reaches over and grabs her hand kissing each knuckle.

We pull up to Trent's house which is 10 minutes from where I live. He owns his own construction company at age 26, so he clearly makes enough to live alone, but ever since he moved here he's always had a roommate. That was until Mike, his friend from DePaul, stopped paying his portion of the mortgage and "accidentally" lost the money to pay the electric bill. He really was a winner. I think maybe Trent learned his lesson with the roommate situation and now just tries to focus on raising Jason.

His place is definitely a bachelor pad. A ranch brick house, 2 car garage, 3 bedrooms, 3 baths with an entire wall made up of windows that lead to a deck with a hot tub, overlooking his enormous yard. With his building expertise he also added an extra living space that has been turned into a game room. It has a pool table, a huge TV, every game system you can think of, and surround sound which is currently blasting Bruno Mars, my other baby daddy.

Erin and Walker take off towards the kitchen and I spot Trent talking to a few of his friends.

Trent is a handsome man. Ok, scratch that. The man is a walking billboard for hotness and has starred in quite a few of my fantasies during my sessions with B.O.B. (Battery Operated Boyfriend, in case you were wondering.) He and Erin are 2 years apart and look almost identical with the exception of her huge boobs and his 11-12 inches over her 5 foot

3 frame. His brown hair just long enough to grab onto, brown eyes the color of chocolate, and every inch of him cased in muscle. He screams male. From what I can tell, his dating life, or should I say sex life, is far from lacking. Construction does a body very good.

"Noe, where have you been? It's been months since I last saw you. I was having withdrawals," Trent yells from across the room, apparently already drinking as he staggers towards us and throws his arm around my shoulders. He smells like cologne and looks sexy as hell in a red polo shirt and khaki shorts. I can't help the rush of heat that spreads throughout my body when he touches me. He is seriously sizzling.

"Oh, you know, working corners, slappin' hoes and binge drinking. The usual." He rolls his eyes, used to the crazy shit that comes out of my mouth.

"Speaking of prostitutes, what the hell are you wearing?" His eyes take in my very inappropriate attire, clearly unhappy.

"Shut the hell up, Trent. I'm a grown ass woman and I make this outfit look good," I angrily state. "Even a man like you can appreciate it."

His eyes, looking hungry, run up and down my body. I feel exposed and turned on.

"Noe. I'm serious, I really have missed you." He places a hand on each shoulder and leans in so we are breathing the same air. Brushing my collarbone with his thumb he whispers in my right ear. "You look fucking amazing."

Uh, what? He is definitely drunk. In all the years I have known Trent he has never said anything like this because if he had I sure as hell would remember.

"Thanks. I think."

"You're welcome," he says quietly, and pulls back, looking at me for a dangerously long time.

"SHOTS! SHOTS! SHOTS!" Erin announces as she brings 3 shot glasses from the kitchen, all with what I can only assume is tequila. She loves tequila. Tequila, however, does not love me. Tequila makes my clothes fall off. Tequila makes me fall into Trent's roommates' beds.

"I don't think so Erin. If you are taking shots I need to be able to drive home," I say pushing away the glass she has shoved in my face.

"Live a little Noelle! One shot won't kill you. Plus Walker offered to drive," she says, shoving it back towards me.

"I don't mind Noe," Walker says appearing

next to Erin, kissing her jaw line. "I love getting Erin drunk."

"Ok, one shot. But then I'm done." *What can I say? I'm easy.*

With a roll of her eyes she hands me and Trent a shot each. "To hot guys from Starbucks that grab Noelle's ass!" She says a bit too loudly, glancing over at Trent.

What was that about?

A weird look flashes quickly across his face while I give her a death glare. Damn Erin. I had almost forgotten about him. Almost.

"To hot guys from Starbucks," I toast anyways, lifting my glass. Trent rolls his eyes and takes the shot with Erin and me.

"To sexy girls that try taking sneaky pictures of hot guys at Starbucks." My knees buckle when I feel his hot breath on the back of my neck, mid-shot.

Oh, crap!

I turn and am met with the fierce green eyes that belong to Jace, the Starbucks god.

The tequila burns as I spit it out all over his face.

Trent looks between the two of us and says hesitantly, "Noelle, this is my new neighbor,

Jace."

You've got to be kidding me.

Acknowledgements

Joshua and my beautiful children...Thank you for having patience and understanding through this whole process. No matter what my dream is you have always been behind me. My time was taken away writing this book and you stood by and supported this one hundred percent. I don't know where my life would be without you all but I do know it would be empty. I love you with all my heart and I hope I make you proud.

Valerie Callow...There are no words to express my gratitude for a friend like you. Who knew moving across the street from you I would find a best friend, confidant, shoulder to lean on, person to vent to and cry to as well as share books with and travel with. Ensuring my happiness is not your job but you chose to make it so. I truly mean it when I say you are the greatest friend a person could have. I wouldn't have started this book without your encouragement. This is our baby. MFE!!!

Elizabeth Froelich...Thank you for putting up with all my craziness and making sure I looked like I knew what I was talking about when it came to your edits. No one will ever know that I suck at punctuation and grammar. You are the best and I wish you lots of luck in your own writing journey! Love you.

Sydney Lane...One of my fellow author mentors. You didn't have to go out of your way for me but you did and for that I am grateful. My endless questions were met with "happy to help" and "no problem". You are seriously one of the nicest people I have never met and I cannot wait until I can hug you and give thanks in person. I look forward to sharing more projects with you.

Krista Elder. My fellow ZIN. That nerve wracking day in October 2012 was met with one of the biggest smiles I have ever seen. Since then you have continued to be on my side through my ups and downs. I'm so joyful to call you a Z-sis, beta reader, and great friend. You were the first one to claim Walker as your book boyfriend. I hope he continues to be throughout your reading journey. I love you!

Amber Boyd...When I needed help you stopped what you were doing and offered to jump in.

That meant the world and since then I've continued to rely on you for your honesty and advice. Thank you for all that you have done. Who knew Vegas was the place to meet some of the greatest people! Love you!

Amanda Maxlyn...I am so proud to call you a mentor. Who knew that a lunch with another author I would come out friends with a sweet and amazing person? I am so ecstatic that I get to be in your life and your writing journey. I am so proud of what you have accomplished and cannot wait to read more of what you have in store.

Kelsi Foltyn...One of my favorite cousins. Thank you for putting up with me constantly changing my mind and then going back to what I originally wanted and then changing my mind again. Thank you for your thoughtfulness and understanding. I wish you lots of luck in your upcoming nuptials and a lifetime filled with happiness. I love you!

April Gordon...You are one of the funniest women I have ever met. I am so glad we bonded over Gavin Blake. My author picture is stunning and I wish lots of happiness to you in your new adventure in Florida. Miss you!

Adrienne Scales...For showing me that my first book I started sucked and giving me a harsh realization that I needed to SHOW and not TELL. If it weren't for you I would have never started over with a second book. Thanks for always being patient and answering my million and one questions.

TBY Family...There are so many to name that it just seems unfair to list them all. You all rooted for me from the beginning. My life will never be the same since I walked in the doors of that gym and that Zumba class and was graced with all of your friendship. Thank you for believing in me. I love you all. You truly are my VA family.

Heather Davenport...For putting my Cover Reveal and Blog Tour together. For getting answers to questions even if you had to ask around. I appreciate your tolerance and advice. I'm so lucky to know someone like you and thrilled to spend our weekend in Philly with you!

Jenn Mooney....Thank you for jumping in as a beta and falling in love with Erin and Walker. Your ego boosting messages catapulted me into finishing the book. Thank you for doing this for me even though we have never met.

Grandma Beeman....Because according to Aunt Randa you would be proud of me for doing this. I hope that is true even if Grandpa is standing next to you in Heaven telling you it's smut.

To my Mom, Step-Dad, Alyssa, Kaleigh, Nikki, Keith, Holly and John. I love you all and I don't think I tell you enough. You are the foundation of who I am today. I truly hope you are proud.

Louisa at LM Creations...No words. My cover is fantastic and you have been so patient with me. I'm in love with your work and I cannot wait for my readers to see what else you have in store for the Unexpected Series. I hope to meet you one day!

Angel's Indie Formatting...For being my savior and helping me format this in no time!

UNEXPECTED

Made in the USA
Lexington, KY
06 August 2014